WORTH THE WAIT

LOVE AT FIRST SIGHT
BOOK FOUR

KARLA SORENSEN

WWW.SMARTYPANTSROMANCE.COM

COPYRIGHT

Print Edition
ISBN: 978-1-959097-01-3

CHAPTER 1

IRIS

*B*efore she died, my grandma taught me a lot of valuable lessons. The first and foremost was that even the shittiest day could be improved by a hot cup of coffee and somethinghing sweet on the side.

I was testing the limits of that lesson, and had been for about the last six months.

Walking into Donner Bakery, a few steps behind my much younger, much more energetic brother, I thanked my lucky stars that no one ever seemed to pay us much mind. Because the day had started shitty, moved to shittier when he spilled his bowl of cereal down the front of my shirt, and I realized just a touch too far down the road that I'd forgotten to so much as run a brush through my hair before we left.

At age ten, with the kind of restless energy that reminded me of a corked-up champagne bottle shaken a bit too hard, Theo couldn't hide a single thought or feeling once it took root. And judging by the look on his face at the current moment, he was very impatiently waiting for his exhausted sister to catch up to him.

His eyes—blue to my hazel green—took an unimpressed look from the top of my messy ponytail down to my paint-splattered sneakers. "You sure you wanna go in there like … that?"

At the rate we're going and had been going for a while, we just might prove Grandma's lesson wrong yet.

"Yes," I told him. "I'm working after this, and there's no one I need to get dolled up for while you go to school."

"Summer school is bullshit," he said.

As the curse echoed across the sidewalk, an older woman sitting at one of the tables gave us a dirty look. I stifled an eye roll. The least of my worries in the past year was his minor language infractions. Many, many more of my sleepless nights came from the fact that he'd just flunked fourth grade, and if he didn't want to be held back, the boy currently waiting for his chocolate hazelnut croissant needed to work his energetic ass off for the next couple of months.

I yanked the door open and gestured for him to go in. "Well, let's remember that the next time you decide to hand in a blank test."

"Testing is even bigger bullshit," he stated. "And making me sit down with a stranger to do homework and talk about my feelings is the biggest *bullshit* of all. Don't they tell us not to talk to strangers anyway?"

If anyone in this town had watched me closely in the two years since Theo and I moved back, they would've seen a remarkable increase in the bags under my eyes and the number of weary sighs that came out of my mouth. In truth, they'd started accumulating two years earlier than that, when my half-brother was dropped off on my doorstep by an unsmiling case worker because our mother had landed herself in jail.

Again.

But I'd take every wrinkle, every inch of exhaustion, every gray hair he'd eventually cause me to have the swearing little hellion under my roof. Moving back to Green Valley, putting down our roots in a place where we actually had a small support system in Grandma and her friends still felt like a brand-new transition most days.

It was why I could walk into a place like Donner Bakery, looking a bit more *homeless chic* than I typically preferred, and no one paid us much mind.

"He's not a stranger," I told Theo. "He works for the school. Or the county. Or whoever is starting this program for stubborn, argumentative geniuses like yourself who've decided that standardized testing is bullshit," I hissed down by his ear.

He laughed.

We stood in line, and because I couldn't help myself, I swept my hand over the dark mop of his hair, pushing it off his face. As I expected, Theo rolled his eyes and knocked my hand away.

"You need a haircut."

He shoved the hair back the way he wanted it. "I like it long."

Shaking my head, I studied the curve of his downy soft cheeks, the way my touch had him blushing a little. Simple affection was something that had taken him time to feel comfortable with. And even with four years together under our belts, I typically waited for him to initiate affection outside of small touches like that.

It was another way Theo and I were alike. If I thought about it too long, it might just break my heart into a million little pieces, scattered in a messy heap, where no amount of hot coffee and banana cake could fix it. When your earliest years are spent dealing with the fallout of someone selfish, someone who could never inhabit any role except the victim in the situations of their own making, it didn't make for a warm, fuzzy upbringing.

Hugs were hardly the norm. Kisses on the forehead or someone rubbing your back when you didn't feel good—neither Theo nor I experienced much of that in our earliest years.

I'd needed someone to show me what normal, safe love felt like too. But luckily for Theo, he was learning it from me much earlier than I'd ever experienced it.

The line shuffled forward. "I mean it, kiddo," I told him. "It's a big deal they're giving you this opportunity. You have to promise me you're gonna try. Don't shut down just because you don't want to be there."

He groaned dramatically. "Can we talk about this after I get my croissant?"

"No, because once you get your croissant, you'll tell me you don't want to talk about it because it'll ruin your eating experience." I gave him a pointed look. "Like you did yesterday when I tried to bring this up."

"We could've talked about it last night, but it's not my fault you dump me on Maxine and work all the time."

His sullen tone and pouty lip had me emitting a dramatic groan to match his. Because what a steaming pile of horseshit he was feeding me. Theo loved when Maxine babysat because he got to play basketball with the boy who lived across the street, and she gave him free rein of his handheld video games, something I did not allow when we had evenings together.

Gently, I set my hand on his back and curled my palm around his skinny shoulder. "I know you're kidding, but working like this at night won't always happen," I said. "This is..." I shook my head while I chose my words carefully. "It'll be different when the store opens."

"You don't even have your building yet."

My eyebrow quirked. "Minor details. You know what I mean."

A quick glance at my face, and Theo nodded. "Set hours."

"Only open past five two nights a week, and hiring employees for those nights is my first order of business. It won't stay like this."

His eyes were serious, so big and trusting when he repeated the phrase that had become our mantra the last four years.

"Swear it?"

I held my hand over my heart. "On the only thing it would hurt to lose." I leaned down and dropped a kiss on the top of his too-long dark hair. "You and coffee, kiddo. Nothing else is worth swearing on."

He grinned, crooked and sweet, and I still marveled at how quickly I'd take a bullet for someone I'd only known for a handful of years. When the women in front of us took their coffees and small paper bags of pastries, we shuffled to the glass display case.

The girl who always helped us, with her wide happy smile and curly brown hair, started reaching for the chocolate hazelnut croissant before Theo could say what he wanted.

"Morning!" Joy said. She set the croissant into a bag and looked at me with wide, expectant eyes. "For you this morning?"

I hummed, scanning the immaculately filled case.

The morning *had* improved just by walking through the bakery doors, and I had to smile because I wished Grandma was still around. If she was, we'd go to her house with an extra cup of coffee, the blueberry muffin she loved, and we'd talk about those two things. The smell and the taste and the anticipation of both made the whole day look brighter.

"I think I'll have the blueberry today," I told Joy.

"Your grandma loved those." She sighed.

"Wouldn't it have been cheaper to like, bake them herself?" Theo asked.

Joy laughed, a delightful chiming sound that brought a smile to my face.

"We're doing our civic duty by coming here," I told him. "Supporting the local economy."

He snorted, shoving half the croissant into his mouth in one bite.

"How about another one of those too, Joy."

She slid one in with my muffin, turning to fill a to-go cup with the French vanilla I favored. I paid while she fixed the lid on the top.

"I heard you say something about summer school?" she asked, handing me the curled-up paper bag.

"It's bullshit," Theo proclaimed.

The woman behind us in line sighed heavily.

Joy smiled. "School was the best," she said. "I remember wishing I could go all year round because I just loved learning."

Somehow I managed to smother my smile at Theo's pained facial expression.

"Is it one of the Green Valley teachers helping out?" she asked.

I shook my head. "A new program they're starting. I think the county department of education is behind it. They've got enough kids dealing with back-sliding in the summer, they want to see if this can help mitigate the fallout when they return to school."

And ... kids acting out because they feel their safe, secure world is on the cusp of exploding later in the year, but ... that wasn't something I was getting into with Joy from Donner Bakery. My brother and I were dealing with similar feelings as we crept steadily closer to when Nellie hit her release. The difference was that I'd learned how to cope with those massive, overwhelming feelings.

Thank you, therapy.

But Theo, even if I'd managed to get him to agree to therapy, refused to talk to anyone.

Instead, the feelings built like a pressure cooker, and considering his body was the thing holding all that pressure, it was no surprise to me that he'd allowed school to become his release valve.

"I think that sounds great," Joy said. "Do you know who your summer school teacher is?"

Theo shrugged lightly. "Never met him. My teacher from last year called him Mr. B. Said he's real smart or something. Used to be a teacher."

I let out a slow sigh. "Speaking of, I should get you over to the school. He's probably already inside waiting for you."

Theo shook his head, flaky pastry crumbs sticking to his lips. "We don't start the one-on-one until lunchtime. We have stupid reading groups first, then some science crap outside."

Joy coughed politely, a smile stretching her cheeks. "Sounds fun!"

Her voice was so bright and as sweet as any of the confections she was packaging up in pretty little bags and boxes. For a moment, I wondered if she'd want to work at the store once I opened, if I could lure her away from sugar-topped muffins and cakes and cream puffs. She knew everyone. Everyone knew her.

And I was still a bit of a question mark in town—which was lucky for me—only a select handful of people had made the connection to the skinnier, sulkier teenage version of myself that lived with my grandma for my high school years.

And even fewer than that knew why I'd been there in the first place.

It was best to keep it that way, and best that the people who did know, well ... they probably didn't want much to do with me. Given I was the reason their son hightailed it out of town and rarely came back.

But those were memories that needed about a dozen donuts and a few extra croissants for good measure.

We said our goodbyes to Joy, and Theo was quiet as we walked to the car. Quiet on the short drive to his school.

A handful of cars were in the parking lot, and I glanced worriedly at the time.

"Need me to walk you in?" I asked. "I'll leave it up to you."

He stared at the school, and I held my breath that he'd ask me to. I was working on it, leaving him choices that would make him feel in control in situations that stressed him out.

His face firmed up in resolve, and I caught him letting out a slow, measured breath, something else we were working on. "No, thanks."

I nodded, fixing my face with an encouraging smile. "You've got this, T."

Again, the crooked grin had my heart swelling. "Will you come in when you pick me up?"

Don't cry. Don't cry. Don't cry.

"Absolutely." I managed it without so much as a single waver to my voice, and for that, I was pretty damn proud. "I should probably like, meet the guy who's gonna save your ass from repeating fourth grade anyway."

He rolled his eyes before he got out of the car, and I was still smiling when he disappeared into the front doors of the school. With a deep breath, I laid my head down onto my hands where they gripped the top of the steering wheel.

Maybe it was the muffin or the coffee, maybe it was because my sainted grandma—may she rest in peace—was looking down on what I was trying to do with Theo, how I was trying to build a life for us in a place that held my only happy memories. For that one moment in time, I was able to lift my head with a bone-deep certainty that I could do this.

I *had* to do this.

CHAPTER 2

HUNTER

*T*he halls of Green Valley Elementary school hadn't changed much since my own time there. They felt smaller, of course, because of how much I'd grown. But even with fresh coats of paint, new lockers and desks and tables, the smell was the same. It reminded me of a time in my life that was so much simpler, something I couldn't recognize because I wasn't sure anyone could at that age.

Back then, I never had to think about anything that weighed on my head now.

Now, I wondered how I'd ended up back there. In the place that I'd left more than ten years ago, the place I'd avoided because it hurt too much to be.

Now I had an ex-wife who showed as little reaction to our divorce as she had to our wedding, and to the slow acceptance of reality that she'd married a man whose heart would always be with someone else.

I had a former job that I loved while I was in it, that I'd walked away from because the halls of that school held all the memories I'd made with the person I'd married.

Even though these halls were deeply embedded in the memories of my youth, they were free of any true heartbreak. And that's just about the only reason I agreed to the job. They were empty and quiet because it was the beginning of summer, and only the small handful of people involved in the new summer program was required to be in.

When I closed my eyes, the squeak of my shoes on the gleaming floor reminded me so much of my old school in Seattle that I had to fight a wave of trepidation at the massive changes in my life in just a few short weeks.

As I turned a corner toward the upper elementary wing, my eyes scanned the nameplates outside of the small offices, and I slowed my steps when I reached the correct one. The door was cracked, and I tapped a knuckle against it.

"Come in," a voice called.

"Tracy?" I asked.

The woman at the cluttered desk smiled, glasses wedged firmly into the graying cap of hair on her head. "Hunter? My Lord, look at you." She laughed, standing with an outstretched hand. "How long has it been since I've seen your face?"

I rubbed a hand along my jaw, one that desperately needed a shave. "I was probably twenty? Maybe twenty-one."

She sighed, gesturing for me to take a seat in the wine-colored chair wedged into the corner of her windowless office. Her desk was stacked with papers, a couple of lamps set behind them to create the illusion of light and warmth in an office that was just shy of a jail cell. And this was the counselor's office, I thought with a pang of sadness, again thinking of the school I'd left. Private schools weren't necessarily leaps and bounds nicer than public schools, but the place I'd left ... that I'd run for the past few years ... it wasn't just a private school. It was a prep school for the wealthy of Seattle. Our school counselor's office had a wall of windows, a leather couch with plush white pillows, and a small water feature she'd set in the corner to help students relax when they came to speak to her.

"Well, you've sure grown up in the past twelve or so years," she said. "And I hope I'm not being rude, but what on God's green earth made you take this job?"

I laughed under my breath. "Thought maybe you'd let me warm up a bit first before asking the big questions."

Her eyes were warm, and I could see why she'd do well with the younger students. "I could've asked you about your divorce, but that felt like I'd be taking a turn past rude and heading straight into sinful gossip."

"I appreciate that." The chair in her office was soft and comfortable, and I rested an ankle over the knee of my other leg, thinking about how I wanted to answer her question. She'd been a new teacher at the high school when I left and one who encouraged me to pursue my love of reading and education. "The short answer is twofold. I was ready for a change, get back to the source of why I wanted to be a teacher in the first place. And two, my sister-in-law is having a baby." I smiled when she nodded. Nothing was a surprise in Green Valley, not if your family had roots in the town. "My mother called me on the right day to ask if I'd consider coming back for a while. I signed a resignation letter and packed a suitcase to be here when I become an uncle for the first time."

She hummed a happy sound. "Your parents are good people. And they'll make excellent grandparents."

"And Connor has cemented himself as the favorite son because he stayed right down the road where she can visit that baby any time she wants."

"I don't know. You must've gained a lot of motherly favor by coming back."

I conceded that with a nod. "She did make me pancakes and bacon for breakfast this morning, which my father glared at the entire time he ate his egg white omelet and bowl of fruit."

Tracy laughed. "I'm sure she loves being able to fuss over you again."

That was the truth. I'd only been home for three days, spending the first two of them catching up on the sleep I missed in my drive from Seattle to Green Valley. And every time I surfaced, there were hot, homemade meals, a few tears, and more hugs than I'd received in the past five years if I thought about it.

"She does. When I told her I could grab something from Daisy's on my way out here, she asked what she'd ever done to offend me so badly that I needed someone else to make me breakfast."

Tracy gave me another smile before her eyes turned thoughtful. "What about the long answer? About why you're here."

It was my turn to hum. A hollow ache clicked on in my chest like someone had it hooked to a light switch. It appeared like magic like it always did when I thought about the mixed feelings I had in returning to Green Valley. Twelve years earlier, I'd left this place that I loved because the one person who held my heart had asked me to go. Had asked me to stop loving her.

11

I'd done the first. I'd never be able to do the second.

Staying was impossible, if it meant seeing her face around every corner. I'd heard she left. My mom mentioned it in passing about a year after I'd moved to Seattle. *She* was so tangled up in the long answer. Of why I'd left. Why I was back. Why I'd married someone I knew wasn't right for me.

None of those felt like safe topics.

I held her gaze steadily. "We may have to save that for a day when we feel like some sinful gossip."

Her answering laughter was loud and brought a smile to my face.

"Who am I meeting with today?" I asked. The county had assigned me a handful of students, and today I'd be meeting my first.

She let the subject change slide, pulling a bright blue folder from the top of the stack next to her. "Theo Rossman."

I took the folder and flipped it open, my gaze tracking down blank test scores, teachers notes about outbursts in school. Despite those things, he had years of performance prior that showed signs of a bright kid. "What happened this past year?"

"I don't know all the specifics. The couple of times I've had Theo in my office, he shut down faster than I can blink. He lives with his older sister right now. There are some legal troubles with the mom." She paused, trying to choose her words carefully. "She's a repeat offender. The sister is the only stability he's ever had, and she does well ... considering she never expected to be a single parent to her younger brother. If I remember right, the mom's sentence is up sometime in the next year or so, but I might be wrong about that, so don't quote me."

"He's scared," I guessed.

She made a sound of agreement. "Some of his outbursts at school have definite roots in feeling out of control. But really, he's a good kid," she said. "Smart as a whip and has a mouth on him like a twenty-year-old college boy."

I laughed. "Great."

"No one here wants to see him repeat a grade. He's got enough to worry about, and that's part of the problem. How do we help him figure out how to regulate all those big emotions, those fears, and then sit down and take a test when we've got thirty other kids who need our attention too?"

Just about every school in America faced this same problem to varying degrees. And the access to that kind of help was so much easier for the kids at the school I'd left. Their parents made a phone call and had an appointment with a pediatric therapist within the week. Had them signed up for karate or taekwondo the week after that because their friends said it worked wonders for their kid's anxiety. But in a place with higher poverty levels, it wasn't so simple.

"Today is mainly an intro day, right?"

She nodded. "They're doing some group activities now. Their parents know it's a shorter schedule while we ease into the program. And I can't tell you how lucky kids like Theo are to have you willing to put your background to use like this."

Her words echoed on a loop while we reviewed a few more students—one in the lower elementary and two in middle school. But my focus for the day was Theo.

Tucked against the inside flap of the folder was a picture of a boy with bright blue eyes and a gap-toothed smile.

Tracy walked me down the hallway toward the playground, where the kids were working on a science scavenger hunt led by a college student who was part of the program. As the kids wandered the space, I held up a hand to shield my face from the sun while I tried to pick him out of the group.

He was by himself, paper clutched in his hand, kicking lazily at a clump of woodchips by the base of the slide. His hair was dark and long, flopping over his eyes, and his shirt was large on his thin frame. He was tall and gangly, a lot like I'd been at his age, and I tried to think about how I might've felt if I were him.

Theo noticed my approach and gave me a quick, nervous look before turning his attention back to the woodchips. I took a seat on the nearby bench, spreading my legs out and dangling my clasped hands between.

"You must be Theo," I said.

He shrugged. "Yeah."

I held out my hand. "I'm Mr. B. It's a pleasure to meet you, sir."

At the adult greeting, he glanced up in surprise but cautiously took my hand in his.

"You done with the scavenger hunt already?"

He shook his head. "Haven't started yet."

"Why not?"

He blew out a slow breath. "Because I think they're stupid, and I don't need to search around for a worm to expand my brain or whatever they're trying to get me to do."

I tried not to smile. "That so?"

"I promised my sister I'd try, and I did. Until they handed me a list that a *five*-year-old could check off in like, ten minutes. If I'd known I was signing up for kindergarten crap, I never would've agreed to come."

He said it with so much disdain, like there could be nothing worse than being five. And it was right there, all over his face, that this was not a kid who'd need me to tiptoe through warm-up questions. A lot of adults missed that. Most kids approached you in the way they wanted to be approached. They'd show you exactly what kind of interactions would mean the most to them if you're willing to pick up the signals.

Theo Rossman needed a direct, firm approach because it was the exact way he greeted a new authority figure.

I sat up, crossing my arms over my chest. "Kids learn important stuff in kindergarten, you know. It's foundational. You can't learn anything else without knowing those things."

He stopped just shy of rolling his eyes. "I know how to read and write and shit."

At the slip in his language, Theo's eyes darted nervously in my direction. But I didn't correct him.

I tilted my head. "How about you and I come to an agreement, Theo?"

"Here we go," he muttered.

"I won't get you in trouble for your language, which is a pretty big deal, considering what I did at my last job."

14

He eyed me warily. "What was that?"

I leaned forward and held his gaze. "I was a principal."

Theo swallowed audibly. "Like, a real principal?"

"Yup."

"You suspend anyone?"

"Of course. They had to break some pretty big rules for that to happen, though."

"They're not gonna suspend me for saying shit."

I let my brow rise in brief concession. "Probably not."

"My sister told me it's fine if I don't get straight A's as long as I don't get suspended. And she knows I'm trying." He crossed his arms over his chest like I'd done. "I'm not sure you're giving me that great of an offer."

"You sure you're only ten?" I asked.

He gave me a quick grin.

"Okay. How about this—I know you want to be treated like an adult because you're using adult language, and you clearly don't want to be here, so I won't treat you like a little kid. But you've gotta level with me. This won't work otherwise. I know you know how to read and write and shit. I've seen your test scores from the past couple of years. You're a smart kid, Theo."

His mouth popped open when I cursed, but he didn't interrupt, and for a kid acting out, whether it was from fear or stress or a need for attention, that was a big deal.

"You don't have to tell me why you're turning in blank tests, but it's gonna piss me off if a smart kid like you throws away your education because of something going on inside your head."

Theo went as still as a statue, blinking hard when I didn't continue. "I don't think teachers are supposed to talk to kids like that."

"I'm not your teacher," I said. "Right now, I'm just the guy who's supposed to make sure you don't have to go back to fourth grade. And that means honesty from both of us. And trust." I stood from the bench and held out my hand again.

"You can trust me, Theo. But only make a deal with me right now if I can trust you the same way."

It never occurred to me, as a teacher and then later as an administrator, to talk to kids like they didn't have the same struggles as adults. They understood stress and fear and anxiety, albeit on a different scale, with different language behind it.

That scale changed as you grew up. Your responsibilities took on a different face, and you knew how to label those struggles. But to them—at their age—the responsibilities still felt like the whole world was pressing down on their shoulders. It didn't help if the adults in their life pretended otherwise.

So I knew I'd won something big when Theo Rossman stuck his skinny arm out toward me.

He gave me a firm handshake, his cheeks turning pink when I returned it.

"You sound like Iris," he said quietly.

My heart skipped unsteadily in my chest at his use of that name.

"Who's Iris?" I asked calmly. So very, very calmly. I'd only met one person in Green Valley with that name. And as far as I knew, she'd never come back. Not that anyone had told me, at least.

"My sister. I live with her." He tucked his hand back in his pocket, his face softening as he answered. His love for her, even if it wasn't *my* Iris, was immediately clear.

Behind my ribs, I felt a hot squeeze of pressure while my mind absolutely fucking *raced*.

"I knew an Iris once." I watched his face as I said it. "She'd probably be about thirty-two now."

His eyes narrowed, mental calculations evident in his face. "I think that's how old my sister is."

My breathing was choppy, my lungs struggling to pull in enough oxygen. "The Iris I knew ... her last name wasn't Rossman."

He kicked at a stick, so blissfully unaware that all my insides were jolting with unchecked pulses of electricity at the mere thought of it being her.

"Yeah, she's my half-sister. She had a different dad, so she has a different last name."

"What's your sister's last name?" I asked, fighting the urge to grab him by the shoulders and shake the truth from his mouth.

At the sound of a car, Theo's attention was pulled to the parking lot. In an instant, he transformed. Wide smile and happy, bright eyes as he waved at the driver of a beat-up-looking SUV. "That's her. Iris Black."

I swiped a hand over my face and tried to check my breathing.

Check my pulse.

My ability to stay fucking *conscious*.

This was it. All the sleepless nights I'd wondered if I'd ever see her again. Wondered how I'd ever walked away from her, why I believed her when she said she didn't have room for us in her life. If respecting her choice would damn me to a life that would always feel a little empty. Where every day held a slight edge of grief, something that might have worn down over the years but could still damage me if I caught it in the right way.

The last time I saw Iris Black, she wept as she told me to leave. That she couldn't —wouldn't—make room in her life for some great big destined romance. That she couldn't—wouldn't—believe that it was true.

The last time I saw her, I told her I'd love her for the rest of my life, whether she was in it or not. And I walked away all the same.

And there it was.

A gentle snap, a whisper-soft snick of something sliding back into place underneath my ribs. The shift of something that had been out of place since the last time I saw her. The realization came as quick as a thunderbolt and just as powerful. As I slowly turned toward the parking lot and she stepped out of the car, I knew this was the reason I'd come back to Green Valley.

It was her.

The one I'd loved since the moment I saw her.

Who I hadn't seen in twelve years.

The one staring at me like she'd just seen a ghost.

CHAPTER 3

IRIS

*E*ven in the years apart, I held on to one unrelenting bit of truth—I'd always know him. Would always and immediately recognize him. Something happened in my body when he was around. Something at the cellular level, even if it didn't seem scientifically possible.

But that man, the one standing tall and strong and unsmiling next to my little brother, had a way of rearranging the universe around me. I breathed differently. My heart beat to a rhythm unique to him.

And I'd forgotten.

I'd forgotten the cut of his jaw. The piercing eyes.

Hunter Buchanan was the most handsome son of a bitch who'd ever walked the earth, and even worse, his looks paled compared to the heart he had in that big, strong chest.

My body stayed locked in place, the car door a strange barricade while I tried to unlock my frozen hand from where it gripped the metal frame.

His mouth moved, but I was just a bit too far away to hear his voice.

"Iris."

It was the only thing he said. His dark eyebrows bent in confusion, a big hand coming up to swipe over his mouth.

Oh. I laid a hand over my heart and tried, with ice-cold desperation, not to burst into tears. To dive back into the car, peel out of the parking lot in a trail of burning rubber and dramatic smoke. The single thing that kept me from doing it was Theo.

My brother was, and had been for years, my anchor. No matter what was going on around us, he was the thing that kept my head above water and what I'd work myself to the bone for.

I pinched my eyes shut. It felt like I'd been standing there for hours, trying to gain control over the thrashing of my heart, but only seconds had passed. When I opened my eyes, Theo was looking up at Hunter, saying something with a big, happy smile on his face.

One meeting, and Hunter had my brother—my wary, smart-ass brother—eating out of his hand.

I blew out a slow breath and managed to pry my hand off the car frame. Hunter cataloged every movement with a banked hunger in his eyes, and that—oh, that look in his eyes—had my stomach trembling.

With shaking hands, I smoothed back the stray wisps of hair as it swept over my face. My ponytail was a little sad after the past few hours of doing some sanding and cleaning. No doubt there were bags under my eyes from the choppy sleep I'd managed the night before. Normally, it didn't bother me, but suddenly, all I could think of was how I might have changed in his eyes.

The wrinkles that hadn't been there before.

The curves that appeared in my mid-twenties.

And make no mistake, I had never felt the need to look perfect for any man. Not even this one. But there was a very particular sort of awareness when you walked toward the first—the only—man to truly love you.

Hunter's eyes tracked down the front of my T-shirt, his lip quirking to the side when he saw what it said.

The fanfic was better.

I'd had the shirt for approximately eighty years. I'd washed it a thousand times, and the hem and the collar had holes. Exactly what every woman hoped to be wearing in such moments.

Each step I took, my heart settled a bit, and my breathing came more easily. That damn, damn shifting again. Like just breathing the same air as him had something easing into a place of peace.

Asshole.

He wasn't, though. He wasn't even close.

Without a word traded, without a single idea of what he'd been through or what I had been through, in turn, I took one look at his face and knew he'd let me walk straight into his arms without hesitation.

He'd let me notch my head under his chin like I used to, wrap me up in his embrace—a safe haven I hadn't felt since the last time he held me.

And that was why I used those last few steps, that immediate truth of what I could see in his eyes, to slap down a wall.

Brick by brick by brick.

The only way I could survive this, whatever would come from it, was by keeping Hunter very firmly locked into a box reserved for my past.

"Iris!" Theo exclaimed, running the last few steps toward me for a boisterous hug. I slid my hand over his back and gave him all my attention. "Mr. B said he knew you! How crazy is that?"

I pressed a fervent kiss to the top of Theo's hair and, again, pinched my eyes shut.

Should've bought a few extra baked goods.

A hysterical-tinged laugh almost crawled up my throat because the idea that they would help anything was panic attack-inducing. When Grandma gave me that particular tidbit, she did not mean moments like this.

"So crazy," I said quietly. I hugged him a bit too tightly, and he groaned.

"I can't breathe."

I attempted a smile, and if he noticed the tight edges, he didn't show it. "Sorry, kiddo."

He gripped my hand, something he rarely did anymore, and dragged me the last few steps that separated Hunter and me.

The man facing me had smoothed out his facial expression and curbed whatever I'd briefly seen in his dark eyes.

"Iris."

The box where I'd put him rattled and roared, and it took everything in me not to react to the sound of his voice. Deeper than the last time I'd heard it and full of ... everything. In my brother's grip, my hand went clammy and cold.

"Hi," I whispered.

His jaw clenched.

"How do you know Mr. B?" Theo asked. The tension in our little circle was so thick I could hardly breathe, heavy with unsaid things and a million questions and racing emotions, and God bless my little brother, he was completely fricken oblivious.

Hunter recovered first, sending Theo a warm, contained smile. "I knew your sister a long time ago. We were in high school when we met."

Right. A simple polite answer was good too.

My rule, the one Theo and I established the day he moved in with me, was that there were no lies between us. Our mother lied almost every time she opened her mouth, and it was a vow we'd held strong to in the four years he'd been under my care.

If I'd answered him privately, it probably would've been a bit too honest.

How did I know him?

I knew Hunter Buchanan as the only man I'd ever loved and the hardest goodbye I'd ever said in my entire life.

But sure. Meeting in high school was a good answer too.

"High school?" Theo asked. "Wow. Iris is like, old now, so that was a really long time ago."

22

Hunter huffed out a soft laugh when my cheeks bloomed hot.

"Thanks, Theo," I said gently. I squeezed his shoulder, and he laughed.

Hunter's eyes locked with mine. "I haven't seen her since I left to finish college out of state."

I couldn't *breathe* when he looked at me like that. And I really couldn't breathe when his gaze slipped from my face and landed unerringly on the ring finger of my left hand.

When he found it empty, the relief was immediate and palpable. His broad shoulders dropped a solid inch.

I knew he'd married. And I knew he'd divorced. This is why my gaze stayed far, far away from his ring finger.

"I thought you were," I started, clearing my throat when it went a little bone-ass dry. "Were a principal or something."

He nodded. "I was."

"He doesn't look like a principal," Theo muttered. "They're usually old and scary."

Hunter laughed, a rich, deep sound that tugged deliciously at the hair along the back of my neck. "I was ready for a change," he said after his laughter faded. "And I was ready to live by family again."

I nodded. In my couple of years back in Green Valley, I'd done an A-plus job of avoiding the Buchanans. Even if his parents were really the only ones who knew anything about our history.

"Are there a lot of people in your family?" Theo asked.

Again, I closed my eyes. This kid would break my heart someday, more than it had already ever been broken. More than anything, he wanted a big family. He wanted me to get married and have a dozen babies just so he could feel like we were a part of something other than the meager family history we did have.

"I do," Hunter said. "My parents, two brothers—Connor and Levi—and a couple of cousins who live here in town. My brother Connor is married, and Levi is engaged, so I've got a couple of sisters-in-law, and in a month or so, I'll be an uncle for the first time."

My heart did a weird flippy flop, this one squeezing with a slight tinge of long-ing. Never did I ever need to think about Hunter holding a baby. That did not help to keep boxes of the past locked and quiet and in the back of my head where they belonged. When he'd left, we'd been too young to even think about such things. But now ... now I wasn't young anymore.

I was a single woman, staring at a man who most likely still loved me, with a metric fuck ton of complicated reasons I wasn't available to be with him. And thinking about him holding a baby with dark hair and dark eyes was enough to make me burst into tears.

Honestly. I'd been around him for ten minutes. If I was being graded on keeping my head straight, I would find a grade lower than F on my report card.

"We need to go, Theo," I said quietly. "We'll be late for dinner at Maxine's."

"I thought that was on Wed—"

I cut him off with a squeeze of my hand. "No, I think you forgot we changed it."

He gave me a look but wisely didn't argue. Oh, I'd hear it from him when he real-ized just how full of crap I was.

Because I was running. From the hot man who rearranged atoms and molecules and caused heart palpitations.

Hunter's eyes searched mine when I allowed my gaze back to his face.

Theo's voice broke through the sweat-inducing eye contact. "Miss Tracy said you need to trade phone numbers with Mr. B because..." He stopped, saying the words that he'd committed to memory. "Summer school should include parental interaction." He glanced back up at me. "And you're the parent. Sort of."

I arched my eyebrow. "Sort of?"

Theo grinned, and the sight of it had the squeeze on my rib cage easing.

Without an apologetic look at Hunter, I tilted my head at the car. "I left my phone in the car, so..."

He nodded, pulling his phone out of the back pocket of his dark jeans. I caught the slightest tremble of his hand while he typed in my number, each long, perfect finger hitting the screen slowly, deliberately. Then he read it back to me to make sure it was correct.

Was it a thousand degrees outside?

My back was pooling with sweat, just knowing he had a way to contact me. That I'd have a way to contact him. It was so much easier to keep the thought of him far out of reach because I wasn't on any social media, except for the account I was starting for the store.

"Got it," he said, his voice a quiet, low rumble. When he tucked his phone away, he gave me another long look.

My heart sped up, so I tore my eyes away.

"See you in a few days?" Theo asked Hunter. "We meet again on Friday, I think."

Hunter nodded.

"And you promise, no kindergarten shit?"

"Theo," I hissed.

But Hunter simply smiled. "No kindergarten shit."

My mouth fell open.

My little brother smiled like the cat who got the friggin' cream, and Hunter laughed quietly at the expression on my face.

I gave him a look. "I hope you don't make a habit of encouraging ten-year-olds to swear."

"Only the really smart ones," he answered smoothly.

Theo laughed.

"And no," Hunter added. "I don't."

The air around us felt dangerous, charged and heavy with that flirtatious edge to his voice. And I fought the urge to run as a result.

"Well," I hedged, "I guess we'll see you later."

Hunter gave Theo his fist for a bump, and his eyes glowed with promise when they locked back onto mine.

"I look forward to it," he said. The deep surety of his voice yanked at the baby-fine hairs along the back of my neck.

And during the entire walk back to my car, I felt his eyes on my back.

CHAPTER 4

HUNTER

I wasn't entirely sure how long I sat on the playground bench after she left. But the moment her car disappeared from sight, my legs gave out, and I sank down onto the sun-warmed wood.

At first, I replayed each second of the interaction, filtered ruthlessly through what I could remember of her facial expressions. Cataloging the change in her face in the last twelve years.

The play of light off her dark hair, those dark greenish-brown eyes. In the sun, they always looked more like ivy, the kind that wrapped around the tree trunk outside my parents' house. Elbows braced on my legs, I sank my head into my hands and fought against a rising panic that that one interaction would be it.

That she'd disappear, and I'd never see her again. I'd been gone for so long now, and as much as I thought I'd remembered, as much as I thought I'd never forgotten what it was like to be around her, I had.

Or maybe forgotten was the wrong word.

My memories were dulled with time and faded in a way that I couldn't fight.

And her sudden reappearance—a bright clash of light and sun when I was least expecting it—was jarring in its intensity.

The longer I sat, the easier it was to smooth that intensity down. My brain sifted back further to the memories I didn't revisit as often, simply because they were too painful.

Iris walking in the rain, a book clutched to her chest, and a wary look permanently etched onto her face.

The way the sight of her pushed and pulled at the core of me. Something I'd never really believed was possible until I met her.

My soul mate. The one I'd always love.

Our first kiss behind the tree where we met when my hands shook at the feel of her soft lips and the sound of her quiet moans.

The days we spent lying out under the sun, her head tucked against my chest while I read out loud.

The sweet early days when I never doubted the future that we'd share.

With my hands clutched tight into my hair, those were the only memories I'd allow myself. For now.

Anything else—the way she felt underneath me, the explosive passion we found as the weeks and months and years passed—was impossible to think about.

My phone buzzed in my pocket, and an immediate irrational thought zapped me into movement.

What if it's her?

But at the sight of a text from my brother Connor, I managed a short laugh at my own expense.

Iris didn't have my phone number yet, but she would soon. When I could trust myself to reach out and not sound like a complete fucking head case.

Connor: Up to shoot some hoops with your brothers?

Connor: Levi thinks you can beat me, and he's so insufferable about it that I can't wait until you feel more settled.

Me: You're on.

. . .

Maybe it was habit after years of living away from my family, but I didn't tell my brothers about what happened. I wasn't quite ready to share the news about Iris's appearance in Green Valley and my role in her brother's life as a result. Not in a significant way, because I wasn't even sure what it meant.

I knew what it meant to me. It was a second chance. An opportunity that I never thought I'd have again.

But I didn't know what it meant to her. And that was equally important.

I was able to channel all that jittery anticipation into our game, where I absolutely destroyed Connor in a game of one-on-one. Levi earned twenty bucks off my win, and I got a body full of aching muscles for the next two days.

I helped my parents make dinner, where Connor and Sylvia joined us. And I lounged in my chair on their back deck and quietly watched my younger brother dote on his pregnant wife.

I was impossibly happy for them. And I wanted what they had so badly that my chest ached from the force of it. I wondered if it would've felt so bittersweet to watch them if I hadn't seen Iris.

The following morning, I went for a long run, my lungs heaving as I sucked down the humid morning air. I pushed my pace faster than normal like I was trying to drain all the anticipation out of my body. Knowing she was around. Knowing she could be anywhere in this relatively small town.

Something urgent under my skin pushed me to action.

Pushed me to find her. Talk to her. Look her in the eyes and see what I could find buried in their depths.

I showered.

Dressed.

Stared at my phone and thought about messaging Iris. But every time I pulled up the screen, something stopped me short.

The surprise was gone for both of us.

After surprise came awareness. The anticipation that I couldn't shake.

And as I drove to the Bait and Tackle to pick up a few things so I could join my dad for one of his early-morning outings, I knew that the anticipation would never fade.

Not as long as I knew she was here.

Every errand, every outing held a tenor of premonition.

The store was busy when I entered, and still, my gaze swept over every person that I could see. Bobby Jo MacIntyre, one of the few familiar faces I knew, gave me a friendly, close-mouthed smile as I wandered down the first aisle.

"Hunter," she said. "Haven't seen your face in a while."

"No, ma'am." I gestured to the line at the register. "Business seems to be doing well."

"No complaints from me." She studied my face. "My daughter told me you'd be back in town soon."

I nodded. "I haven't had the pleasure of seeing Magnolia yet," I admitted. "Her trip out west with my cousin overlapped with me getting back into town."

Bobby Jo raised one eyebrow. Honestly, she looked like she hadn't aged in the past twenty years. "My daughter on a hiking trip is something I still can't quite reconcile." She shrugged. "Love makes you do crazy things, I suppose."

As she said it, and I managed a short laugh in response, the doors to the shop swung open. Theo ran through, heading straight for the fridge of bait. The doorway behind stayed empty. My breath stalled somewhere in the bottom of my lungs.

Iris walked in with a battered ball cap covering her head and her legs bare. The faded green of her shirt hung over denim cutoffs, and I noticed a tiny spot of ink on the inside of her right wrist.

Something about that small tattoo was intoxicating, something I didn't know was there before just now. My entire being was drawn to her. Like she'd flipped a force field on just by walking through the door.

"Can I help you find anything today?" Bobby Jo asked, unaware that I'd briefly forgotten I was right in the middle of a conversation.

Tearing my gaze away from Iris, I gave her a distracted smile. There was no idle chitchat from Bobby Jo, which I appreciated. Especially now that I felt the tug to the opposite side of the store. "Just ... looking for a new pole."

She nodded. "We've got a few of those for you. Holler if you have a question."

I had a lot of questions, but none of them could be answered by Bobby Jo MacIntyre.

Letting out a slow breath, I didn't even pretend to look at fishing poles. Didn't pretend to study the reels or bait or lures filling the rows of the store.

All the questions I wanted to ask Iris, now that the surprise and awareness and anticipation melted into something else, crowded my brain.

I wanted to know what her home looked like.

Whether she still slept curled up on her side with her hands tucked under her pillow.

I wanted to know what she was doing with her life, where she spent her days, and if it was something she loved.

And beyond those things, I wanted to know—with a heart-rattling desperation— if she was wondering the same things about me.

My mind raced, thinking of what to say first, how to approach her now that I was expecting the gut punch impact of her gaze on mine. But Theo beat me to it.

"Mr. B!" he yelled.

Iris spun, the small fishing pole in her hand whipping around with such force that I had to duck to avoid getting smacked in the face.

I laughed under my breath, and with a sweet pink tinge to her cheeks, she carefully set the pole back on the display. "I'm so sorry," she breathed. "I didn't ... I wasn't expecting you."

Tucking my hands into my pockets, I jerked my chin toward the poles. "Didn't know you could use those as a weapon, too."

Iris breathed out a laugh. "I'm very talented that way."

"Iris is taking me fishing tomorrow," Theo proclaimed. "But my pole broke."

"Ahh." I crouched down next to him, touching the side of the bait container he was holding. "What are you trying to catch with those?"

He cracked open the lid, eyes lighting up at the wiggling bodies of the night-crawlers pushing through the black dirt. "Usually, we get bluegills. Some trout. Once I caught a catfish, though." Theo closed the lid again. "I've never caught a pike. Those are big."

"They are," I agreed easily. "Pike don't go for the worms, though," I told him. "I'd get one of those lures over on the end if you want a pike. The soft ones that look kinda like a minnow."

Theo waited for his sister to nod her agreement, and he took off.

A quick glance at Iris as I straightened to my full height had my heart pounding in my chest. The look in her eyes was warm, the tips of her ears were pink, and I knew for a fact that her ears only did that when she was flustered.

What she wasn't doing was running. She wasn't shutting down the conversation.

It was an opening. A chance to see whether that opening was something I could walk through and if she'd walk through it with me.

"Where you taking him?" I asked, leaning my shoulder against the bait fridge so I could turn more closely toward her.

Her eyes stayed locked on Theo, where he asked Bobby Jo about the lures, then they flipped back to me. "Bandit Lake. He likes the view there best."

"It's beautiful, that's for sure," I murmured.

I wasn't talking about the lake. Iris's gaze stayed locked on mine for a long, breathless beat before shifting away.

It was, by far, one of the cheesiest, most cliché moments I could've conjured. And the way the pink on her ears shifted to the tops of her cheeks, I couldn't find a single shred of regret.

I opened my mouth to ask her something ... anything, just keep the conversation going, and Theo yelled her name.

"I got a good one! You ready to go? I'm *starving*."

Iris smiled. "He's always starving. He'll eat me out of house and home when he's a teenager."

"How long has he lived with you?" I asked. I needed one—just one—of my questions answered. It would tide me over until the next opportunity.

Her eyes went warm again, something soft and wonderful shifting in the finely carved features of her face. "Four years."

"He's lucky to have you."

Iris closed her eyes at the sound of my voice. "I'm the lucky one," she said quietly.

"Iris," Theo said. He widened his eyes dramatically. "Can we go, please?"

She gave me a rueful smile, and it was the slight hesitation before she left that had me taking a step closer.

"It feels good to run into you, Iris Black," I told her, voice low, meant for just the two of us.

The breath she exhaled was nothing but a short, shocked puff of air.

Hell, I couldn't believe I'd said it either, but it was the pink-tipped ears, the warm look in her eye, and the fact that she didn't run. There was no way I couldn't say it.

When she turned with a slight shake of her head, I knew there would be no loaded answer in return. No whispered goodbye heavy with subtext. And that was okay.

Surprise and awareness and anticipation.

Those three things dominated the next few days. As did more frequent run-ins with Iris. Each one stacked little bricks of happiness and peace inside me, rebuilding a foundation that had been decimated in her absence from my life.

When I pulled up next to her car at a red light on Main Street. Her amused little smile when I rolled down my window and said her music was too loud.

When I went for a run, and she was pumping gas, her eyes locked momentarily on my chest. Her cheeks were bright red when I waved.

When I left church with my parents, and she was getting out of her car a block away. They didn't see her, busy talking with their friends.

But I did.

And I saw how she tucked her hair behind her ear, eyes tracking over the suit I wore to appease my mother. And I saw how she increased her speed as she walked in the opposite direction but offered a small glimpse over her shoulder to see if I was still there.

The surprise never faded.

The awareness was a hot and relentless pressure against my rib cage.

And the anticipation was the most delicious sort of foreplay she and I had ever engaged in. Like each little moment, she trailed her fingers along my skin, teasing me with glimpses of her own.

Monday morning rolled around, and I had time to kill before I needed to be at school. On my bedside table, I rifled through the stack of books there and decided that a visit to my favorite building in town was a perfect way to start the day.

The library had grown substantially since I lived in Green Valley, and I took in the building with a pleased smile as I walked through the doors. Inhaling deeply, I couldn't help but equate the smell of books, the quiet, hushed atmosphere with the place where my love of learning—and teaching—had been born. And I couldn't help but equate it with memories of Iris.

I wandered the adult fiction section, trailing my fingers along the spines of the books, occasionally stopping to pull one from the stack so I could read the back cover. Nothing caught my eye, and I moved to the next aisle, studying the titles of a popular thriller series, when I caught sight of her through the stacks.

A smile pulled at my lips.

The surprise was pleasant and warm.

Keeping my steps slow and steady, I walked down the aisle and watched her through the opening above the books. Her fingers tracked over some of the copies in front of her. She was looking for something too.

Awareness caught at the back of my throat when she carefully tugged a small book from the shelf. The cover was in muted creams and browns, the same version she'd been holding the day I saw her for the first time. Next to it was an identical copy, and I held my breath as she flipped toward the back of the book.

I knew what she was looking for.

My heart thundered while the pad of her thumb skimmed past the pages in search of a small note scribbled on the last page.

Iris got to the last page, and there was no note. Her brow furrowed, and when her shoulders slumped, I knew she was seeking out memories, running through pieces of our past in the same way I was.

The awareness melted away.

Anticipation.

It bubbled dangerously under my skin, and my hands shook from the effort it took not to rush toward her and cup her face in my hands. To suck on her bottom lip and slide my tongue into her mouth and curl my hands around her waist as she pressed against me.

I turned the corner, found her standing alone in the row.

Iris froze, her eyes widening when she saw me there, shoulder braced on the shelf next to me.

"You're reading my favorite book," I said quietly.

The first words I'd ever said to her. And she remembered, based on the slow tightening of her hands on the paperback.

"This book," she started, her eyes taking on a luminous glow, "is overrated nonsense."

The first words she'd said in return.

I laughed under my breath, walking toward her in slow, measured steps.

I should've known when she said that to me, all those years ago, that Iris Black would be the death of me. That she'd challenge me within an inch of my sanity.

Iris inhaled deeply when I stood beside her, carefully taking the book out of her hands.

35

I ran my fingers over the letters of the title.

The Alchemist.

It wasn't necessarily my favorite book anymore. My tastes had changed since I was an eighteen-year-old, but at the time, the simple message felt as close to life-changing as anything I'd ever read. That achieving your dreams was as simple as following your heart. And the fact that Iris had been holding it in her hands, reading it underneath a big, sprawling tree when I saw her for the first time, seemed like destiny.

"Still hating on *The Alchemist*?" I asked.

She bit down on her bottom lip, but she couldn't stop the edges of her smile. "My opinion remains... unfavorable."

I made a wounded sound.

"Is it still your favorite?" she asked.

I shook my head. "I've read a couple that have knocked it down a peg or two."

Her pink lips curled in a pleased smile. "Which ones?"

The fact that she asked was good.

Another opening. Another opportunity.

I named off a couple of titles and saw the interest spark in her eyes when I mentioned a fiction title she must have enjoyed.

Iris gave a knowing nod. "So you have better taste now."

My laugh was hushed and quiet, and when I glanced down, I saw goose bumps sprinkled over her arm. My eyes closed as I breathed her in, tilting my head toward hers. Iris had never smelled flowery or heavy with perfumes.

It was clean and fresh, and being this close had my body reacting like she flipped a switch.

"Oh, I think my preferences have stayed just about the same," I said, my voice dragging meaningfully on the words.

Her exhale was unsteady. "Hunter," she whispered.

Someone cleared their throat in the aisle next to us, and Iris took a quick step away from me. As she did, I saw the tips of her ears turn a flushed pink, and her fingers unconsciously went to the necklace hanging around her throat.

It was the vintage emerald her grandmother gave her when she turned eighteen. And when she was nervous, she worried the gem between her fingers.

I didn't want to make her nervous, but I couldn't help the bright, hot flare of hope at her reaction either.

"Is Theo with you?" I asked.

She took another steadying breath, her gaze flipping briefly up to mine before she replaced the book on the shelf. "He's in the kids section. Picking up a book that Miss Tracy recommended."

I nodded. "That's good. I'll make it a point to ask him about it later."

Iris was clear-eyed when she took another step away, adding some pointed distance between us. "I should get Theo over to the school," she said quietly.

With a quick glance at my watch, I made a split-second decision. "I can take him if you want. I don't mind getting there a bit early."

"That would be great," she said, a cautious smile lighting her features. "I'll go tell him."

She brushed past me, a soft whisper of her hair tickling the side of my arm, and I had to brace my hand on the bookshelf at the feel of it. When I opened my eyes, I studied the second copy of *The Alchemist*—the one she hadn't checked.

Carefully, I pulled it down, flipping through the pages until I reached the back. My breath whooshed out of my lungs when I saw my handwriting, small blue letters that I'd printed on the page.

Whatever path I'm on, every sign in my life will lead me back to you. HB+IB

When I wrote it to her, I thought it was a clever little message to a woman who had my heart. Something we could laugh about, given her distaste for the book. But as I traced my fingers along my own handwriting from all those years ago, I couldn't help but question how all this would play out.

If it was enough that she was here. That I was here, too.

She returned with Theo, and there was no hidden longing in her eyes now. Something shifted in her body language, and I couldn't help but wonder if me catching her in that aisle, with that book, had been a bit too much vulnerability than she'd been ready to share.

"Thank you for bringing him," Iris said. "I really appreciate it."

"Of course." I smiled at her brother. "Ready?"

He sighed. "I guess."

Iris nudged him as I laughed. I tried not to watch her walk away but failed.

Theo was giving me a curious look. "How'd you know Iris again?"

I cleared my face and set a hand on his thin shoulder. "We met while she was living with your grandma. The first time I met her, she told me she hated my favorite book."

His laughter dispelled some of the lingering unease I had at the way we parted.

Theo followed me to the counter so I could check out my new books, and I rolled the entire interaction around in my head. I wasn't sure exactly what came after the anticipation. But I had the feeling we were building to it, one way or another.

CHAPTER 5

HUNTER

*W*hen she picked up Theo that afternoon, Iris stayed in the car with her phone pressed against her ear. My disappointment was strong.

I waved as he left, and she lifted her fingers off the steering wheel to return it. It was too bright for me to gauge her facial expression, and I thought about the library again.

So few words traded, but they meant something.

I just wasn't quite sure what.

Pursuing Iris was a natural instinct when I saw glimpses that she might be feeling some of the same things. But I wouldn't find much success in building a new relationship with her if I kicked down doors and made grunted, domineering proclamations that she was mine and I was hers. That was the fastest way to catch Iris Black's kneecap in my balls.

Pursuit of the woman you loved was a bit more nuanced than that, especially when you had our history.

Close to a week after I'd seen her the first time, I found myself sitting on the same playground bench, the sun beating pleasantly down onto my back, while I tried to untangle it all.

My phone buzzed, and I smiled when I saw Connor's name.

My middle brother had a knack, it seemed, for knowing when my head needed a break.

Connor: I've learned a valuable lesson the past seven months.

Me: What's that?

Connor: When your wife is pregnant with the first grandchild, she's the golden ticket.

Connor: Anything she wants, Mom delivers.

Connor: Sylvia made a passing comment to Mom about how good her meatloaf sounded, so ... Mom has now made enough to feed 18 grown men. You better be home for dinner. I know you're done with tutoring soon.

Me: Did Sylvia ask for that too?

Connor: Ha. No. She's more concerned with the meatloaf than you. I'm the one who wants my big brother there.

I smiled, typing out a quick response that I'd be there. The house would be loud and chaotic, and it was exactly what I needed after the strange rhythm of my day. The rhythm of the whole last week, really. And I needed some time with my family to help with that. For my whole life, I'd been the quiet brother. The one who'd more often than not be sitting on the outskirts of the action, probably with a book in my hand so I could pass the time without having to talk to anyone. But the longer I'd been away, the more I missed the craziness.

As hard as it was, I pushed off the bench and tried to set the memories of Iris aside, trusting that I hadn't messed anything up with our interaction earlier.

Driving to my parents' house, I wondered what memories she was allowing herself.

If she allowed any, after I'd caught her seeking out that particular book.

I knew her—no matter how many minutes and days and weeks had passed—and Iris had an incredible talent for compartmentalizing. I used to imagine that her brain was divided into some elaborate filing cabinet, with locks and passwords and magical barriers that kept each section separate.

The more important a memory and the more damage it might do, the further she was able to push it back.

I just never thought I'd be one of those things. Until the day she asked me to leave her alone. When she asked me to walk away from her.

Anger toward Iris was something I'd left in my past, and I had to swallow back the bitter taste of it before it could creep up my throat.

As I pulled into the driveway and navigated past the line of cars, my brothers—Levi and Connor—were already here, as was my cousin Grace. Her boyfriend Tucker's truck was in the street.

Before I joined them at the main house, I let myself into the converted garage apartment that I was temporarily calling home. It was dark and quiet, and for a moment, I sank down onto the gray couch just like I had the wooden bench.

This time, I pulled up a blank text thread and carefully typed in each letter of her name. For many years, something this easy, this simple, was completely impossible. Until now, I wasn't sure what to say, or if it was the right time to initiate this kind of communication.

Me: It's Hunter.

Sixteen-year-olds could text with better tact, and just sending those two words had my stomach in knots. But what else could I say?

You are the most beautiful thing I've ever seen.

Tell me we have a chance.

I still love you.

I blew out a self-deprecating laugh. Probably just a bit too much. Despite that, I wanted to send her something true. Something of substance.

. . .

Me: It was good to see you today. It always is.

Before I could send anything else or crush my phone under the weight of how stupid this all felt, a knock on the door preceded my two brothers barging in.

"Thanks for waiting for an invitation," I said wryly.

Connor ignored me, flopping into the chair on the opposite side of the room while Levi took the corner on the far end of the couch, stretching his long legs in front of him.

"We all learned the hard way to use the lock," Levi said, folding his hands over his stomach. "Mom walked in on me and Joss one too many times."

Connor laughed. "Same. Sylvia swore she needed therapy."

I smiled. "I didn't see Joss's car outside."

My little brother grinned widely at the mention of his fiancée. "She's working. Started at a youth center in Knoxville a few days a week."

"Good for her."

When Levi and Joss had moved out to Seattle, Joss was practically a stranger to me. But it didn't take long to see how perfect they were for each other. They'd been best friends for years, my little brother pining over her like a fool, before they'd finally turned to more.

Maybe I was biased in how much I loved my future sister-in-law because she reminded me of Iris in so many ways. A little prickly when she didn't know you, a lot mouthy when she did, and underneath all that, a giant heart for the select few people who'd earned the right to it.

"Why are you over here in the dark while there's beer and meatloaf at Mom and Dad's?" Connor asked, tossing a foam football in his hands.

For a moment, I wondered if I could tell them. If I could manage it without sounding crazy, the one man in the Buchanan family who'd voluntarily walked away from his one true love.

It was an unspoken topic in our family that my parents never broached. They'd left it untouched because I'd asked them to. And one thing I knew, no matter what we'd been through and how long I stayed away, was that my family loved me.

It was all those years of respect, that love, that had me leaning my head back and closing my eyes. I took a deep breath.

"I saw her today. I've seen her a few times this week, actually."

The room went deathly quiet. Connor stopped tossing the football.

Levi blew out a slow exhale. "Like ... *her*? Iris?"

Would I ever get used to hearing her name again? The impact of it was bone-deep, like a tuning fork hit at just exactly the correct pitch, something loud and pleasing and exactly right.

"Yeah." My voice was hardly audible. "Her ... brother, he's one of my students at the elementary school this summer."

"Holy shit," Levi breathed.

I opened my eyes and found them both leaning forward, gazes locked on mine, full of sympathy and concern.

Connor's face held the slightest shadow of guilt. "I wondered when you'd run into her. Didn't think it would be so soon."

Levi glanced at him. "You knew she was back?"

Connor nodded. "We all did. But ... she was kind of a forbidden subject, you know?"

"Mom tell you not to tell me?"

He shrugged. "When Iris moved back with her brother, you were still married to Samantha. No one had to tell us to do anything."

I swept a hand down my face.

"I'm sorry. Maybe we should have said something."

I shook my head. "Nothing to apologize for."

He sighed, visibly relaxing. "Good. Now you can tell us what all this excellent brooding is about."

"That's not..." I huffed. "I'm just thinking."

Levi chuckled. "You're so good at it, Hunter. Connor has the charm, I have the looks and the athletic ability, and you have the dark, brooding mysterious thing. Can't escape our natural talents in life."

Connor chucked a pillow at him, which Levi caught and lobbed straight back at him.

I wanted to feel the same lightness as my brothers, but I couldn't bring it up to the surface. And they realized it as they settled back into their chairs.

"I'm sitting in the dark *thinking* because I don't know how to do this," I admitted steadily. "I don't know how to be around her and pretend I don't love her so damn much—still. Even after I walked away for a fucking *decade* simply because she asked me to leave her alone."

Connor covered his mouth. Levi dropped his head.

"I'm sitting here because I don't know how to walk into that house filled with perfect matches. People who love each other in exactly the right way, are matched in exactly the right way, knowing that *my* match is out there. She's out there, within reach, but she knows I'll never force her. I won't disrespect the space she asked for. And as a result, I will sit here in this dark fucking room and wonder how the hell I'm supposed to do this without losing my mind."

"Shit, Hunter," Connor said. "What are you gonna do?"

"What can he do?" Levi asked. He'd raised his head, and in his eyes, I saw the man who'd loved his best friend for years. Until she was ready to love him back. "We all know that this love at first sight crap isn't easy or romantic or perfect for everyone. Connor, what happened with you and Sylvia? It wasn't like that for me. It's not like that for Hunter. He doesn't know how she feels after all this time. There's not always something to be done, at least not right away."

"Not right away," I repeated, chasing it with a dull laugh. "Twelve years, Levi. That's how long we've been apart."

Again, we lapsed into silence. They couldn't give me a clear answer, but it did help to know that they knew and could imagine how hard this was. And how it felt like a miracle just to have her in my life again.

Levi reached over when my phone screen lit up, tilting the screen toward him with a slight grin.

"Looks like you may not have to wonder what to do for much longer," he said.

My heart thudded wildly when he pushed it toward me.

Iris: I think we should talk.

Iris: Can you meet tomorrow morning?

Me: I'm free.

Me: Just tell me when and where.

Levi looked over my shoulder. "You don't sound too eager at *all*."

"Shut up, Levi."

He laughed.

"Should I have suggested somewhere specific?" I looked back and forth between my brothers.

"Somewhere with privacy," Connor said.

Levi nodded. "Good call."

Me: What about the park down the road from the elementary school?

Iris: I was thinking Donner Bakery. I'll grab one of the tables toward the back by the windows.

Iris: 10, if that works for you.

Me: I'll see you there.

"Maybe no privacy then," Levi said.

"Can you stop reading my texts?"

"What did she say?" Connor asked.

"Donner Bakery," Levi answered. "At ten o'clock," he added meaningfully.

Connor winced.

I looked back and forth between them. "What? Why is that significant?"

"It's always busy in the mornings." Levi gave me a pitying look. "She really doesn't want to be alone with you."

"I'm so very glad I decided to confide in you two."

Levi stood, slapping me on the back. "I know you are. Come on, big brother. Let's get you a beer and some meatloaf. We won't tell Mom yet because she'll start crying."

"And then Sylvia will start sympathy crying," Connor added.

I rolled my eyes.

Even though they ribbed me ruthlessly until the moment we walked into the house, I felt that thing again. Something that had been off-kilter was slowly sliding back into place.

This time, it was my family. And tomorrow, I'd have another chance with her.

For what, I wasn't sure. But even if I had to take that chance in front of the entirety of Green Valley, I would.

CHAPTER 6

IRIS

*W*hen I was fifteen, fresh under my grandma's roof, she caught me crying underneath the blankets of my bed. They were new blankets too, pretty and bright and covered with flowers that she thought I'd like.

She tugged them back where I had them covering my head and didn't say a word when I swiped at the evidence of my breakdown, angry at being caught. Not angry with my grandma. I was never, ever mad at her. She'd done nothing but take me in, give me a hug, and make me feel safe for the first time in my whole damn life.

But I still wasn't sure I was ready to tell her what had me hiding underneath that pretty blanket covered with flowers.

"You wanna tell me, or should I guess?" she asked.

I sat up in the bed and twisted my hair over one shoulder. My pitiful sniffle must've given her the answer she was after.

"It took me years to accept that my daughter would never change." She sighed. "I gave her more chances than I should have, but I think that's what we do when we love someone who struggles with something we won't ever understand."

The tears started fresh again because even at fifteen, I'd lost count of the times I'd made excuses for my mother. Lied for her because she begged me to. I'd given her chances too. Maybe just as many as my grandma had.

"It's okay to be sad that she's paying for the consequences of those struggles, Iris."

I remember turning toward her, tucking my legs up against my chest. "I'm not crying because I'm sad."

My grandma watched with those steady eyes. "All right then. Where are they coming from?"

With my pinky finger, I traced the image of one of those petals. Later that night when I tucked myself into bed and pulled the covers tight, it would brush right up against my face. "I'm happy," I whispered.

Her mouth popped open, a gentle O of surprise.

"I thought I'd be sad," I told her. "I thought I'd worry about my mom if she ever got arrested. But now that it's here..." My voice wavered. "I'm just really happy I'm here. I know I should probably feel guilty for how good it feels, but I don't. I don't *ever* want to go back with her."

In the five years I lived with my grandma, it was the only time I saw her shed a tear. She wrapped me in her arms, held me so tight, and when she pulled back, cupping the side of my face, she told me something I'd often remember as the years passed.

"Sometimes that happens, Iris. We can think all night and all day, about how it'll be when something big rolls up on us. But once it's there, no amount of thinking can prepare for how we'll feel at that moment." She smiled. "I'm happy you're here too. But then, I always knew I would be if I got the chance to have you. *That*, I was prepared for, my little flower."

Seventeen years had passed since she told me that. The truth of it hadn't faded, no matter what I'd gone through. Maybe because she said it at such an impressionable age, I'd let those words stamp somewhere under my heart.

I could think and think and think, and the big things in life could still knock the feet out from under me.

Like the appearance of one Hunter Buchanan. I'd prepared myself to lay awake all night, thinking about what it would mean and how I should feel, knowing I'd see him the next day. But his text caught me just on the edge of all that thinking, right before I could dive too deeply into it.

I couldn't prepare. That was the truth. Neither one of us could.

After only a handful of run-ins, it was so painfully obvious how little we were prepared to be around each other again.

He still wanted me. He was doing nothing to hide it.

And it was very evident that something was knotted inside my chest, something he could tug on with very little effort. But I wasn't sure I was ready to sway helplessly in his direction just yet.

All we could do was try our best not to let our past consume us and smooth out a way to coexist. Because my brother needed someone like Hunter far more than I wanted to hide from the way he looked at me.

Hide from the way he made me feel.

Which is how I found myself at the back corner table at Donner Bakery, resisting the urge to check my reflection in the small round mirror from my purse.

What I'd see in that mirror hadn't changed from the last time I looked. Thirty-two seconds earlier.

As I blew out a nervous breath, Joy approached with a small plate in one hand and a to-go cup in the other.

"Thought I'd bring it over so you didn't have to get up," she said.

I gave her a warm smile. "Thank you, Joy."

The plate held a pair of blueberry muffins, and the sight of those innocuous baked goods sitting side by side had my heart galloping at an unnaturally fast speed.

"Your hair looks beautiful today," she said. "I don't think I've ever seen it braided back like that."

My hands touched the edge of the braid where it hung over my shoulder. "Just ... had a bit too much time on my hands this morning, I guess."

"Your makeup looks real nice too," she added. "And with that white shirt, your eyes just..." She made a soft *pow* sound, complete with hand gestures and wide eyes and everything.

Was it too late to run?

I rolled my lips between my teeth and managed an awkward smile of thanks. "I always look like this in the morning," I said weakly.

Joy eyed the second muffin. "Uh-huh."

With a groan, I dropped my head into my hands. "I don't think I can do this."

"Oh, come on now. It can't be that bad." There was a soft, unsure hand patting my back. And I imagined Joy's sweet smiling face was frozen in some sort of "how the hell do I get out of this" expression. Her voice dropped to a whisper. "Is it a ... date?"

I managed a strangled whimper.

I didn't know what the hell it was or what I wanted it to be, and that was so much worse.

But before I could answer, his voice—deep and steady—cut in. "Just coffee with an old friend."

My head snapped up.

Joy's gaze bounced between us, her mouth hanging open at the sight of Hunter Buchanan.

And what a sight he was.

Not once in the three years we spent together had I ever seen the man wear a leather jacket, but he was wearing the holy hell out of one now. Underneath it was a light gray Henley stretched across his chest with muscles I'd also never seen in the three years we were together. And his jaw, still covered in that dark stubble, was tight as he looked down at me.

Joy recovered first. "Can I get you anything? A coffee?"

He gave her a polite smile. "Whatever she's having is fine. Thank you."

What *she* was having was a mental breakdown, but I didn't think he'd want one of those.

While he took his seat, I managed a slow, slightly unsteady exhale.

Grandma's words rolled through my head like a storm cloud. We can think all night, and all day, about how it'll be when something big rolls up on us. But once it's there, no amount of thinking can prepare us for how we'll feel at that moment.

There weren't enough words in the English language to describe how it felt to sit across a table from Hunter. And it was definitely nothing I was prepared for.

So I decided to go straight to the heart of it.

"You caught me mid emotional meltdown," I said. "Didn't mean for you to see that."

Hunter settled in the chair, his eyes gently roaming my face. When he was done, he made a soft humming noise. It wasn't an answer but more like a pleased sound, something happy and content.

"What did you want me to see instead?" he asked.

I took a slow sip of my coffee while I decided how to answer. Looked like there would be no simple pleasantries. But I'd expected that. Because since day one, the man had an uncanny knack for knowing exactly what was in my head. What words I wasn't saying out loud. After less than a week of circling each other, we'd already settled into that same pattern.

Joy returned with his coffee, giving me a tiny wink of encouragement when she set it in front of him.

"Anything but that," I admitted. "I didn't think much beyond looking a bit less like you just rolled out of bed this time."

His eyes warmed. "Wouldn't have bothered me."

Right. None of that.

It was the warmth in his eyes, and the immediate rattling of the box of memories that had me clearing my throat.

Hunter and beds. I had a lot of memories combining those two things.

We'd waited until I turned eighteen. Pushed every line, every invisible boundary, and every one of the bases until we were about out of our minds from waiting.

The night he slid between my legs, kissing me sweet and slow and with so much hunger I almost cried, Hunter made a sound deep in his chest that still haunted me in my dreams. Before I'd met him, I expected short, messy, and unsatisfying for the first time. And what I found instead was so much more. So much better.

After that night, there was no shortage of flat surfaces that that man hadn't mussed up my hair and clothes on.

"Hunter," I said quietly, "before last week, I hadn't seen you in twelve years. A lifetime for both of us."

He accepted my words with a nod.

"I'm sorry about your grandma," he said. His dark eyes were so earnest, so kind. "She was a hell of a woman."

"Thank you." I took a sip of my coffee and felt the sting of her loss all over again. "I'm sure we could sit here all day, talking about how our lives have changed since then. What you went through. And me too." I waited while he took a drink of his coffee and then set the cup back down. "But I don't know what purpose it would serve. Or if we can even manage to sit here and fumble our way through a recap of a dozen years."

Hunter swallowed roughly. "Not even out of friendly curiosity? You have a brother who didn't even exist when I left. That's a pretty big life update to skip over."

The thought of Theo brought the first real smile to my face. "He was a gift I didn't expect."

"Your mom is..."

He knew so little. I'd told him so little. Out of embarrassment. Insecurity and shame, rooted deep in who I was. A laundry list of reasons, all of them contributing to the end of our young relationship, the one where he'd promised to love me for the rest of his life. And I pushed him away because I couldn't bear the thought of him shouldering any of it. Of her.

"My mom is out of the picture," I said. "Has been for the past four years."

Understanding filled his expression. "When you got Theo."

I nodded. "I didn't even know about him until he was two."

Hunter studied my face, weighing the truth of my answer, and thankfully, he decided not to ask anything further.

"He loves you."

I laughed. "The feeling is very mutual. I'd do anything for him."

Hunter held my gaze. "Even have coffee with your ex."

My cheeks went warm. "Even that."

That had him looking away with a pained look in his eye.

"Theo needs someone like you," I told him. "I'm a single parent, working myself to the bone to provide for the two of us. Programs like this will help make sure his education doesn't suffer, simply because I'm burning the candle at both ends. So yes, I'm willing to meet you for coffee to figure out how we can do this in a way where neither of us gets hurt. Where Theo doesn't get hurt either. Because no matter how hard it might be for me to sit here, for you too, I'm guessing..." My voice broke. "I will do it because my brother needs me to."

Hunter studied me.

He always gave me that look, deep and searching, when he was fascinated by something I said or did. The silence stretched out long and slow, warming underneath that gaze of his. I wondered if it would always be like this when he and I were together. Loaded with subtext. Heavy with an unspoken longing.

When he spoke, his voice was rough.

"What do you need from me?" The words came up slowly like it pained him to say them out loud.

I swallowed the lump in my throat, blowing out a slow breath of relief. "Can we ... I don't know ... be friendly?"

Hunter swallowed too. "Friendly," he repeated.

"Friends," I amended.

"I've never been just friends with you." He shook his head. "Not even at the beginning."

"I know," I said quietly. "I know what I'm asking."

It was a big ask, too. But if the last week proved anything, it was that we had a tendency to circle each other unconsciously. He was in my orbit now, and I was in his. It was that thought that had me remembering that stupid book he loved. And why he found me in that library in the first place, caught red-handed as I strolled down memory lane.

Thinking about signs and omens about the things we were meant for.

I hated the idea as a teenager, that someone could simplify finding happiness that way. If it had been so easy to make your dreams come true, I would've been able to wish myself away from Nellie Black, and that sure as hell hadn't happened. I knew why Hunter found that book so appealing. But he'd always been the optimist in our relationship, coming from a good family of good people who loved him unconditionally.

"But it's what you want?"

What did I want? I could conjure a mile-long list of all the things that fit under that category. Financial security for Theo and me. A successful business would allow us some much-needed stability to carve out a future in a place that was slowly feeling like home. I wanted a family of my own—someday. And I wanted to bottle the way Hunter Buchanan made me feel because after so long of *not* having it, these tiny pockets of time with such big, big feelings were rare and precious. Something I wanted to clutch to my chest to keep it safe.

But I couldn't admit any of that to him. It was too soon. And I had too much to untangle before things like that could be said.

"I have a thousand balls up in the air, Hunter. I can hardly count all the things I'm trying to juggle. I can't handle any extra pressure on what I'm feeling or not feeling."

Briefly, he looked away, his jaw clenching while he thought. "And you think I'll pressure you?"

It was the easiest question to answer. I thought of all the days and nights we spent together. The way he explained the permanency of his feelings. The way he respected the more natural progression of mine.

And because I couldn't help it, I thought of the way he walked away. Simply because I asked him to.

"No, I don't," I said. When his gaze returned to me, I didn't blink. I didn't look away even though my cheeks went hot, my heart weightless at what I saw in his eyes. "But I can't ignore the way you're looking at me right now either."

At my softly spoken admission, his eyes went molten hot, searing in their intensity. His brow furrowed like he was trying to pull all that emotion out of his gaze.

Trying. And failing.

"I don't know how not to," he admitted. Hunter set his elbows on the table, resting his head in his hands for a moment. With his attention pulled down toward the table, he said, "I don't know how to look at you any other way, Iris."

My heart had barely survived him the first time around. His love, so intense and deep and real, was a dream to someone like me who'd experienced so little of it. For a while, I thought it was because of how young we were. That with age, our love would've mellowed into something more normal.

But I knew, sitting there, that it wasn't true. It wasn't our youth or our inexperience.

We didn't know how to be anything else with each other.

Intense and real and deep. It was all of those things. Might still be.

And lying about it, even now, didn't help. Because even if he wasn't pointing it out, I felt that I was looking at him similarly. With my heart pouring out of my eyes because there were too damn many things we weren't ready to say out loud yet. And an ocean of complications that kept us from acting on it.

"But for you," he said, lifting his head, "I will try."

My eyes fluttered shut, relief and a desperate urge to run battling mightily in my chest.

"Thank you."

He let out a slow breath. His eyes cleared of some of that intensity. "You're welcome."

Gently, I nudged the plate in his direction. "Blueberry muffin?"

Hunter gave me that small secret smile, the one that was crooked and imperfect and slid right into my aching heart. "I'd love one."

CHAPTER 7

IRIS

*M*axine Barton—my grandma's best friend, and the only family we had left in Green Valley—was very much like a barnacle stuck to the hull of a ship. Adds character, doesn't seem too bothersome in theory, but won't do anything it doesn't want to do, and God help anyone who tries to remove it.

When I walked into her house, she and Theo were in the kitchen, and she was bossing him around in a way he pretended to hate.

"Theo, don't think I don't see what you're doing."

He groaned. "I'm stirring it like you did!"

"You keep mixing it that much, and it'll crumble all over high heaven, and not much makes me crankier than crumbly cornbread."

I leaned my shoulder on the doorframe and watched the two of them where they stood with their backs to me in the kitchen. When Grandma died, Maxine told me, with her characteristic stubbornness, that we were her family now, and that was that. We didn't have a choice in the matter, which was fine with me because even if she was the grumpiest, feistiest octogenarian on this side of the Mississippi, she was ours. And I wouldn't trade her for anything.

On the days she watched Theo in the summer, Maxine had started working through all of my grandma's best recipes. Because Theo didn't have nearly as many years with her, Maxine was determined to keep some of those good family traditions alive.

Apparently, today was Grandma's Southwest Cornbread.

Theo set the wooden spoon down and made a gagging sound when she told him to open the jar of pimento strips.

Maxine clucked her tongue. "Oh, hush. Pimento is a gift from God Himself."

"It looks nasty."

From where she was sitting in her walker, Maxine saw me out of the corner of her eye. She winked. "Your grandma used to eat that by itself every morning. Said it kept her legs strong."

My brother sniffed at the pimento and lost a little color from his face. "Seriously?"

Maxine nodded, eyes wide and guileless. That should've been Theo's first clue. If Maxine Barton said anything looking like a perfect angel, it was the surest sign that she was full of shit.

"Don't you listen to her," I said, pushing off the wall and joining them. I squeezed Theo's shoulder and gave Maxine a chiding look. "Grandma only ate pimento in this cornbread, and you know it."

Theo pushed the jar away. "Gross."

"How was your ... meeting?" Maxine asked.

At her tone, I gave her another look. Theo had no clue what my first appointment had actually entailed. And if it were up to me, it would stay that way. The last thing I needed was him putting some "are you my new dad" fantasies onto Hunter's shoulder.

I narrowed my eyes meaningfully. "Fine."

She sat back in her walker with a shit-eating grin on her face. "Just *fine*?"

Theo looked up from the pimentos. "I heard Hunter got blueberry muffins too. Just like you!"

My mouth popped open. "How did you—?"

"Maxine's neighbor, the old one who always tells us who she saw in town, stopped over when we were sitting on the front porch."

"The old one," Maxine muttered. "She's two years younger than me."

Theo laughed, and I pressed a hand against the sudden pressure that was dead center on my chest.

Once. I sat with him *once,* and the town's busybodies started paying attention.

I took a seat at the small, worn table in her kitchen. "Raelynn was feeling chatty today, was she?" I asked.

Maxine eyed me over the rims of her glasses. "She was. Theo was good enough to let her know why you were meeting with him, though."

"Did he?"

Theo nodded. "I told her Mr. B is my tutor or whatever, and you're just doing your parental involvement so I don't flunk out."

"You're not going to flunk out."

"I might," he said seriously. "I skipped a lot of tests."

I gave him a tight smile. "I remember."

The conversation paused while Maxine showed him how to spray the bread loaf tin, and then he carefully held the mixing bowl tucked against his body while scooping the cornbread dough into the form. While she gently corrected his technique, I ran a hand over my face and tried to dissect body language or accidental touching or anything gossip-worthy while we'd sat at the back table.

I'd picked that table because it was the one that would afford us a modicum of privacy but still be public enough that I hadn't worried about big emotional outbursts or, like, fearing I'd do something really stupid like stick my tongue down his throat because he looked so handsome. And because he stared at me the way he did. And because I'd been just a little bit lonely for the past few years.

But no matter how I viewed our interaction at the bakery, I couldn't come up with anything that warranted juicy storytelling. Then again, that was a small town for you. Anything out of the ordinary was exciting, and even the boring stories got spread around like they were front-page news.

The juiciest part was the fact that it was Hunter, and he was home. Not just home but had an empty ring finger and looked like sex on legs.

While they shuttled the bread tin into the oven, I let my forehead rest in my hands and heard Maxine suggest that Theo go play basketball across the street. Once the screen door slammed shut, I lifted my head.

"What did she say?"

Maxine waved that away. "That old busybody needs a hobby. She came strutting up my driveway, or as much as she can strut with those ugly white shoes she always wears." Her steel-gray eyes met mine. "I'm more concerned with what *you* have to say. How did it go?"

I sank back into the chair. "I told him the truth. I don't have room in my life for anything beyond friendship."

Maxine scoffed.

"You sound like that cat that comes around every night. The one you pretend to hate."

"I do hate it. If I don't leave that food out, it makes a horrible racket."

"The fancy expensive cat food you order online?"

She gave me a look. "Nobody's gonna accuse me of animal abuse by feeding it that dried-out crap they sell at the Piggly Wiggly. If I had to guess, those bags expired about three years ago."

"Mmkay."

"And don't change the subject, Iris Black. I'm not the only one pretending here."

"What am I pretending about?" My hands lifted in a helpless gesture. "I'm trying to start a business from the ground up. Every penny of my savings is tied up in this. I have custody of my little brother because my mom is a selfish piece of shit who will get out of jail sometime in the next year and probably try to manipulate her way back into our lives." I shook my head. "And that's the best-case scenario. Worst case is she tries to take him back. Where, pray tell, do I have room in my day-to-day life to pick back up with any man?"

Maxine's eyes filled with pity and resolve.

I hated both reactions for very different reasons. Anyone's pity made me want to hiss and scratch like that orange cat she bought food for. There was nothing about the life I'd built that was worth pity. I had a home—the one my grandma had left me when she died. I had a dream that was slowly becoming a reality. And I had more than one person who loved and supported me.

My life, by any worthwhile definition, was overflowing with riches.

And the resolve, I hated for an entirely different reason.

"All your complications are real enough," she conceded. "And what a hardship it must be, to have someone like Hunter wanting back into your life."

"Don't patronize me," I told her.

"I'm not." She set her soft, wrinkly hands on the handles of her walker. "He's a whole bundle of complications in his own right. I know enough about your history with him, so there's no point in arguing that."

When she paused, I gestured for her to continue. "Get it all out while I'm listening."

She stood from her walker and joined me at the table. Her hand settled on top of mine. "There's no life in the world that doesn't have enough space for someone who truly loves you. Because that's the thing about Hunter," she said. "His presence wouldn't make things harder. It would make everything better. Maybe not easier. But you'd have another set of shoulders to carry the load."

My nose tingled, and I didn't want it to. I didn't want to hear all her solid reasons for why I was simply running scared from what he made me feel. The bigness of it.

"It's not that easy," I whispered.

"Nothing ever is, little flower."

She rarely used my grandma's nickname for me, and it almost made me lose my tenuous grip on my emotions. "He was everything to me, Maxine."

Her face gentled, something it didn't do often. "I know."

"I can't ... I can't go down that road again unless I know..." My voice trailed off.

"Know what?" Her fingers tightened over mine. "Because it sounds to me like you know an awful lot already."

Her gentle poking at my emotions had me up and out of my chair. "I've hardly seen him, Maxine. It's been twelve years. He was married, and now he's not, and there's no way I can know *anything* with certainty."

I was breathing hard. My hands were trembling.

It sounded crazy. Probably because the way we'd felt about each other had always seemed too intense to be real. To last.

But no matter how much I wanted to deny it, Hunter Buchanan was under my skin, and nothing I did had ever dislodged his grip on my heart. I'd hoped that distance would do it.

It didn't.

And then when I heard he married, my heartbreak—anger at myself and him— hadn't done it either.

But as each month rolled over and another year ticked away, the passage of time allowed me to ignore it. I hadn't boxed Hunter in the back of my mind intention- ally, but after a few years, all my memories of him got tucked away out of some sense of self-preservation.

It was a good thing he couldn't read my mind. Because if he knew just how easily he'd be able to consume my life and my head and my heart, I had a feeling that he'd be relentless in his pursuit of me.

Maxine must have seen just how close I was to an epic sort of meltdown. She went for the pitcher of tea sitting next to her, reaching over to the cupboard next to the table and pulling out one of her sea-green drinking glasses. Wordlessly, she poured me a healthy serving and patted the table's surface.

"Come on now," she said quietly. "Take a few deep breaths and have some tea. You'll feel better."

I did as she asked, and after a few sips and a few lungsful of air, I did feel calmer.

"Just promise me something," Maxine continued. "I know you're waiting for that space to open for your store, and that means you've got a little bit of room on your plate."

Any argument I might have made died a quick death when I saw the look in her eye. Maxine Barton, who kept her soft mushy heart locked up tight behind all her attitude, damn near looked like she was about to cry.

"I do have a little room," I agreed. "For now."

"Don't push him away." She clasped my hand. "Your grandma made me promise I wouldn't let you get lonely and cranky like me."

I laughed through my blossoming tears.

"You don't have to jump in headfirst, honey. But don't lock him out either."

"I asked him if we could be friends. That's a start, isn't it?"

Maxine studied me, eyes thoughtful. "Do you think you can be?"

"I don't know," I admitted. "We should be able to, right? It's not like we don't have things in common."

"Yeah," Maxine drawled. "I remember catching you two in all the ways you found common ground. He might be the most attractive man to walk the planet, but I don't ever need to see his pants around his knees while you two go at it against that tree in the backyard. I was scarred for life, young lady."

I groaned, covering my face. "Maxine."

She laughed. "Is that not helping?"

Dropping my hand, I pinned her with a glare. "What do you think?"

Her face smoothed out, the smile fading away. "You loved each other an awful lot to try to be *friends* after all this time."

"What else can I do?" I shrugged. "I can hardly ask him if he still loves me. If all those feelings are still there for him like they were before."

"Why not?"

I gaped at her. "Because it's been twelve years. I hardly know what I feel about seeing him again, let alone what I want to do about it."

"If you say so," she muttered quietly.

"I'm not eighteen anymore." I gestured weakly toward the sound of Theo dribbling a basketball, shouting out the imaginary score of whatever game he was playing. "It's not just me that I have to think about. I have to be smart about all this, no matter how he spins my head around."

Maxine conceded that with a nod.

Blowing out a slow breath, I thought about what she was asking me. If I really believed we could be friends. How it might look different than what Hunter and I talked about. About whether that was what I wanted.

Could. Should.

Wants and needs.

Those spun around in my head too.

And as I cataloged the differences between them, my phone started ringing.

I tugged it out of my purse, where I'd set it on the floor, and my heart made an excited roll.

"It's that real estate agent," I whispered. I punched the screen to answer. "Hello?"

"Iris, hope you're doing well."

I gave Maxine a hopeful look. "That probably depends on what you're about to tell me, Marie."

"That corner spot by the Bait and Tackle?"

My breath caught in my throat. "Yeah?"

"Lease will be open again next week."

"Next week?" I said on a rushed exhale.

She hummed excitedly. "They're moving to a larger space, and the one they wanted just came open. We negotiated a mid-month move because I told them I had a very eager future tenant for the space."

"Marie, I could kiss you right now."

She laughed. "Just thank me by getting all your ducks in a row at the bank."

I'd been waiting—to the point of insanity—for that particular space to open downtown. The location was perfect. More parking. Next to a staple business in town which would provide exactly the kind of foot traffic I was hoping for. Because it was on a corner, it had double the number of windows as a normal retail location, and with the second-level apartments and the houses just down the street, I could finally, finally imagine the way all my planning would come to life.

"I'll go tomorrow," I promised.

"It'll need work."

I nodded. "I know. I'm ready for it."

All the extra shifts and counting each dollar we spent on groceries, refusing to make any updates to Grandma's house because I knew my savings were better spent on starting my business, it came down to this. And in my nest egg, I had exactly thirty thousand dollars to transform the corner spot of my dreams.

My mind raced with all the things I had to do before going to the bank to finalize my small business loan. On the other end of the phone, Marie told me she'd email me all the lease information for the space. I'd need it for the loan application.

When I hung up, Maxine was smiling. "Sounds like you got your store, little flower."

I laughed breathlessly. "I think ... I think I did."

She squeezed my hand again, and as she did, I realized what that phone call meant. The breathing room in my life had all but disappeared.

"I won't lock anything out," I promised her.

"There are worse things in life, you know," she said.

I sighed because there was no point in asking her to elaborate.

"He's smart. Funny when he wants to be. Loves you more than that old bat next door loves to gossip. Handsome as the devil."

I smiled. "You don't have to sell me on him, Maxine."

"And," she continued, "he looks like he could break that sturdy old headboard in half without a whole lot of effort."

With an embarrassed groan, I dropped my head onto the table. "I beg you, stop."

Her eyes were shrewd when I raised my head. She knew, as well as I did, that even if I'd promised to give him a chance, I just added one more giant complication onto any possible future with Hunter. Green Valley was no longer a resting place while we made plans.

I wasn't going anywhere. But I wasn't entirely sure that Hunter could say the same thing.

CHAPTER 8

HUNTER

"*A*re you sure we're allowed to do this?"

I hid my grin, passing the basketball to Theo. He dribbled, attempting to send the ball between his legs, but he wasn't quite tall enough and only managed to trip over the ball. His cheeks went a little pink, but I didn't comment on the slipup. We'd done good work already, sitting at one of the picnic tables by the playground and working through some math worksheets.

I shrugged, snagging another ball from the rack we'd pushed outside. "No one told me we had to sit at a desk all day."

Eyeing me for a second, he pushed the ball up into the air with a grunt, smiling when it bounced off the rim and rolled through the net.

"You're not like most teachers I know. They're usually full of rules."

Setting the ball on my hip, I watched him move around the court. "I like rules, but I think methods should be flexible, and I'd rather figure out what way you like to learn best. If someone sitting in an office in there has a problem with it, they'll let me know."

He considered that, attempting another shot. "Kinda like ... it's better to beg forgiveness than to ask for permission."

"Exactly." I stood at the free throw line and tossed a ball in, glad I wore a T-shirt as the sun beat down on us. "That's a good correlation."

I set my ball down and motioned for him to try to make a shot. It wasn't really a fair matchup. I'd hit my full height of six-three by my sophomore year of high school, and even though Theo was tall for his age, I still had a pretty distinct advantage.

Just as I had the thought, he pivoted around me, moving a hell of a lot faster than my mid-thirties body would allow. The ball banked off the backboard and dropped through, pulling a victorious whoop from Theo.

"Speaking of methods," I said, "how'd you work through those last couple of math problems?"

He shrugged. "My brain just knows it."

"That's impressive." I caught the ball when he tossed it to me, dribbling a few times between my hands. "Still have to be able to show your work."

Theo rolled his eyes. "You sound like my last teacher."

"If you know the answer, why not at least put that down? You'd get partial credit, instead of nothing, which is what you get when you submit a blank test."

I passed the ball back, and he dribbled with a bit more ferocity, taking a shot that whiffed through the air, straight past the net.

"Because that's stupid. If I know the answer, why do I only get full credit if I show them eighteen different ways to get there? It's a waste of time."

"You know what else is a waste of time?"

He glanced over.

"Repeating a grade when you know all the things you're supposed to know in order to move on." I tapped his forehead. "It's all right there. You just need to slow down and think through the steps."

Theo dribbled more slowly.

He wasn't the first kid I'd met who struggled with this part of school. It wasn't just about having the knowledge—it was teaching them how to deconstruct the pieces already there. And with Theo, I had a feeling that this small rebellion was rooted elsewhere. We'd spent half the day together, and so far, I'd resisted the urge to ask about his situation with Iris. Or even ask about Iris in general.

Did she still have a stack of books next to her bed?

Did she still lay awake when it stormed?

But I kept all those questions locked tight because the absolute last thing I wanted to do was make Theo feel like he was simply a pawn in my desire to get to know her again. He was so much more important than that, and even the small glimpses of honesty he was giving me, I already knew him to be a smart and thoughtful kid.

It was no wonder Iris was willing to rearrange her life for him. When we were together, our age kept us from thinking too seriously about things like kids or the size of the family we might want someday. But I'd always known Iris would make the very best kind of mother. She didn't love easily or indiscriminately, but she'd walk through fire to protect the people who found a spot in her heart.

For a while, I'd been one of those people.

But a lack of love had never been our problem. It was believing in it. A trust that it was real, that it could last.

Something about my certainty terrified her. Maybe if I'd had even the smallest shred of doubt, if I verbalized that it was hard for me to believe too, she wouldn't have pushed me away the way she did.

Maybe. But I couldn't be sure of that either.

As Theo and I shot around and talked through math problems, I realized just how much he was like his sister. And I couldn't help but wonder if Iris saw the similarities.

"What are we working on next time?" he asked.

I took another shot, accepting his high five when it sliced through the net. "Reading comprehension."

"Ugh."

"Nothing to groan about," I said. "Just two guys talking about the stuff they read over the weekend. I put a couple of books I want you to try in your backpack."

He perked up. "Are they the comic books ones?"

I shook my head. "Nope. If you want to read those after you're done with the chapter book, knock yourself out."

Before he could argue, Iris's vehicle pulled into the parking lot a few minutes before the end of the tutoring session. My heart took off, something I wasn't even attempting to control anymore. Her eyes were hidden behind large aviator shades, and it made her look like she did when we were nineteen and twenty. All that dark hair was swept off her face, and when she exited the car, I could see that she'd anchored it in some sort of complicated-looking knot at the base of her skull.

My eyebrows popped up when she closed the car door because this was Boss Iris, a look I'd never seen on her. Her long, long legs were encased in snug-fitting dark pants, and a matching slim-cut blazer was buttoned over a pale-yellow shirt. On her feet were spiked heels, and everything about her walking toward us was confident and powerful.

I tried—very hard—not to gawk.

Every new side of her felt like a vital piece of information, something I needed to keep tucked safely away for future reference.

"Why are you wearing *that*?" Theo asked.

Iris laughed, and her smile made my ribs squeeze tight.

I elbowed Theo. "You're supposed to tell her she looks beautiful."

He wrinkled his nose. "She's my sister."

Iris carefully removed her sunglasses, and her gaze on mine felt like a hot touch down my spine.

Friendly, I reminded myself. Be friendly.

"Then you can tell her she looks nice," I said. "Even sisters need compliments."

He sighed. "You look nice, Iris."

"Thank you."

"But ... why *are* you wearing that? You don't even dress up when Maxine makes us go to church."

She tucked the sunglasses into a small leather purse hanging over her shoulder. "I had that appointment at the bank, remember?"

"Ohhh yeah. Did they give you your money?"

I watched her carefully, wishing I could ask ... everything.

Her answering smile was slow and so happy that it was impossible not to smile along with her. "They did," she said.

He whooped, running to her, throwing his arms around her waist.

When she returned his embrace, her eyes closed as she pressed a kiss to the top of his head. Another side. Another piece to cherish.

Theo, arms still around his sister, gave me an excited grin. "Iris is opening a store, and now she can buy the space."

My head went back. "Seriously?"

She nodded, cheeks pink. "Yeah, just by the Bait and Tackle."

"What kind of store?"

Bored with the topic change, Theo sprinted back to his ball and began practicing his layups.

Iris took a few steps closer. "Sort of a jumble, I guess. I've been reaching out to local vendors for the last six months or so. Lotions, lip balms, face creams. Small home décor items, like signs and baskets and artwork." She ticked off more items on her hands. "Scarves from a woman in Merryville. Earrings and bracelets from a guy who lives just outside of town. And just a couple of weeks ago, I signed a contract with Lavender Hills Farm. She has teas, honey, dried lavender, and other stuff."

Talking about it, she was glowing. Was it too much to ask that I could just ... sit and stare at her all day?

It probably was, because she averted her eyes for a moment, and I had to wonder if I was looking at her in that way she mentioned. But it was impossible to keep my heart out of the equation, even if I'd never go against my promise not to pressure her. Seeing her, a woman with a plan and a vision, felt like a full circle moment. Because I'd known her as a teenager, on the cusp of adulthood, without any idea what she wanted to do. I'd always been the one with the plans. Teaching was the seed planted in me long before I met Iris. And it was one more thing that always made her feel ... behind me, in some way.

My voice was a little rough when I spoke. "And you have a location now?"

She nodded. "There were a couple of empty storefronts downtown, but ... this was the one I've always wanted. Corner lot. Better parking. Tons of windows."

"One of the thousands of things you're juggling," I said. It made a lot more sense now, and I hated how much I understood.

Iris exhaled a soft laugh. "Yeah."

"I can't even imagine how hard it's been to get this started."

Theo interjected. "She works all the time."

"Not all the time," Iris said. "But I have been doing as much work as possible so I wasn't starting from scratch once I got the location."

"You should show him the counter you're building!" Theo dribbled past us. "It's so cool."

She gave him a look. "I'm sure he doesn't care to see it. Plus, we have to go soon."

"You're building it? Don't remember you using many power tools."

"I've learned a few things over the past twelve years," she said, eyebrows arched slightly.

The gentle jab at how long I'd been gone hit where she'd intended, directly in the center of my chest. "I have no doubt," I said quietly.

Iris squinted off beyond the playground for a moment, and in the gesture, I saw her regret. She'd never been able to hide her emotions, at least not from me. But there was nothing for her to regret.

"When do you sign the lease?" I asked.

She shrugged off her jacket, tucking it over her arm, and my eyes traced the delicate line of her collarbone where it stretched underneath the buttery yellow of her tank top. The delicate silver chain of her grandma's necklace was nestled against her chest, the emerald tucked safely underneath the shirt's neckline. There was no fidgeting today.

"Early next week," she answered.

Before I could ask another question, Theo passed me the basketball. "Can I play for just a few more minutes? Mr. B promised we could play a game of PIG when we finished our work."

"Did he?" She slid me a sideways glance.

I held up my hands. "I'm a man of my word."

My answer had her face going serious, maybe just a little sad. "I know you are," she said. As my mouth opened to reply, she blinked, turning her attention to her brother. "One game."

He whooped.

Iris interrupted. "On one condition."

Theo and I traded a look when she kicked off her heels. My smile started somewhere deep in my chest long before it ever touched my face.

"We can play with three people, right?" she asked, setting her jacket on top of the discarded shoes.

I passed her the ball, laughing softly when she spun it in her hand. "It's been a while since we've played," I murmured, risking a step closer.

Her chest rose and fell on a sharp inhale. It was all these different sides to Iris that had endlessly fascinated me. What did she hear in my voice?

Hope? Because that was there.

So was desire.

They both scared her, no doubt, but she didn't back away. And she wouldn't, because even if we were still dancing around the truth of our relationship, Iris was one of the bravest people I'd ever met.

"You two used to play basketball?" Theo asked, skepticism heavy in his tone.

She sent her brother a close-lipped smile. "A time or two."

"Every night," I corrected. "Or just about."

It was the closest hint I'd dropped about our past relationship in front of Theo, and his gaze darted between us, trying to puzzle something together. But he didn't comment on it.

Other kids arrived at the playground, running past us with shrieks of delight as their tutoring finished for the day. Theo sent a longing look at a few kids who were yelling his name.

"Ten minutes, and we have to go," Iris said to her brother. "But if you want to play with them instead, you may."

Our game forgotten, Theo tore off toward his friends, and Iris laughed when he tackled one of the boys with a violently happy greeting reserved for the very young.

"He's so smart," I said. "Knows just about everything I throw at him."

She glanced toward me, basketball still in hand.

"Does he challenge you at home?" I asked.

Her answer was immediate. "No. He's just ... a great kid, you know? He minds well. Only argues when I make him go to bed," she said with a smile. "He's not disobedient or reckless."

I hummed. Theo was his own little puzzle, and the educator in me couldn't resist trying to fit the pieces together.

"Should I be worried about him?" she asked. "More than I already am."

"I don't think so." I held my hand out for the ball, and she tossed it to me. I dribbled a few times, tossing it up to the basket. Iris caught the rebound and stepped back, feet bare against the asphalt, and sank an easy basket. "The issue isn't what he knows. It's why he's acting out at school and nowhere else."

Iris passed me the ball, but I propped it on my hip, tugging up at the front of my shirt to wipe at the sweat on my face. Her eyes locked onto my stomach and darted away.

Friendly, I reminded myself.

Friends occasionally studied their friend's collarbone. How they looked wearing tight black pants. And the way the light hit their hazel eyes. Just like others would study their friend's abs when their shirt hem lifted a touch too high.

I cleared my throat, and she blew out a slow breath. "What did his teachers say?" I asked.

She made an exasperated sound. "They always said the same thing. He's polite and respectful, until he's not. He's smart, until he refuses to answer questions. And I don't blame them for hitting a wall. They've got dozens of other students who need help. But he just ... he's so stubborn, and he won't tell me why he's doing it."

"He probably doesn't know." I dribbled the ball. "Or can't verbalize it."

"Miss Tracy said something like that."

"Emotional regulation is difficult at this age," I told her. "And if Theo is feeling stress or anxiety from some part of his life, he'll exert control where he can find it. Unfortunately for teachers and parents, that usually comes in the form of outbursts. Acting out. And turning in those blank tests, it's an attempt at control." I turned my focus to the boy in question. "It's up to the people in his life to figure out why he's pushing this particular button. Then we can give him the tools to manage it."

I wasn't sure if Iris heard her own background mirrored in what I was saying about Theo. But as the words came out, I thought again how similar they were. I knew her mom struggled with mental health issues. Her incarceration was the reason that Iris was living with her grandma in Green Valley. And I was the button she'd pushed when the rest of her life spun out of control. Not that she'd shared much with me. Bringing up her mom was the quickest way to ensure that Iris locked down all her emotions.

The good and the bad.

It was what she'd had to do to survive.

Iris blew out an unsteady breath, glancing at the watch strapped around her wrist. "I should go. I've got ... a never-ending list, it seems."

"Right." I set the basketball down, tucked my hands into my pockets and faced her. "I'm around during the week."

Her eyebrows rose slowly.

I held her gaze. "If you want to talk about Theo. Or need help with anything."

My attempt at stealth sucked because she gave me a tiny smile. "I've got your number."

Nice try, Hunter.

"Congratulations on the store," I said. "It's amazing."

She smiled so wide and so happy, my heart ached. "I can't believe it. Iris Black ... Green Valley business owner."

It would've been so easy to stand there all afternoon and ask her questions to ease into this friendly new space. It was something we'd never, ever done. Be friends.

"I can see it." I took a deep breath. "Maybe you can hire me to restock your shelves when the school fires me for letting my students play basketball all afternoon."

She laughed. "I don't think I could afford you, Hunter."

Maybe she couldn't, but I just might work for free if my only payment was hearing her say my name every day.

Iris was putting down roots, probably for the first time in her life. And I'd just torn mine up, unsure of what came next. It was a strange reversal of fortune from where we'd been as teenagers.

I wasn't sure what it meant for us now. If there was even the possibility of an *us* to consider.

CHAPTER 9

HUNTER

I didn't notice at first. Not when I put the creamer in my cart or the coffee that I preferred. It was somewhere around the produce section that I felt the eyes on my back.

When I turned, overly ripe bunch of bananas in hand, no one was staring.

But when I made a circle around the bags of apples, I heard my name whispered by two women standing in front of the deli counter.

Then I heard "divorce."

Followed up with something about muffins at Donner Bakery.

There was a lot about Green Valley that I missed in my time living in the Pacific Northwest. This was not one of them. It didn't matter where I went in Seattle. No one commented about my comings and goings. Or my pastry preferences.

I settled my gaze on the two women. "Can I help you clear anything up?" I asked.

They snapped to attention, shifting their focus to the spiral cut ham in front of them. One sniffed haughtily, glaring as I started pushing my cart again.

A voice came from behind me. "You know they'll just start telling everyone at their knitting circle that you're a giant horse's ass, right?"

I turned. Maxine Barton, someone I hadn't seen in at least five years, was studying the ears of sweet corn.

"I don't think I'll lose any sleep over that, Miss Barton."

Her steely eyes met mine. "No, I didn't think you would, Mr. Buchanan." She jerked her chin in their direction. "The one with the snooty-looking face is my next-door neighbor, and I'm pretty sure I knew about your *blueberry muffins* before you'd finished the last crumb."

"I sure didn't miss this," I told her.

"You missed a few other things, though."

At her loaded tone, one of my eyebrows arched slowly. "You trying to make a point? I thought you were supposed to start with polite small talk when you hadn't seen someone in years."

She waved that away. "Polite small talk is a euphemism for horseshit if you ask me. If I want to know how someone's doing and get an honest answer, I'd listen to all the gossiping. I certainly wouldn't ask you to your face."

I laughed. "No?"

"Nah. Because you know what you'll say? You'll say, 'Oh, I'm good. Family's fine. Glad to be back, etcetera etcetera.'"

Leaning my hip against the sweet corn bin, I studied her openly. "You know people answer that way because it's expected. We don't ask how someone is doing because we want the naked honesty. You ask to be polite."

"A waste of time," she said. "I might very well be dead soon, and if I am, you won't remember me fondly because I'm polite."

"That is true." I crossed my arms over my chest. "At this point, I'll remember you for calling me a horse's ass by the sweet corn, and that's much, much better."

"Don't you put words in my mouth, young man. You're handsome enough that I'd let you get away with it, and then I'll tarnish my reputation as a crotchety old woman who doesn't like anyone."

I smiled. "It's good to see you, Miss Barton."

She eyed me over her glasses. "I'm not going to waste any more time because while I understand why you'd want to spend your morning talking to me, I don't much feel like beating around the bush."

"I should've had more coffee before this grocery store adventure," I muttered under my breath.

Maxine ignored me. "If you leave the Piggly Wiggly and head over to the hardware store, you just might catch Iris while she's shopping for paint for her new store."

I narrowed my eyes. "Are you doing some secret meddling, Miss Barton?"

"Nothing secret about it. I'm standing here telling you where she is, what she's doing, and if I'm correct, her ex-boyfriend is helping her out."

Her ... I couldn't even *think* the word. My chest felt tight, and I pressed a fist to my sternum while I blew out a breath. Honestly, Maxine Barton made my head spin just a little bit.

"I ... what?"

"Don't play dumb, young man. I know you were valedictorian and made dean's list and all that." She picked up a couple of ears of corn and tossed them in a bag in the main basket of her cart. "Iris can't make heads or tails of you being back, and I damn well know that you still think the sun rises and sets with her."

I blinked. Then blinked again.

"You're trying to help me get her back?" I asked, just to be perfectly clear.

"I'm not trying to help *you* do diddly squat, Buchanan." She pinned me with a level stare. "Iris is the closest thing I've ever had to a daughter. When her grandma died, I promised my best friend that I'd look out for her. And looking out for her means sometimes she needs to be reminded of the things that will make her life better, even if they seem tied up in too complicated of a knot to untangle."

I swiped a hand over my mouth and studied her.

It was the perfect description for Iris and me. And everything Maxine was saying were things I'd already guessed to be true. We'd always jumped straight into the deep end. We bypassed all the niceties and polite beginnings Maxine mentioned as a waste of time.

"She asked for space," I heard myself say. "To be friends."

"I know what she asked for."

"Yet here you are."

She eyed me. "Friendship holds a lot of different meanings, young man. I don't think I need to tell you that."

"You don't. But friendship with an ex usually has a pretty slim definition."

"Pfft. My ex-husband and I were friendly for years until he died. We got along just fine in the bedroom, and that's about all that mattered to either of us once those divorce papers were signed."

I pinched the bridge of my nose. "I wish I didn't know that."

Maxine started pushing her cart away, stopping to slap a hand against my chest. "I don't know how they did things up in Seattle, but the friends *I* know would have no problem helping me pick out some paint colors."

———

Staring at the doors of the Eager Beaver Hardware Store, I couldn't bring myself to push them open.

Without overthinking it too much, I pulled out my phone and hit the number for my parents' house. Mom picked up on the second ring.

"I know you don't miss me so much that you're calling me from a trip to the Piggly Wiggly."

"Do you need anything from the hardware store?" I asked.

On the other end of the phone, my mom went quiet. "Umm, not that I can think of?"

Scratching the side of my jaw, I was reminded of how badly I needed to shave. "Not even a box of light bulbs or batteries or anything?"

My mom sighed. "Hunter ... I've got a very good book waiting for me and about an hour before your father comes home and will undoubtedly interrupt me. If you need a reason to go in there, just buy me whatever you'd like."

She hung up on me.

With a shake of my head, I tucked the phone away and strode through the door. Given it was a Saturday, the store was busy, and absently, I snagged a small basket. My eyes scanned the rows as I wandered, but I didn't see her long dark hair anywhere. A young couple stood in front of the paint chips, discussing which yellow was "butter-ier," and I blew out a hard breath.

"Idiot," I muttered.

Knowing Maxine, she probably sent me over to see if I'd react like Pavlov's dogs with the ringing of that stupid bell. It was the idea of Iris, a trigger embedded deeply, that I'd had a reaction before I even recognized how illogical it was.

That's when I saw her. She'd been crouching down, studying something at the bottom of the aisle, and when she straightened, her hair fell in a soft sweep over her shoulder.

No power suits today, but this might be even better because it was the Iris I'd fallen in love with.

Ripped jeans encased her legs and a worn T-shirt that she'd probably owned for decades. From where I stood, it looked like a concert T-shirt, some rock band that was probably little known. If I asked her about it, she'd be able to tell me their entire discography, why mainstream music had overlooked them.

As she studied the back of a small yellow can, a tall lanky guy approached her. He reached for the can she was holding, and even though it felt like a form of self-flagellation, I studied them through the rush of blood in my ears.

An ex, Maxine had said.

He wore a worn leather tool belt, a simple gray shirt, had shaggy dark hair and a beard. He wasn't as tall as I was, but he was roped with muscles, and when he said something to Iris, she laughed.

I rubbed at my chest. I shouldn't be there. Shouldn't be studying this other piece of her life that I didn't deserve to know.

He put the can back and grabbed something else, setting it in the cart next to her.

She moved to the side, pulling a few paintbrushes off the display in front of her, checking prices before she tossed them in her cart. The guy's phone rang, and he tucked it against his ear before walking away from Iris.

Indecision had me frozen, and my instincts warred mightily.

Iris turned, angling toward me when she picked up a gallon of ceiling paint from a large stack next to the paint counter. That was when she looked over, head snapping in a double take when she saw me there. Her lips fell open in surprise, only snapping shut when I gave her a rueful smile.

"Hey," I said, approaching slowly.

She tucked a piece of hair behind her ear. "Hunter."

Her eyes moved to my empty basket, and I felt that irrational panic again, that I was making an utter fool of myself. But then again, I'd always felt like a fool for how much I loved her. How was this any different?

"My mom needed light bulbs," I said. "And batteries."

Iris's lips curled into a slow smile. "I think you're in the wrong row for those."

My face felt warm, and I nodded. "Yeah. Seems like it." She tapped her fingers on the handle of her cart, and I peered at the contents. "Looks like the recipe for a great Saturday."

She exhaled a laugh, picking up the can of varnish. "Right? I have a friend helping me build my checkout counter in his shop, and it's finally ready to be stained."

"Let me know if you ever need an extra set of hands for heavy lifting," I said. "I'm not very good at painting, though."

"I remember," she said, a dimple peeking from her cheek as she grinned. "The walls in my old bedroom continue to bear witness to your shame."

I smiled. "Still?"

"Why I wanted that color, I'll never know."

"It was awful."

She laughed. "It wasn't that bad."

"It made that entire upstairs hallway look purple," I said. "I thought your grandma was going to have a seizure when she saw it."

Iris shook her head, but her smile stayed wide and happy.

"But you kept it?" I set a hand on the shelf. "I'm surprised you didn't paint over it."

Iris wrinkled her nose. "I don't go in there much."

We'd spent so many hours in that small room. The day she wanted to paint it purple, I'd tried to talk her out of it. But she was determined, and I could never say no to her. Especially when, our hands and arms splattered with deep lilac, she pushed me down on her bed and stripped her shirt off. Showing me something she'd learned in a magazine, she had me seeing stars and swallowing my groans when she swiveled her hips over me, the naked stretch of her back facing me while I gripped her hair in my fist.

I could hardly remember whatever *Cosmo* called that particular move, but it got a gold star from me. We'd been ravenous during that phase of our relationship, once Iris tiptoed into adulthood. The single greatest skill we honed for a solid year was how to have sex quietly enough that her grandma didn't hear.

Such excellent thoughts to have while I stood in the paint aisle at the Eager Beaver, about Iris's proclivity for the reverse cowgirl.

I forced my brain somewhere a bit safer, picking up on something she'd just said.

"You and Theo live at her house?" I asked.

She nodded. "I inherited it after my grandma died, and I haven't really done any updates. Every penny has gone right here." She touched the cans in the cart.

Before I could answer, the ex reappeared, an affable smile on his face when he saw me. "Sorry about that. Had an ... unexpected call."

Iris gestured in my direction. "Grant, this is Hunter Buchanan. Hunter, this is Grant Simmons."

If the name meant anything to him, he didn't show it. His smile was warm and kind, and even if I hated imagining them together, I found it impossible to dislike him on sight. We shook hands, and I noticed Iris's cheeks were pink, her eyes landing anywhere but on me.

"Welcome back to town," Grant said. "I did some work for your parents a couple of months ago, and your momma couldn't stop talking about you moving back to Green Valley."

"Yeah, she's pretty pleased with herself right now."

Grant scratched his chest, giving Iris an apologetic smile. "I hate to do this to you, but I just had something come up, and I've got to run."

Her eyebrows shot up. "Now? I thought you were going to drive me out to your shop."

Grant looked over at me, face innocent. A little too innocent. "Would you be willing to take her home?"

Iris narrowed her eyes.

I looked between them. "Yeah, I'm free today."

He clapped his hands. "Perfect. I owe you, Hunter."

Iris pursed her lips. "Who called you?"

"Hmm? Oh, it's ... it's no one."

"Grant Michael Simmons," she said.

His face flushed bright red. "I gotta go. It's ... an emergency."

Grant Michael Simmons was a shit liar. He looked like he wanted to crawl in a hole.

"Uh-huh."

I smothered a smile.

Grant shook my hand again, and I couldn't help but wonder exactly how Maxine had pulled this off. But I'd bet every penny to my name she was behind it.

Iris huffed, moving to the cash register to pay for her items.

He smiled. "I really do owe you."

I studied his face. "I think maybe I owe Maxine too?"

He held up his hands. "I have no idea what you're talking about." He clapped a hand on my shoulder. "Take care of her," he added meaningfully.

I scratched the side of my face again as he left the store. Iris was pocketing her receipt when I walked up behind her. My hand hovered over the small of her back, and before I could overthink, I settled it on the soft cotton of her shirt. Through that thin layer, the heat of her skin seared my palm. "I've got it," I told her quietly, my mouth close to her ear as I slid the heavy box under my arm before she could lift it.

She froze, and my hand fell away.

That one touch sent awareness zapping white hot under my skin, and I wondered if it did the same thing to her. From the day we met, we'd always had that electricity. Something impossible to contain once we'd tapped into it, let it flow free between us.

I'd never felt it before, and I'd definitely never felt it since.

Iris finished putting away her things, tucking the paper bag of her brushes and roller covers around her wrist. When she glanced up at me, her eyes were wary by this unexpected time with me.

"I'm parked around the corner," I told her. "Just let me know where we're going."

She let out a slow breath. "The store, if you don't mind. I was going to head back to Grant's shop to work on the counter, but I might as well bring this stuff over now. They're letting me in early even though I'm not signing the lease until Monday."

"Beauty of a small town," I said.

It was only a couple of blocks, and I fell in step beside her, relishing the way her shoulder lightly brushed mine as we walked. The air was warm and damp, and she gave me a shy look when she motioned down the block.

"Just tell me where to go," I said quietly. "I'll follow your lead."

She gave me a loaded look as she turned the corner toward her store, and that was how I found myself walking through downtown Green Valley, staring down the first time I'd be alone with Iris Black in twelve years.

85

CHAPTER 10

IRIS

*T*here were two versions of me when I got nervous. Most often, I clammed up tight, didn't talk much, and allowed the people around me to carry the conversation while I watched. And the second version—apparently —came out in situations such as this.

This being the single thing I was trying to avoid the moment I saw him standing on that playground.

It was the nervous that came from being alone with someone who posed the greatest kind of threat to my heart.

And that nervous had me talking. A lot.

It was *awful*.

Hunter set the box of paint and stain down on the floor just inside the door, and listened to me ramble about how I wanted to transform the store. Where I planned large circular tables in the middle, each vendor with their own display, nothing to block the natural flow of walking through the space. The walls would be a warm white, all my tables a light oak, the floors would be laid in a herring-bone pattern, only covered in two places with patterned rugs framing a seating area. The jewel of the store, right in the middle, would be the vintage green couch I'd found in Nashville.

"It's exactly like the one my grandma had." I heard myself say. "I remember walking into her house the first time and thinking it was the most beautiful piece of furniture I'd ever seen. Rolled arms, brass nailheads, tufted along the back."

He smiled. "Where is it now?"

"A *really* expensive consignment boutique in Nashville." I closed my eyes. "I put down a deposit. They said they'd hold it another couple of weeks until I knew I had the store secured. If I think too hard about how much I'm about to spend on an old couch, I'll have myself committed."

For a moment, I stared at the space on the floor where it would go. The emerald green would be the centerpiece, the first thing anyone saw when they walked through the doors. I blinked rapidly.

"What?" he asked.

"It makes it feel like my grandma will be here," I admitted. When my nose started tingling, a dangerous precursor of tears, I changed the subject.

And he let me.

He'd always been so good at that. He'd level those dark, steady eyes on me and listen with rapt attention at whatever I felt like saying. It used to be books, something we had in common, and movies and music. Us.

And now, despite all the time we'd spent apart, he was doing it again.

I found my voice trailing off when I reached the plans for the bathroom, because honestly, I had to dredge up my dignity somewhere. He tilted his head. "You've been planning this for a long time," he rumbled.

I exhaled a laugh. "A solid year now. I worked at a place like this in Knoxville for a couple of years, right after I got custody of Theo."

His gaze tracked over my face. "Tell me why you loved it so much."

He'd always done that too, ask endless thoughtful questions, simply because he wanted to know what was going through my brain.

Turning in a slow circle, I studied the dust-smudged windows, the battered floors, and nicked walls. "You know how I used to love walking through the farmers' market?"

He hummed. "Every weekend."

"The store reminded me of that. But all together, where the vendors could really settle their stuff in, see people fall in love with what they made, what they were passionate about. And after some time, townspeople would just come and hang out, see what was new even if they didn't mean to buy anything." I smiled at the memory. "It wasn't a small town place, but it reminded me of one. The rhythm to it. The way life just ... meandered through. And I thought, maybe I could do that here."

"I think it sounds amazing," Hunter said quietly.

Where some men were loud and pushy, where they thought taking up space meant to dominate everything around them, Hunter had always been the opposite. His strength wasn't like a bomb. It was the steel foundation that held everything up around it. Implacable and unmovable. His quiet had always drawn my eye to him when we were in the same room.

It was what made me trust him so many years earlier. Why I sat and talked to him for hours the first day we met. Why only about a week later, I let him cage me up against the tree and kiss me until I saw stars. Why I'd slid my hands up into his thick, soft hair and held on for dear life, swallowing his groans as he pushed a big, hot hand up underneath my T-shirt and traced the line of my back. There'd been no going back after that.

A patch of sun streaming through the front corner windows made me stop and tilt my face to the heat. It calmed a bit of that nervous energy he whipped up in me.

"What are you going to call it?" he asked.

I had to blink out of the heated memories and focus on the present.

"Black's Southern Staples, I think." I touched my hand to the window and imagined the clean black lines of the logo there.

I dared a glance in his direction, and he was watching me, a small curve to his lips and warmth in his eyes that had my tummy fluttering. I pressed a hand to my stomach, and he noticed.

"What is it?"

With a soft huff of laughter, I gave him a look. "Come on. This is what I was trying to avoid." My hands gestured weakly in the space around us. No more than five feet between where I stood in the sun and he took up space in the middle of the empty floor. It felt like a mile. And it felt like nothing.

His jaw tightened when I said it. "Being alone with me?"

I nodded.

"Why does that scare you?" he asked, taking a step closer. Then he stopped. "I made a promise, and I meant it. I won't pressure you."

"I know, but—" My voice cut off, and I pressed my hand harder against my weightless stomach. "Maybe I'm realizing that being friendly with you..."

His brow furrowed when I stopped. "What?"

My voice was just above a whisper. "I don't know how to do it. We've never known."

"I'm *trying*."

I took a step. "I know you are. I can see it."

He laughed, a dry sound. "I hope so. That wasn't easy for me in the hardware store."

My head reared back. "Because of Grant?"

Hunter's eyes darkened. "Come on, Iris. Don't play that game."

The air around us trembled, an omen of all the things we hadn't said yet. The reckoning that we'd yet to have.

"I'm not playing *anything*. You have nothing to be jealous of," I said. "Grant and I ... we were friends for a while. Dated for maybe six months before we realized we were better off as we started."

"Nothing to be jealous of," he said disbelievingly.

My chin rose a notch. "No. Nothing."

"Did he kiss you?"

I snapped my mouth shut, face hot and my heart thrumming.

"Does he know what sounds you make when someone bites on your lip in that way you like?"

My stomach shook.

He took a step. "Did you sleep with him? Let him see you naked in the daylight? I am jealous of all those things because they're *all* I've thought about."

The rope holding back my temper frayed. "I don't have to answer that because you do not get to question me on the choices I made while you were gone."

His eyes flashed like a rumble of thunder. "You asked me to go," he ground out. "You begged me to leave you alone because you couldn't stand the thought that I was trapping you, that we had no choice in any of this." Hunter pointed an angry finger at his chest. "It doesn't matter how I fell in love with you, Iris. How quickly it happened. I had a choice, I made one with you, and you damn well know you did too."

My eyes burned hot, and I wanted nothing more than to tip my head back and scream. My memories of Hunter, the good and the bad and the wonderful, they pushed forward with violent, desperate hands, straining to come to the forefront where I could no longer ignore them.

"I did," I said, keeping my voice even. It was the only calm thing about me. My heart thrashed and jolted under my ribs, and my skin vibrated at his nearness. "I had a choice, and in your absence, I chose to move on, and that is not something you get to play caveman about."

"Caveman?" Hunter repeated. He tilted his head to the side. "A caveman would've tossed you up over his shoulder and ignored every protest out of your mouth." He moved closer. "If I was acting like a caveman, I would've done so many things differently."

His voice was low and dangerous, and when the tenor of it changed, I knew the line between us had shifted to something more precarious. It was whisper thin, sharp as a razor.

A part of me, one I'd never admit out loud, that wanted him to do exactly that. Some dried-up section of my heart that craved the intense way he'd always loved me. To see him fight for me because he couldn't *not* fight for me.

"I think you know exactly how I feel," he said softly.

I rolled my lips between my teeth. Frantically, I shook my head.

A lie.

He knew it. So did I.

We were so close now. His scent surrounded me, sharp and masculine and clean. "Tell me, Iris," he said urgently. "Tell me if you'd want to hear about my wife."

At that word, my breath escaped in a sharp hiss. My hands trembled.

"Would you be jealous?" he asked. His eyes, his voice, his body language— every inch of him was tense with misery. He wasn't doing this to punish me. If anything, it hurt to say, and I knew that too. "Would you want to see us talking? See her make me laugh?"

A tear slid down the side of my cheek before I could stop it.

Without knowing her name, what she looked like, whether she was the reincarnation of Mother fucking Teresa, I wanted to rip every hair out of her head. The monstrous green feeling inside me had claws and snapping teeth, something snarling and ugly.

I *hated* her.

Simply because she'd had him in a way I never did. If I admitted that now, there'd be no stopping the reaction. I wasn't sure I'd want to stop anything, if I actually said the words out loud. I'd want his hands digging in my hair, his tongue sweeping into my mouth. I'd want that million-pound groan of relief yanked from his chest and the press of his big body on mine. I'd want him to push me back against the wall. Yank my thigh tight up against his waist.

I'd want him to bite down on my lip like he said because he knew exactly how to suck it into his mouth. Make me feel like he was about to devour me whole.

I'd want his skin hot and hard under my fingers, mine wet and waiting under his. Bruised lips and muttered curses while we discovered each other again.

If I even hinted that he was right, we'd fucking *explode*. Nothing would stop us from crossing that flimsy invisible barrier I'd erected.

And that was why I kept the words in.

I'd never harnessed every shred of my self-control like at that moment. Not even when I asked him to leave.

Hunter was so close. When his hand rose slowly toward my face, I didn't pull back. His brow furrowed when he brushed his thumb against the wetness on my face.

My eyes fluttered shut, and I laid my hand on his warm, hard chest.

Our light touches were a stark, violent difference from the thoughts running through my head. The same ones were likely running through his too.

He exhaled rough against my face, his breath hot and minty. I'd taste it on his tongue if I let him kiss me right now. And if that happened, I'd fall. I'd fall into him with everything inside me because I didn't know how to love this man in halves.

Something deep in my chest cracked open when he slid his hand farther against my cheek, tangling his hand into my hair. Against the crown of my head, his lips mouthed my name, and my fingers curled into his shirt.

"I can't," I whispered. My voice wavered on the words, and he set his forehead against mine.

Hunter didn't pull back right away, and I didn't either. It felt too good, this selfish moment, of knowing that it still felt like this between us. I wanted to dive into it and forget everything else whirling around in my head.

"You can," he said gently. After he said it, he settled a featherlight kiss on my skin. "But you won't. And there's a difference."

He pulled away, stepping back until my hands fell limp by my sides. His face was stony, all emotion tucked away and out of sight.

"I'm sorry," I said.

He wiped a hand over his mouth, studying me intently. His hand dropped, and he shook his head. "Maybe you're right, Iris."

"About what?"

Hunter looked up at the ceiling. "All of it. Maybe it's impossible for us to be anything outside of how we started. How we're..." His voice trailed off, and his jaw locked tight over the words.

How we're meant to be.

I could've filled in the words, but I didn't. It wouldn't help.

"Now what?" I asked.

He dropped his chin to his chest. "Do you want me to find a different learning specialist for Theo?"

Immediately, I shook my head. "No. He likes you, he listens to you, and I won't take that away from him."

Hunter nodded, exhaling loudly. "Good. I like him too." He smiled, boyish and crooked, and I had to look away.

"Thank you for carrying the paint for me," I said.

He studied me before speaking again. "Aren't I supposed to drive you home?"

I glanced outside. "I think I'll walk. You know it's not far. Might do me good to get some exercise."

That jaw clenched again. But he didn't argue. "All right."

Hunter paused at the door, gave me an inscrutable look over his shoulder, and left without another word.

I sank down onto my haunches, digging my hands into my hair while I tried to steady my breath. The universe seemed determined to shove him in my path, and I still didn't know what the hell I was supposed to do about any of it.

CHAPTER 11

HUNTER

*I*t didn't take me long after my incident with Iris—the one that had me restlessly tossing and turning in bed as I imagined what could've happened if she hadn't pulled away—to realize that my time in Green Valley looked a lot more like a temporary landing spot when I removed her from the equation. Conceding the power she held over the view of my own future wasn't all that difficult, because I'd made peace with that almost immediately upon falling in love with her.

And that, thanks to my family history, happened the moment I met her.

I'd been able to push it aside for self-preservation purposes, just to see if I could make a life without her in it, but now it was front and center. The thing I thought about above anything else.

It wasn't like I couldn't function without her in my life.

I could.

Everything was just ... less.

I was able to go fishing with my dad just as the sun was dawning in the sky. We caught a few small fish, releasing them back into Bandit Lake.

I was able to help Levi clear some overgrown landscaping in the backyard of the home he and Joss had bought, close to Merryville. Normally, they'd be right in

Green Valley, but they'd found a house already fitted with a wheelchair ramp, widened doorways on the inside, and a newly renovated kitchen. That meant they could move in immediately since Joss needed a house that was fully accessible. It allowed him easy access to his new job at the University of Tennessee, and they were close to family.

I took a Sunday evening to play basketball at the park with Connor and Levi.

I met another student, worked with her on some of her fluency issues, and another new student after that, who struggled with math and science. I wouldn't be seeing Theo until the next day, and in the few days I spent after I last spoke to Iris, everything felt muted.

My world wasn't suddenly drained of color because of what she said. All the things I did in the days between, I enjoyed myself. I loved the time spent with my family, but thoughts of her were always on the edges of my consciousness.

When I arrived home from my last tutoring session, a free evening stretched ahead of me, and I found myself wishing I had something to keep me busy. My parents lived about ten minutes outside of downtown, on a large plot of land that stretched behind the house. Years earlier, they'd converted a free-standing garage into a full apartment. Whenever someone in our family matriculated back home, it was a landing spot of sorts. Levi lived there first, while he went to college, a place where Joss could visit him with ease because he'd built it to accommodate her wheelchair.

My cousin Grace lived there next when she arrived in Green Valley, but quickly moved in with her boyfriend Tucker Haywood. After Grace, it was home to her twin brother, Grady.

Grady suffered the exact same fate every Buchanan had before him, falling head over heels almost immediately upon arriving in Green Valley. He and his fiancée, Magnolia MacIntyre, lived in a house just outside of the downtown area.

And now, it was mine.

When I pulled up, parking my car just next to the front door, I stared at the building and had a horrible thought.

It was where the Buchanans stayed until their love lives shifted into place. *We* might fall in love quickly, but it wasn't so seamless for the other person. There were always conflicts, bumps in the road to our collective happily ever after.

My bump was just ... bigger. Spanned the greatest amount of time. Had the most complications.

The more I thought about it, the more I wanted to burn that garage down.

When I got out of the car, my mom's voice came from her favorite spot on the wraparound porch.

"I hear you," she said. "But you know it's not that simple."

She had the phone up to her ear, a stack of binders and papers strewn out on the table next to her rocking chair. I waved, and she motioned me over.

Her eyes studied my face as I approached, and I wondered if she could see my sleepless nights stamped there. When her face took on that worried mom look, I got my answer.

"I'll see what I can do," she said. "But you've got to give me a little time." She nodded. "All right. I'll call you when I get something settled."

I took a seat in the rocking chair on the opposite end of the table and let my eyes close.

"You look tired, son of mine."

I turned my head toward her. "I am."

Her brow furrowed. "Should I be worried about you?"

That drew a quiet laugh. "Isn't that a part of the parenting gig?"

She hummed, pushing her rocking chair into motion again. "Sure is. When you and your brothers were babies, I thought it would get easier. That as you grew and gained your independence, I'd worry less. That I wouldn't lose sleep over what you were going through, but sometimes ... I think it only gets worse."

"How so?"

Mom thought for a moment before answering. "When your kids grow up, you gotta let them go. All the things you used to have in your control, that's gone. But the love isn't. And that love makes you want to protect people from anything that could cause harm. What makes you want to wrap them up and keep the worst parts of the world away."

"But you can't."

She shook her head. "All you can do is offer advice when it's asked for, support when it's needed, and a good ass-kicking if one is warranted."

I laughed, and she gave me a small smile.

"I never needed an ass-kicking," I said.

Her eyebrow lifted. "Maybe you were too far away for me to try."

"Touché."

A car drove past the house. Mom lifted her hand in a wave, and the driver hit the horn in greeting. I shook my head.

"What?" Mom asked.

"Still getting used to it here." I settled my hands onto my stomach and stretched my legs out, crossing one foot over the other. "Nobody honks at you in Seattle unless they're thinking about running you off the road."

She laughed. "You think you're gonna be here a while?" she asked.

No one had asked me that outright. All I knew when I left Seattle was that I needed a change. I needed somewhere to clear my head because trying to live a happy life without the person I loved hadn't quite worked out.

And I knew that my family would love nothing more than if I settled here. But I wasn't sure if that was possible, not if Iris dug in her heels. Her ability to do that was obvious. Painfully, heartbreakingly obvious.

So I answered carefully. "I don't know yet."

"Your contract with the county is ... six months, right?"

I nodded. "They'll assess extending the grant at the end. But even if they do, it's not a long-term option for me."

"Do you want to find another principal job?"

I blew out a breath. "I don't know. I loved my school in Seattle. But I don't think I want to stay in administration. I miss seeing the immediate impact of working with the students."

"Maybe you could teach at one of the schools here," she ventured.

"Maybe."

Watching Iris live a life outside of me. It sounded like a great way to lose my mind.

"I know you haven't brought it up to me," Mom started. "But your brother slipped up the other day and told me Iris's brother is one of your students."

I cut her a look. "He slipped? Or you beat it out of him?"

"You accusing me of prying, son?"

"Yup."

She clucked her tongue. "This is why adult children are no easier. Because you make horrible assumptions about the woman who gave birth to you."

"One can't help but notice you're not denying it."

"Fine." She held her hands up in surrender. "You win. I saw them whispering about something, and I heard her name."

I hummed. "Doesn't it feel good to admit the truth?"

Mom made an offended scoff, and I grinned.

"What do you want me to say, Mom?" I asked, resting my head on the rocking chair so I could look at her fully. "Talking it to death doesn't help. There are so many things about me and Iris that can't be changed, and every time I say it out loud, I have to feel it all over again."

"No one's asking you to talk it to death, but the two of you always thought you had to bottle it up and tuck it away somewhere it couldn't hurt you. That doesn't help either." She smiled sadly. "Just one of the ways you and she were two peas in a pod. You feel things so big that once you let it out in the open, it swallows up everything else in your life."

"And that's our issue right there," I said. "She has too many important things on her plate. Risking those things getting swallowed up isn't an option for her."

"Her brother," Mom said.

I nodded.

"He's such a precious boy. Breaks my heart thinking about what they've both been through with that mother of hers."

My gaze sharpened. "How do you know so much about it? I didn't think many people in town knew about her mom. I hardly know the details. She always shut down when I tried to talk to her about it."

"You know I'm friendly with Maxine." Mom smiled. "Or as friendly as Maxine is with anyone. And Iris's grandma was such a good person, raising Iris like she did. That poor girl could hardly talk to anyone at the funeral because she was so heartbroken. Theo didn't know their grandma as well, of course, but I'll never forget the two of them holding on to each other at the front of the church."

Mom stopped, dabbing at the corner of her eye.

Questions tingled at the tip of my tongue. And one by one, I swallowed them down. Asking for all the details wouldn't help because imagining her in a somber black dress, saying goodbye to the person who raised her when it mattered most, would only ignite a helpless sort of rage.

I hadn't been there for her when it happened, and I couldn't undo that, no matter how much I wished it.

"I don't need you to talk it to death, son." Mom's gaze settled on some birds fluttering around the bird feeders she had in her garden. "But I hope you know that I'll always listen if it helps. No matter how much or how little you want to share. You've always been my quiet one. Just like your dad. And he doesn't talk his thoughts out much either."

I smiled. "I think we traded about ten words when we fished yesterday."

"Sounds about right. And that's okay. He talks when it matters, and the words he gives people ... they mean more because of it."

Mom knew Dad so well, knew all the ins and outs of the way he was, not wanting to change the ways they differed. And the only person I'd had that with was Iris.

It was always a bone of contention with my ex. Samantha wanted to talk through everything, which was fine. But when I didn't reciprocate, she always felt like it was a personal slight to her. When I didn't share all my thoughts, share the things I was going through as I processed them, it started a cycle of frustration and anger, and eventually, resentment that we could never quite pull ourselves out of.

When we reached that last stage, the resentment, it only caused me to shut down further. Share even less.

Signing our divorce papers was a relief for both of us.

"It's not that I don't want to share things, Mom." I chose my words carefully. "The first time with Iris, I thought it was forever. That you'd get to know her, make her part of the family as time passed, and she would trust us enough to show you the things I knew about her."

"But then you left," she said quietly.

I nodded. "Because she asked. In the end, she couldn't even trust me, let alone all the rest. She couldn't trust that I'd stay, or that I meant what I'd said."

"She's had a lot of reason not to," Mom added in a gentle tone.

My jaw clenched tight. "I know. But then, talking about all the rest—Samantha, and what a stupid fucking idea it had been to marry someone else, I couldn't do it." The words stalled, and in the silence, my mom didn't even chide me for my language, which is how I knew how important these conversations were for her. And how much I'd deprived her of them over the years. "How was I supposed to come back and celebrate the fact that the universe seemed to drop Iris right in front of me after all the years, all the damage we've done to each other? I didn't even know how to talk about it. I'd gotten so used to not sharing."

It was more words than I'd shared with her about the things hiding in my heart, probably since the very beginning. And while she sat in her white rocking chair, I saw the quiet tears tracking down her face. Maybe it was that piece of parenting she mentioned. She couldn't do anything about what I was going through, except sit and listen and let me know she loved me.

And today, it was what I needed more than anything.

So I talked. Told her about Theo. About our conversation at the bakery. The empty store.

Seeing Grant. What I said to her about Samantha, which had my mom pressing a hand to the space over her heart, humming in sympathy for both of us. And now, this place where I wasn't sure how it would all play out.

"Goodness," she said, once I'd finished. "You've been keeping a whole bunch inside that head of yours."

"Seems so."

She handed me a glass of tea, condensation dripping down the sides. "It's mine, if you aren't bothered by my germs."

Gratefully, I took a sip, settling it back onto the table where she could reach it.

"I'm not gonna tell you what to do or judge why Iris is so hesitant to dive back into a relationship with you because I can understand where her heart's at."

I could too. That was the very worst part of all.

It was the knowledge that our feelings were still there. Still very real and just as powerful as they'd been before I left. But acting on them would have repercussions that she wasn't quite ready to deal with.

"And as much as I want you to stay," she continued, "I know why it would be hard if she can't move past all those complications."

Another car passed. Another wave from the driver.

"I'm in no rush to decide," I told her.

"That's good." Mom leaned over, patting my hand where it sat on the arm of the rocking chair. "Either way, I don't think it'll take long to know. You two never could hide what you're feeling. For better or worse."

I hummed. That was the truth. Everything about our relationship was set to a higher intensity, like a knob got cranked a few notches further than all the others.

"The love is there," she said. "And that's the most important thing. The rest ... yes, it'll still be there. Trust that Iris has learned enough in the last handful of years that she can see past it. And that you have too."

I nodded. "Thanks for listening, Mom." I blew out a hard breath, noticing that the pressure on my chest had eased. "I owe you."

"Oh, my darling son, if you and your brothers owed me for every pep talk, you'd be paying me back for the rest of your life."

I laughed. Mom started clearing up the stack of papers on the table. Her movements slowed, and she gave me a quick look.

"What?" I asked.

Her gaze moved to the binders, her cell phone, then back to my face. "How much is this conversation worth to you?"

"What do you have in mind?"

"I'm on a committee that's organizing a fundraiser for the historical society. We could use a couple of extra bodies to help us on the day of the event."

I shrugged. "As long as I don't have tutoring, I could give you a hand."

She brightened. "Excellent. I'll let the committee know. You'd be a huge help."

"What do you need me to do? Set up on the day of or something?"

"It's on Saturday afternoon. We'll be setting up in the field behind City Hall."

I nodded. "Sounds good. Just tell me what I need to do."

Mom waved me off. "Oh, it won't be anything too complicated. You just show up, and we'll put you where you're needed most."

She dropped a kiss on the top of my head before she left the porch, and if I'd seen the pleased grin on her face as she walked away, I might have worried about what I just agreed to.

But I didn't see it. And if I'd known what I agreed to, I definitely would never have shown up.

CHAPTER 12

IRIS

A lot of things fell by the wayside during the course of the following week.

Sleep was the first.

Keeping our house clean was the second.

Regular showering and clean hair were a definite third.

Home-cooked meals? Forget it. Theo survived on frozen pizza and cereal. Not that he was complaining.

Once the papers were signed for the lease, an approved loan from the bank to get me rolling, and the keys officially in my possession, the real work began. The store was thoroughly cleaned with the help of a cleaning service out of Merryville that I hired. There was so much grime, dust, and debris littering the space that I couldn't start prepping for paint for the first two days.

That was step one, and why I was walking around all week with a limp. My entire body was sore. I'd become a giant ache, muscles that I didn't know existed making me wince as I climbed up and down and up and down the ladder. My dreams, when I was able to sleep, were flecked with a warm white paint color, probably because I had it all over me. Dotting my arms. Splashed on my jeans. On the ends of my hair. Dried underneath my nails.

But the space, after another few days of endless work, looked fresh and bright and airy.

Grant installed the black chandelier in the center of the room, and once I'd finished doing the trim, he and a buddy started laying the floors.

The days passed in a blur, eight of them gone since I stood in the space with Hunter.

Not just stood, I had to admit.

Almost let him kiss me.

Almost kissed him myself, if I hadn't found the last thread of my sanity to hold on to.

Theo continued his tutoring, with Maxine as the chauffeur, allowing me full days to work on the store. It was a clear victory that she'd only made one snide comment when I asked if she could cart him back and forth.

"Someone running scared, eh?"

"I'm not running from anything," I told her, too weary to hide the snappishness in my tone. "I'm trying to get my store up and running. My time and my finances to do so are limited. The longer it takes me, the longer I go without making that money back."

"No need to sass me," she said. "I know damn well what's at stake for you."

"Then don't guilt me. You know it's hard for me to ask for help."

At my admission, Maxine softened. "I know, honey. That's why we'll always do whatever you need."

I didn't ask her who the *we* was. At one time, it would've been her and my grandma. And now ... now I wasn't sure who else would be grouped into that statement.

People had helped me through the week, some hired and, some because they were friends of Grant. Joy stopped by midweek, bringing a large coffee and a box of pastries for the guys laying the floor. Slowly, I was building a safety net in Green Valley.

It was separate from my grandma and independent of the shadow I used to feel about my mom. Even when she was out of jail, this wasn't a place she wanted to be. Small towns, she'd told me once, were the worst because everyone paid attention to the goings-on around them.

What she'd left unsaid was that it made it harder for her to take the things she wanted. Con someone into paying for her life.

That's why she'd moved to a bigger city to find future husband number four. Theo's dad was much older when he hired my mom as his "assistant." Much richer than anyone she'd ever settled in with. He didn't much appreciate that she'd poked holes in the condom. Conveniently forgot the birth control she said she was taking. He wasn't a fan of the fact that she'd slapped his last name on the birth certificate without his knowledge.

And he really, really didn't like it when he caught her embezzling money from his business, siphoning funds into her own account.

It's what landed her in jail this last round. Because it was her second criminal offense, and she'd managed to set aside just shy of ten grand, her sentence was six years with the possibility of early release if she was on her best behavior.

No one in my new safety net, aside from Maxine, had any knowledge of my mom. And if it was up to me, it would stay that way. She had no desire to raise Theo. Not really. He'd always been a game piece she could play when needed. When Theo's dad passed away—from a heart attack, if I believed what was told to me—she didn't have anyone to play those games against.

These were the jumbled thoughts in my head, rolling around between my conversation with Hunter, that I couldn't shake all week while I cleaned and painted and worked my body to the bone.

The guys had finished laying the floor that morning, and because I couldn't do much else until we moved shelves and tables in the following week, I found myself sweeping and mopping the floors while the radio played quietly in the corner. It was nice being in the shop by myself, peeling away the dusty layer until I could see the whole picture come together.

I was wringing water out of the mop when the front door opened.

When I turned, my mouth fell open at the sight of Francine Buchanan and a tall woman with messy blonde hair and the most excellent cheekbones I'd ever seen. Her eyes, though the color was different, were the exact same shape as Hunter's.

"H-Hi, Mrs. Buchanan," I said, settling the mop into the bucket. My hands went straight to my mess of a bun. "I wasn't expecting visitors just yet, so I apologize for the mess."

Her smile was warm. "Nothing to apologize for, Iris. I've been meaning to pop by since I heard the news about your new store. Congratulations."

"Thank you." I blew out a slow exhale. In the years since I'd been back, I'd seen glimpses of her at town events, but all we'd traded were polite, loaded smiles across the room. "I ... it's nice to see you," I managed.

The blonde glanced between us, then stuck her hand out. "I'm Grace Buchanan. Hunter's cousin."

Ahh. That explained the slight resemblance. "It's a pleasure to meet you."

"This is a great space," she said. "So much light."

"That's why I wanted it," I told her. "Other spaces were available, but ... I knew it was worth the wait."

She hummed, pointing at the wall where the sun streamed in. "You could do an amazing gallery wall over there if you're selling any artwork."

"I'd love to someday," I said. "I found a painter in Merryville who's interested, but he hasn't committed just yet."

Grace perked up. "I'm a photographer. I do a lot of families, weddings, and such now, but I still make time to do nature shots too, if you ever want to check them out."

I smiled. "I'd love to see your work."

She pulled out her phone and tapped open a cloud-based storage app. She flipped to the correct folder and handed it to me. I couldn't help myself, gasping when I saw the first shot.

"These are amazing," I said. "I might be tempted to buy that one of the trees myself."

Grace grinned. "Right? I love it too. I do these mainly for myself, but it'd be nice to know they're finding a place in someone's home."

"Do you have a studio in town?" I walked over to my bag, fished out a card, and handed it to her. "If you wanna write your info on the back, I'll email you one of my contracts so you can look it over."

She shook her head. "Thankfully, I haven't needed one. There are so many beautiful places to shoot around here that there's no need. I edit from home and can order all my prints and books online if I need to. Helps keep my overhead down."

With a laugh, I gestured to the work in progress around us. "Like ... the overhead needed when opening up a boutique filled with goods I'm purchasing from local vendors?"

She smiled. "Yeah, like that."

Francine was watching the exchange with a sweet smile on her face. I tugged at the hem of my shirt, wishing I looked a bit less ... unshowered and scraggly and paint-splattered.

I didn't want to be rude and ask, hey ... why are you here? But I had a feeling they weren't here to pitch Grace's photographs. Francine had sought me approximately zero times in the years since I returned.

And she saw the question on my face without me having to ask.

"We won't keep you for too long," she said. "But I wanted to invite you to a charity event we're throwing on Saturday. We're raising funds for the historical society, and I thought you might like to set up a table, tell people about your new shop."

My eyebrows went up. "Really?"

Francine nodded. "Maxine is my co-chair for the event, and well ... we might be biased, but we'd love to give you a leg up before your doors open."

There it was again. The *we*.

My throat went tight at the implication that Francine felt anything about me at all. For all I knew, I was just an ex of her son, something ambivalent in her mind. Or worse, she hated me because I'd driven him away for so many years. I never anticipated support without conditions, simply because she knew I was important to Hunter.

It didn't fit quite right behind my ribs, like I needed to stretch to make room for it. But I wanted to. I wanted to make room for that feeling of welcome so very badly.

"I'd love that," I told her. "I don't have all my inventory yet. A lot of them are waiting to move it straight into the store, but I do have some things."

She clasped my arm, excitement making her eyes bright. "Wonderful. Whatever you have is perfect."

"I'll need a sign or something," I said, mind racing about what I could accomplish between now and Saturday.

"Maybe print up a coupon," Grace said. "Something they can bring to the store when it opens."

Francine beamed. "What a great idea."

I exhaled a laugh. "It is."

The whole exchange had my head spinning a little bit, but I managed to exchange contact information with Grace and a promise to give her one full wall for her photography. She was right. It would be beautiful in the afternoon sun.

"I'll see you on Saturday," Francine said, pausing at the door. "Event starts at three."

"Absolutely. I wouldn't miss it."

Her lips curled; expression pleased as punch. "See that you don't."

Grace gave her a questioning look, but Francine shooed her out onto the sidewalk.

I watched them walk past the front windows, chattering happily with Grace's arm looped through her aunt's. It was strange to think about being included by them.

I'd always thought of Hunter's family as something separate from us.

He and I, the two of us, had formed a *we*. Everyone else in our lives hovered outside that circle. His family was outside of it by his choice, and I definitely never pressed because of *my* family. My background. But it wasn't like that anymore, and maybe that was a good thing. Even without him clouding my thoughts during the past week, I still didn't know what would happen with Hunter and me. I knew we couldn't be friends. That much was clear.

And thankfully, I didn't have to figure out anything else beyond that. At least not yet. But now that I knew he was within reaching distance, I had to decide what we could be.

That was when my phone rang from inside my purse. I blew out a breath and bent over to fish it out. When I saw the number, I could practically see the black cloud as it descended on my mood.

"Hello?" I said.

"An inmate from Davidson County Correctional is attempting to place a collect call. Do you accept the charges?"

A boulder dropped hard, somewhere at the base of my stomach. Somehow, I managed to swallow around it.

My eyes pinched shut, and I couldn't help but marvel at her timing. As always, it was impeccable. Just as I'd been thinking about Hunter's family. Just as I'd been tiptoeing toward a feeling of acceptance. From them. The town. And him.

"No," I said quietly. "I don't accept the charges."

And I hung up.

I picked up the mop and started working on the next section of floor. Deciding what to do about Hunter didn't have to happen now.

Soon. But not now.

I had an event to prepare for.

CHAPTER 13

HUNTER

*T*he field behind City Hall was a hive of activity. Banners strung from wooden poles to the edge of the stage set up in the center of the emerald-green grass. People set up tables and rows of chairs, and a few food trucks pumped delicious smells into the air.

The weather couldn't have been more perfect if they'd ordered it off a menu. A rainstorm the night before pushed some of the humidity out of the air, making it a lot more pleasant to work outside. Through the crowds of people, I thought I saw a flash of Iris's long dark hair, but when I shifted to get a better look, she was gone.

I let out a deep breath. Might as well round out the week without seeing her a single time. After our conversation at the store, it was like she waved a magic wand and disappeared.

A trick she'd honed well. Because it wasn't the first time she'd done it. And somehow, this time stung just as badly as the last. It just wasn't as permanent.

I caught a glimpse of my mom by the stage, instructing two college-aged kids about chair placement, and I heard her drill sergeant tone as I approached.

She rolled her eyes when they took off, and it brought a grin to my face.

"Hard to find good help these days, huh?"

Mom sighed. "Lord. They can navigate all the ticking and tocking like rocket scientists, but you ask them to set up chairs, and they look at you like you're speaking a different language. It's enough to drive a woman to drink."

I set my hands on my hips. "Where do you need me?"

She glanced at my clothes and let out a resigned sigh. "That's what you wore?"

It was my favorite T-shirt, proclaiming my alma mater, and some black gym shorts. On my head, I'd thrown a beat-up Washington Wolves hat on backward. "What's wrong with this? I thought you needed help setting up."

"I said no such thing," she said. "Not my fault if you assumed."

Maxine Barton approached, pushing her walker over the bumps in the grass. "That's what he wore? Jesus, be a fence. Don't you own a nice button-down or something?"

"What is going on?"

The women exchanged a look, and the moment Maxine's mouth stretched into a devious grin, I got a terrible, terrible feeling.

"Someone explain," I managed through gritted teeth.

"Didn't your mother tell you what we're doing for our fundraiser?" she asked.

"No, she did not."

My mom gave me a look. "I don't appreciate your tone, son."

I gave her a look right back.

Maxine cackled. "This is the most fun I've had in a while. Great idea, Fran."

"What idea?" I shouted.

"Lower your voice," Mom hissed. "People are staring."

I glanced around. No one was within earshot, but the idea that a child—even one of the adult variety—would talk back in public was a Southern mom's worst nightmare. "Mother." My voice was calm, quiet, and steady. "Could you kindly explain what I'm doing here? I'd be so appreciative."

She slicked a tongue over her teeth, and her hesitation had something uncomfortable churning in my gut. "We needed one more person for our fundraiser. And you're the perfect ... candidate."

"Candidate for what?" I said. My eye was twitching, I was sure of it.

Maxine patted my chest. "It's an auction, young man. And you are a prime piece of meat that'll fetch big money."

My head cocked to the side. "I'm sorry?"

Mom clucked her tongue. "Calm down. You can offer up handyman services or just a dinner out for a lonely old lady if that's who wins. You could offer up any number of services," she said. "It's not a romantic thing."

"Could be, though," Maxine said breezily. "Depends on who wins you."

I rolled my lips between my teeth and stared down at these two women. They were polite and respectful, God-fearing Southern women, and I was one second away from cussing them out in front of half the damn town.

"No."

Maxine's eyebrows shot up at my tone.

Mom cocked her hip out. Her eyes narrowed.

"Hunter Thomas Buchanan, you don't have much choice."

So maybe she wasn't feeling as polite anymore. When my mother cocked her hip out and used my middle name, I was one shade away from fucked.

"Unless you tattooed it on the front of the stage, I think I do have a choice." I pointed my finger at the crowd. "You cannot auction me off to a stranger without my permission, Momma."

"*Oh*, look who's calling me Momma again." Her eyes widened. "Quite the time to get your full Southern arsenal back."

I pinched the bridge of my nose. "You should have told me."

"You would've said no."

At my incredulous scoff, Maxine laughed. "You have something against preserving history, Hunter?"

I stared at her.

"Pfft. Come on, you know what'll likely happen is some innocent little old woman will bid on you so she can have some help moving boxes or something around her house. You'll be able to raise some money to help us preserve the great history of Green Valley, which is a bonus." She patted my arm, the tiny motion brimming with condescension. "It's harmless."

"Maxine, when you say something is gonna be harmless, we should run in the opposite direction."

My mom laughed. Maxine did too.

Someone called my mom's name, and her attention shifted. I leaned down toward Maxine. "And I know you were the one to call Grant the other day at the hardware store."

Her eyes went wide and innocent and so full of shit that it was a miracle they didn't brown on the spot. "I'm sure I have no idea what you're talking about."

There was a loud burst of childish laughter, one I recognized instantly as Theo's, and I straightened. Because if he was here ...

Iris's laughter preceded the sight of the two of them coming around behind the stage. Her brother was making a strange dancing motion that had her grinning widely.

Theo saw me first, eyes lighting up. "Hey, Mr. B!"

Iris's grin didn't disappear, but it softened, her eyes taking on a wary, uncertain look that I hated.

"Do you miss your tutoring so much that you're following me around on weekends now?" I asked.

He made a scoffing sound. "Yeah, right."

Maxine wrapped an arm around Iris. "Well, little flower, did you find your table?"

Iris tucked a stray piece of hair behind her ear. "I did. It's ... right up front by the stage, isn't it?"

Today, she was wearing faded jeans, torn at her knees, and a sleek black tank top with a swirling white logo over her heart.

Black's Southern Staples.

When my gaze lifted from the design, she was watching me carefully. "Looks good," I told her, tapping at the space over my own chest. "The logo."

"One of Grant's friends has a screen-printing shop. He whipped one of these out for me last night." One slim shoulder rose in a shrug. "Figured I might try to look like a professional for my first professional event."

"Iris has a wonderful view of the whole event," Maxine said.

I narrowed my eyes at her tone. So did Iris.

"It was very kind of Francine to invite me so last minute," Iris added.

A light bulb flickered somewhere in the back of my head, a terrible realization blooming.

"Maxine," I said, "can I have a wor—"

She interrupted before I could finish. "Oh, I think I just heard my name being called. If you two will excuse me."

Amazing how quickly she could push that walker when fleeing the scene of a gratuitous setup.

"What are you doing here?" Theo asked. He was so full of energy he bounced on the balls of his feet while he spoke.

"I, uh, I think I got conned into something by my own mother, Theo."

His eyes widened. "Is it illegal?"

I realized my mistake at his question and the panicked look on Iris's face. "No," I rushed to say. "No, I just meant I didn't know what I was signing up for when I said I'd come help her today."

Iris breathed out slowly, her face a little bit paler than it had been a moment earlier. I gave her an apologetic look. She smiled back, but the edges of that smile were strained.

"What'd you sign up for?" Theo asked.

As he asked the question, a middle-aged woman approached with a giant stack of programs in her hand. They were highlighter yellow, and on her face was a curious smile. "You're Hunter, right?" she asked. Her eyelashes were so long and spidery that they damn near got tangled up in each other when she blinked.

"Yes?"

She pursed her lips. They were coated in hot-pink lipstick. "Excellent," she purred.

Her tank top was bright pink and edged in rhinestones. Stretched across her generous chest was printed *May Contain Alcohol.*

Iris glanced back and forth between us. "Can I see one of those programs?" she asked.

The woman handed one over, but her eyes stayed right on me, tracking down my chest, stopping directly at my crotch. I cleared my throat, and she waltzed away humming a jaunty tune.

I moved toward Iris, reading over her shoulder, and as her finger moved down the line of names up for the auction, I knew the moment she saw mine. Her body froze, and she glanced up over her shoulder, trying desperately not to laugh.

"This?" she asked. Her eyes sparked with unholy glee. "This is what she conned you into?"

I sighed heavily.

The woman with the eyelashes and the lipstick walked past us again, wiggling her fingers in a tiny wave as she did.

I closed my eyes.

And Iris lost her battle. Her peals of laughter were loud and long, and for a moment, she gripped her stomach, bracing one hand on her knee.

"Laugh it up, Black," I muttered.

She straightened, wiping a finger underneath her eye. "I'm sorry," she said with a breathless gasp. "But your face right now."

"Wouldn't you make a face if she was gonna try to buy you?" I whisper-hissed.

I wasn't sure what would come of it, but this one moment, seeing her so happy, laughing like this, it was worth all the scary pink lipsticked ladies in all of Green Valley.

She took a deep breath, finally able to calm her laughter. Theo stared at the program, shrugging because he couldn't see what was so funny.

"I probably would," she admitted.

"You could always give me a pity bid. Make sure Spider Lashes doesn't win me in the end."

Her lips curled in a devious smile. "And ruin the most fun I've had in ages? Dream on, Buchanan."

There was a lightness in her tone I hadn't heard in so long. It had sweet, warm energy pouring through me.

"Fair enough," I said. "But if I disappear one day, make sure to check her basement, if you don't mind."

Iris laughed again, waving at someone who yelled her name.

"I better go," she said. Her eyes twinkled. "Good luck."

I sighed again.

She and Theo walked off toward the front of the stage, and my mom appeared—like magic—once Iris was gone.

I spoke under my breath. "You and Maxine Barton are devious meddlers who should pray for forgiveness right now."

My mom patted me on the shoulder. "I know you're not accusing me of subterfuge, son."

I gave her a look.

She raised one imperious eyebrow. "If you'll excuse me, I've got other things to attend to. You're up last, son. Please don't miss your turn."

"Do I need to go change?" I asked.

Mom patted me on the chest. "You know, I have a feeling it won't matter in the slightest."

CHAPTER 14

IRIS

I should've left when I had the chance.

I should've left when the idea of it was still funny, something I could smile about whenever I needed a good laugh.

It was the first thought that crossed my mind when Hunter walked up those damn steps onto that damn stage, wearing that damn backward hat that made him look young and more handsome than any man had the right to.

Reluctance was stamped over every inch of his tall, muscular frame, and in the tension he held clearly through his shoulders, the stance of his legs, and the tight-fisted way he crossed his bulging arms over his broad chest.

"This is a bad idea," I whispered.

The crowd had been energetic, bidding enthusiastically for any number of the Green Valley male population with their various talents up for sale. Maybe the auction itself was a tad ... archaic. But no one could argue with the results.

Maxine's nosy neighbor, Raelynn, about bankrupted herself (or I had to imagine she came close) when one of the strapping young Green Valley firefighters took his turn. Judging by the panicked smile he sent toward a young, attractive group of women—who'd done their best but couldn't outbid Raelynn—it was obvious he hadn't anticipated that turn of events. She hooted and hollered like she'd just won the lottery, and the poor man's face turned an unattractive shade of red.

Some women around my age won bids on handsome gentlemen serving up everything from romantic evenings to a full day of landscaping services. I was able to mind my own business, *thank you very much*, chatting happily with the people wandering through the event. Theo and I handed out my entire stack of printed coupons, and I sold through half the lavender tea from Lavender Hills farms, plus all the honey brown sugar face scrub I'd brought.

The day was a huge success, no matter which way I sliced it.

Until Hunter Buchanan walked up onto that damn stage.

Maxine had nominated herself the announcer of the event, though a legitimate auctioneer had taken over for each bidding process. But when it was Hunter's turn, she covered her microphone and whispered something to the auctioneer. His eyebrows rose in surprise, but when he swept his arm out to the stage and conceded his spot to her, I knew that devil woman was up to something.

"Ladies," she said, drawing a ripple of laughter from the crowd, "we're going to end this event on a real high note. Fresh back in town, no doubt highly relieved to be free of the Pacific Northwest, is the one and only Hunter Buchanan."

There were whistles and claps, and I tucked my arms around my middle, clenching my fists tightly.

Hunter closed his eyes, jaw rock solid, a muscle ticking ominously underneath that dark facial hair.

"Hunter is a *single* man in his thirties, in possession of *all* of his most important limbs and features," she said. "And whoever wins a day with this highly educated native of Green Valley will learn any number of valuable..." She paused, glancing meaningfully at Hunter. "Life skills."

The glare he aimed in her direction was so dark and promised so much retribution that the crowd roared with laughter. My heart raced under my ribs, skin shrinking as I scanned the crowd to see who might look a bit more eager than others.

Pink sparkly shirt was jockeying herself to the front of the crowd.

So was a willowy blonde with legs for days and cleavage so spectacular that I almost threw up in my mouth.

A couple of college coeds whispered to each other behind their programs, probably pooling all their money, and my skin started tingling.

A stunning Black girl cupped her hand, shouting up to Maxine. "What's he offering? If you win."

Her friends tittered uncontrollably, and I eyed their sorority T-shirts with rage starting to simmer in my blood.

Maxine held up a hand, and everyone quieted immediately. "This particular auction will be ... winner's choice," she said slyly. "How you spend your time, that's up to you."

He leaned over and whispered something furiously into her ear, but she pulled the mic away so no one could hear. Then she shooed him away.

"Ignore him," she said. "He'll forgive me. Everyone does eventually."

"Do we?" someone shouted from the crowd.

Laughter sprang up again.

I was ready to pass out by the time she called for quiet. "Who's ready to start the bidding?"

Prior to Hunter's appearance on stage, most of the gentlemen up for bid started somewhere around $100 and worked their way through the process by a skilled auctioneer until the final price was found. One of the Winstons went for an impressive $2900, the highest winning bid of the day. I think it was the youngest brother and a lucky local named Brooke cheering her victory with fists raised in the air.

Even the significant others of the men who were up for grabs seemed to take the entire event in stride, laughing and catcalling along with the rest of the crowd. Sometimes, they tossed out bids to drive the final price higher, but most seemed perfectly content to allow another woman to purchase time with the man they loved.

So why was I standing by my table, fighting against the icy-cold claws of panic that something irrevocable was about to happen?

Maxine held up the auctioneer's gavel with a flourish, and when Hunter swiped a hand down his face, eyes resigned and mouth turned down into an unhappy, handsome frown, I felt a deep pang of sympathy.

He'd hate something like this.

I might have laughed when I saw it, but this raucous, feral energy aimed in his direction wasn't quite as funny now.

Maybe it was because I was faced with the reality of the years I'd missed. Attention he undoubtedly received—even when he was married. He'd shown up at school wearing his tailored pants, a button-down shirt stretched across his chest, and—with a hard swallow—I pictured the tie around his neck. He'd look sharp. Professional. Endearingly smart. And I'd want to wrap that tie around my fist while he shoved me on top of his desk.

I fanned my face and tried to calm my racing heart.

This was bad. So very, very bad.

Bang.

The gavel came down with a crash. Bidding started fast and furious, my brain skittering frantically as women all through the crowd raised their numbered paddles, and Maxine pointed toward them, shouting to encourage the next bid.

My hand covered my mouth as it went higher and higher.

A hundred turned to five hundred in less than a minute.

Six.

Seven fifty.

The pink-sequined shirt glared at the willowy blonde.

A thousand.

The blonde stared at Hunter, licked her lips, and raised her paddle.

Fifteen hundred.

The group of coeds bent their heads together, and the ring leader raised her paddle.

Eighteen hundred.

My skin was tight, something frantic building, building, building underneath my bones.

Hunter closed his eyes when the pink sequins raised her paddle again.

Twenty-two hundred.

The college girls slumped their shoulders in unison. It was down to two.

Maxine locked eyes with me and raised one eyebrow in a blatant challenge.

The willowy blonde slid her paddle up again, cocking a hip defiantly.

Twenty-six hundred.

Pink sequins screwed her lips together, and my breath stalled somewhere in my lungs.

One of those winners felt like something he'd laugh about later. A little uncomfortable, and he'd no doubt be objectified every second of his time with her. But the second ...

The second was different.

She was young. Probably in her late twenties, if I had to guess. And the only metric I could use to judge was completely artificial.

She was stunning. Well-dressed. Had a big friendly smile that she was now aiming at Hunter like it was a fucking weapon. She probably had a family tree whose roots settled just as deep in this town as Hunter's. She probably saved orphaned kittens and knit hats for babies and had a master's in tantric sex positions.

And the thought of her—of anyone—using such things to gain Hunter's favor had something messy and wild explode through my body.

Because he was *mine*.

My hand shot in the air.

"Three thousand five hundred," I yelled. A thousand pairs of eyes could've turned in my direction for all I knew. The stage could've burst into flames. But I wasn't looking at anything but him.

Hunter's eyes locked onto mine, and I couldn't tear my gaze away.

His chest expanded on a deep inhale, and those lips, those demanding, firm lips, curved into a secret smile that had my heart tumbling head-long in my chest.

"Four thousand," the blonde called out.

"Shit," I whispered.

The blonde never so much as turned in my direction. There was no concern in her tone. I was no threat to her.

But there was a concern for me. I couldn't afford this. I couldn't afford even half of what I'd offered. But logic had flown the coop. It was nowhere to be found.

"F-Forty-five hundred," I said.

She paused, blowing a breath.

"Forty-seven hundred," she countered.

A lower bid. A slight hesitation in her voice.

My stomach somersaulted. I closed my eyes because if I looked at Hunter and saw the unbridled hope in his eyes, I knew what would happen.

I'd never stop.

When I opened them, Maxine was flipping her gaze between us.

"Forty-eight hundred," I said.

The blonde ran a hand through her hair.

Maxine raised the gavel, glanced at Hunter, then back at me.

"Five thousand," Maxine said.

My eyebrows shot up.

The blonde froze.

Bang.

"Sold to me," she said casually. "I'm ready for my afternoon nap, and you two could've carried on all damn day."

Hunter set his hands on his hips and gave her a quick, disbelieving look. She shrugged.

The audience cheered at the stunning total, but the sound was muffled and staticky. All I could hear was the *thud-thud-thud* of my heart pounding in my ears.

What had I just done?

Hunter's gaze landed on mine, unerringly, as he strode toward the steps.

What had I just done?

Theo said something, but my throat was bone-dry, my brain racing uncontrollably. "Stay here," I told him. "I-I'll be right back."

"Iris," Hunter's voice called.

I didn't know where I was going. I didn't know where I could hide from all the questions he'd ask me. What it meant, the instinct I'd just followed.

I just turned and ran.

CHAPTER 15

HUNTER

*S*he was gone by the time I got to the table.

"Do you know where your sister went?" I asked Theo.

He shrugged. "She just ran, like ... that way, I think?"

A pavilion was on the other side of the field, a small brick wall enclosing the restrooms, the pitched roof covering picnic tables for families to sit and eat. And when I glimpsed past the trees surrounding it, I saw a flash of a black shirt, dark hair, and the ripped jeans from earlier.

"Stay here," I told him, eyes locked on the rapidly retreating frame of Iris.

"I will." He sighed, plopping onto a chair next to the table.

I took off, and chasing after her felt an awful lot like someone had just strapped us together and tossed us out of a plane.

This was the freefall, right after the moment of decision, and I let all of that frenetic energy propel me into a run.

"Iris," I called out again. "Wait."

The pavilion was empty, and she'd sank against the brick wall around the corner, her hand pressed to her chest.

"I don't..." she said, shaking her head frantically, "I don't know what I was doing."

Approaching slowly seemed like the smartest thing to do. It was what my logical brain would instruct me to do. But it was the other side of me coming out on top, the one who'd wanted this infuriatingly closed-off woman for so long.

"I think you do," I told her.

Iris pinched her eyes shut. "What did I do?" she whispered.

"Tell me what you felt," I begged.

Her eyes flashed open, hot and angry.

"Tell me, Iris," I repeated.

She straightened off the wall, stalking toward me, and pointed a finger at my chest, stopping just shy of touching me. "You know exactly what I felt, Hunter Buchanan."

I snatched her hand before she could pull it away and smoothed it over my chest. She swallowed a sob.

"Feel my heart right now."

Iris stared at her hand like it was separate from her body, but she didn't say anything.

I laid my hand over the same spot on her, fingers spread on the warmth of her skin, and her eyes fluttered closed. Underneath my palm, her heart thrashed.

"Tell me what made your heart do this," I whispered fiercely, sliding closer, the front of my thighs brushing her jeans. "I want to hear the words."

Iris sagged, her forehead settling onto my collarbone, and finally, she emitted a rough breath. "I couldn't stand the thought of her having you. I didn't even know I was going to speak until the words came out, but I couldn't *not*."

"Why?" My other hand slid around the curve of her waist and up the line of her back until her hair was tangled around my fingers.

Iris's hand moved from my heart, curving around the edge of my bicep, and the light touch of her fingers had me breathing unevenly. Unconsciously, my hips pressed toward her, and she exhaled raggedly when she felt me hard against her stomach.

From a single embrace.

Because it wasn't just the touch of a woman that could do this to me. It was her. Only her.

Iris lifted her head, her eyes pinned onto mine.

"I shouldn't have," she said finally.

My stomach hollowed out.

She shook her head. "I shouldn't have. I was wrong."

Carefully, she extricated herself from my arms and ran a hand through her tangled hair.

For the first time since I arrived back in town, for the first time since I'd seen her again, it wasn't cool, calm logic that pushed my actions.

No.

Now, hearing her say it was wrong, I was angry.

"What's so wrong about it?" I asked.

Her eyebrows rose at the harshness in my tone. "What do you mean? It's unfair... I feel like I'm just jerking both of us around right now."

"You are."

Her mouth fell open.

"When you don't know how to make peace with what you feel," I said, stepping back into her space, "you fight it and fight it and fight it."

Iris's chest rose and fell rapidly.

"And then, when it becomes too much, you react without thinking. You don't ever think through the consequences of what'll come from that action."

"It's not about consequences," she said fiercely. "I don't want to be that person who acts like I'm the only one who can have you, the only one who needs you. Not when I can't make up my mind about whether this could even work."

131

"You *are* the only one who will ever have me!" I yelled. My voice echoed around the open space. "And I wish you'd act like you needed me. Because I know how much I need you." I pressed a fist to my chest. "My heart is racing like this because, after twelve years, I will still take any scrap you're willing to give me. No matter how little you think through what might come next. Don't you see that yet?"

Her eyes filled with tears. "Hunter," she whispered.

"Don't you see?" I said again. As my anger receded, my hands moved up the soft skin of her arms until I framed her face. My thumbs traced over the tears that escaped. "Just this ... it would give me enough to live another twelve years without you. If I thought your life would be worse because of me in it or that you'd have to sacrifice something too big, I'd live on this one piece of time and be okay."

Iris took a deep, courage-filled breath, her eyes wide and so vulnerable that my heart trembled from the force of wanting to make her feel safe. Then she pressed up on the balls of her feet, sliding her lips over mine.

A groan tugged straight from the bottom of my chest, heavy with relief and want and love.

Finally, my soul sighed.

Finally.

I wrapped my arms around her and slanted my mouth, tasting her soft lips in gentle pulls and tugs.

It had been forever. And it felt like no time had passed at all.

Iris's hands gripped tight onto my back while I wound my fingers around her hair. The kiss slid from tastes and sighs into something deeper and wetter when my tongue slid against the seam of her lips.

She opened with a sweet sigh, and her tongue brushed mine. A tease and an invitation.

No hesitation, no questions, as I licked into her mouth. Iris tasted like mint and tea, and the curves of her body pressed tight to mine. She rocked her hips when I tugged at her lower lip with my teeth, sucking it into my mouth, releasing it with a wet pop.

Her eyes were hazy and lust-drenched when she stared up at me. I walked us backward, sliding my hand down so I could grip her bottom with one hand when her back was pressed against the sun-warmed brick.

I mouthed down the line of her neck, sucking at the skin of her shoulder, back up to her jaw.

She whispered my name, and it wasn't a plea to stop. It sounded like a prayer.

I couldn't wrap my arms around her tightly enough. I couldn't touch enough of her skin. Couldn't press my body against hers any more than I was. A kiss that felt like coming home was the only way I could describe it.

I love you, I wanted to say into her skin, but I kept the words inside.

Her hands gripped the sides of my face to drag my mouth back to hers, and she whimpered when I sucked on her tongue. Even when I wanted to, I'd never forgotten the sounds Iris made.

Some nights, during those early years we were apart, I'd lay in bed and torture myself by remembering.

I'd think about the times she was laid out in the bed of my truck, and I'd hold her legs open with my hands, my feet braced on the ground while I tasted her between her thighs. I'd think about the sweet curiosity in her eyes when she explored my body and her pleased sounds when she'd make me explode with her hands or mouth.

There was no sweetness now. It was gripping hands, teeth and tongue and lips. My hand moved up between her shoulder blades because I didn't want her to scrape her skin against the brick. With my other hand, I tugged her thigh tight up around my waist, and she dropped her head back against the wall when I rolled my hips.

"Oh, there," she whimpered.

I cursed under my breath at how good it felt. How good she felt. The warmth of her lips, the silk of her hair, the perfect way she moved with me.

My head ducked down to press sucking kisses against the line of her jaw. She moved mindlessly, trying to seek out her pleasure. And for a moment, I worried I'd revert to high school, messing my pants because a gorgeous woman was rubbing against me.

I might have to send Maxine a thank-you note for the entire fucking auction. I'd pay her back the five thousand with interest. Forever.

My head lifted from her skin so I could watch her face. Iris was flushed a pretty pink up her neck and spilling into her cheeks. Her eyes fluttered open when I stopped kissing her, and she bit down on her lower lip, fisting the material of my shirt and tugging me back again.

"I want to see you," I managed.

Iris whimpered, dropping her head back against the brick. Her back arched, eyes locked onto my mouth.

"Kiss me," she demanded.

With a groan, I took her mouth in a harsh, hard kiss.

There was no finesse in it. Our teeth clashed, and she pulled the air straight from my lungs, our tongues slick and messy as they tangled.

I'd do so much more than that. I'd take her against the wall. On the ground. Anywhere I could lay her out, anywhere I could let her settle on top of me.

That was when Theo's voice rang out beyond the wall. "Umm, Iris?"

We froze.

Her eyes fell closed, and I dropped my forehead to hers.

"Shit," I whispered.

She swallowed, pressing me back to a ... safer distance.

"I'll be right there," she called.

"Okay." Theo cleared his throat. "Because there's like ... a big line of people at your table, and I told them you ran off with Mr. B."

"Dammit," she whispered, scrambling away from the wall. And away from me.

But I understood why.

I curled my hand around the back of her neck before she could flee and gently nudged her chin toward me. "Take a deep breath."

She did as I instructed. The cloud of desire cleared from her eyes, and I saw caution taking a foothold in its place.

But this time, my stomach didn't hollow out. Because I knew. The fact that she'd allowed herself this, even for a moment, was enough.

For now.

Her lips curled up in a sweet smile. "You probably shouldn't walk with me," she said, touching the tips of her fingers to her mouth. I wanted to kiss her there again.

"I don't think anyone will be surprised to see us together after"—I tilted my head toward the stage—"that."

Her smile changed. "No, because of ..." She tilted her head down toward my shorts. "That."

I laughed. "Fair enough."

"Are you coming?" Theo shouted.

"Just about," Iris muttered.

I couldn't help myself. I snatched her mouth in a hard, hot kiss. "Go," I told her.

She started walking toward her brother but paused, settling her hand on my chest. "I have a few ... insane days coming up," she said. "And I think I need to settle my head a little. I'm not hiding if you don't hear from me."

With a kiss on her palm, I nodded. "Okay."

"Oh my *gosh*, Iris," Theo said.

"Settle down," she yelled.

"Are you making out with him?"

Her eyes pinched shut. "I will be *right there*, you little punk."

He laughed, and I could understand her need to step forward with caution. It wasn't just us anymore.

Iris gave me one last smile and walked away.

I sank against the wall when she was gone and rubbed a hand over my chest.

It wasn't perfect.

But for now, I could handle imperfect if it looked like that.

CHAPTER 16

HUNTER

*S*unday came and went without much fanfare.

Church with my family always felt like jumping back in time, taking mints from my Uncle Glenn that had probably been tucked into his pocket for a month, glaring at Connor when he made a paper airplane out of the bulletin and shot it at the back of Levi's head where he sat in the row in front of us.

Monday was about the same.

I worked with two students, met with Miss Tracy about all their progress, and she hinted strongly that one of the middle school teachers would be moving to Michigan at the end of the summer because her husband got a new job, and I should keep my eye out for the opening.

As Monday evening crawled into Tuesday morning, I thought—for the thousandth time—about Iris.

My phone stayed quiet, but I'd expected it to. Twice, my route through town had taken me past the future home of Black's Southern Staples, and it was a hive of activity both times. Workers were installing a lit sign in the front, and I saw at least five people working inside through the windows.

Neither time through town did I see her, and I was forced to acknowledge the same jittery impatience that I felt during the first few months of our relationship.

Who had the strongest feelings from the outset wasn't a secret. She and I had always known that I immediately jumped in with both feet. And as she warmed up to all those intense feelings that I'd been keeping at bay, Iris was finally able to meet me on an equal playing field.

Her intensity matched mine once she trusted me.

Her jealousy rivaled my own once she knew she could act on it without judgment from me. I didn't judge at all. I loved it when she staked her claim because when another woman came a bit too close or flirted a bit too obviously, Iris's feelings about it had teeth. Teeth she'd use on me, a tension-edged reminder that I better not flirt back, even as I held her hair in my hands while she moved between my legs.

Mine had been the same. We'd gone out for dinner once, probably about a year into our relationship, a few weeks after we slept together for the first time. An older guy sidled up next to her while she waited for me at the bar, a predatory gleam in his eye at the sight of her. Iris told him to fuck off when he tried to touch her ass, her words still ringing in the air as I approached.

We'd been mindless against the wall behind the bar, her hand down my pants, mine up her skirt, reminding her with a tight grip and grunted words that she was mine. I was hers.

Our kiss had unleashed so many of those memories that it was hard to even notice that two days had passed while she sorted all the same things out in her head.

But the reminder I needed of our complicated history, and all the things she juggled now, came in the form of her brother on the third day without seeing her.

He was at the playground when I arrived, and his whole body was strung tight with tension as he kicked at a clump of dirt.

"Hey, Theo," I said.

His gaze stayed locked on the ground.

"You ready to work on that research project again?"

His little fist clenched up, and he kicked at the dirt one more time. "I don't want to."

I nodded. "Something else you'd rather work on? We can be flexible."

Gone was the precocious kid from our previous sessions, and I was finally getting a glimpse of what his teachers had seen through the year. "I said I don't want to work."

Taking a seat on the bench, I plucked at my T-shirt. "It's a bit too hot out here for me too. Maybe we can work in the classroom today."

"I did this research project at the end of the year. The first one was stupid too. Why do I have to do another one?"

My eyebrows bent in a V while I studied his facial expression. "What'd you do your first research project on?"

He kicked. Harder. This day had been on the schedule for the past couple of weeks, so it was nothing out of the blue.

"Something stupid," he muttered.

"Try again, young man."

Theo sighed, recognizing my teacher tone, as he called it. "Our family history. Like one of those dumb tree graph things you're supposed to make connecting everyone together."

Realization settled in hard, and I nodded slowly. Of course he hated a project like that. It was no wonder he'd turned in the poster board with nothing on it. Nowhere in his file had it been noted what the topic was.

Theo's family tree, or what I knew of it, would be small. The information sparse, at least the pieces I was aware of.

He had a sister.

A mother who regularly ran into trouble with the law.

And a father who'd never had a role in his life.

"You know," I said slowly, "I don't really feel like working on that project either."

His gaze lifted, wariness in his eyes. "You don't?"

"I think ... that we're intelligent, enterprising young men, and if we want to do our project on something more interesting, then we should."

He'd stopped kicking the dirt. "Like what?"

I stood, snagging a basketball from the metal holder. "What about the history of basketball? How the game started."

He pursed his mouth to the side, catching the ball when I tossed it to him. "That's ... less stupid than the other one, I guess."

"Good."

Theo passed the ball to me, and I ran toward the basket for an easy layup. "Shouldn't we go inside and start?"

"One round of PIG first," I told him. "Expend some of your grumpy-ass energy before we sit down."

He rolled his eyes, but his mouth curved in a smile.

We played for a while, then moved into the library to settle in by one of the computers. While he printed off some pages of research, we talked through how to find information relevant to the project, and the tension left his shoulders and his face. A couple of hours later, once we'd moved on to math, he set his pencil down and pinned me with a thoughtful look.

"Are you dating my sister?" he asked.

I sat back in my chair. "You don't beat around the bush, do you?"

"Life's too short, Mr. B."

I grinned. "Sage advice, young sir." Then I scratched the side of my face. How would Iris want me to handle this?

Evasion. That was how.

At least until I had a better idea of where Iris and I stood.

"You're not done with your math yet."

Theo blew out a raspberry, then quickly scrawled the last two answers by the equations. He slammed his pencil down. "There. Are you dating my sister?"

My eyes narrowed. "What did she tell you when you asked?"

"I'm not stupid. I'm not asking Iris anything. Her face was so red when she came out of that pavilion. And her hair was all messed up."

I propped my chin on one fist and studied him. "I'll tell you one thing, and that's it. But I can't answer any other questions about your sister and me because I think it should be up to her what you do or don't know."

"Fine."

"Your sister and I were in a relationship a long time ago," I said. "Before you were born."

His eyes widened. "You're the ex-boyfriend she and Grandma used to talk about?"

"What'd they say about me?"

"I'm not telling you. You share one thing, then one thing is all you get outta me too."

I sighed. "It's complicated, Theo."

"That's what she always says too."

Before I could respond, the library doors opened, and Maxine pushed into the room with her walker and a shit-eating grin on her face.

"Why does that face make me nervous?" I asked.

Theo giggled.

"I'm here to get the kid," she said. "And collect my winnings."

I sat back in my chair, extending my legs straight out and folding my arms over my chest. "I'll pay you back if it means I don't have to be bossed around by you all day."

"You may want to retract that offer, young man." She tapped her temple. "I don't need your help at my house."

I eyed her. "Where?"

"At Iris's." Her eyebrow rose imperiously. "She's been so busy at the store that her lawn is so overgrown, I half expect a herd of kittens to pop up out of all that grass."

141

Theo grinned, looking over at me with clear excitement on his face.

"She'll be furious," I told Maxine.

"Why do you think I'm not telling her ahead of time? And when I show up with you, she can't kick you out."

I stood. "Wanna bet?" I muttered.

Maxine patted my arm and told Theo she'd wait for him in the car.

We packed up Theo's bags, and for the millionth time, I wondered if there was any way to avoid the way we kept getting thrown together. Not because I didn't love all the opportunities they provided. But something about it felt a bit like we weren't in control of how this was playing out.

Maybe fate had had enough of waiting. Or maybe it was a couple of meddling Southern women who got sick of watching us dance around each other. No matter what force was behind these separate pieces, I decided to roll with it.

Theo slipped his backpack onto his shoulders. "Mr. B?"

"Yeah?"

He swallowed. "If you are dating my sister ... just don't, don't disappear without a word. She's been left a lot. I hate seeing her sad because she'll pretend she's not. And that's almost worse."

With my heart cracking off into pieces in my chest, I held my hand out to Theo. Tentatively, he took it.

"I won't. I promise."

He smiled. "Cool."

"Should we go?" I asked.

"Yeah," he said, bouncing off toward the doors. "She's gonna be so pissed when we arrive. I can't *wait*."

CHAPTER 17

IRIS

*J*ust as I finished brushing through my shower-wet hair, I heard the sound of Maxine's car pulling into the driveway. Theo had tutoring, and my brush strokes slowed as I thought about Hunter.

For the millionth time.

Kissing him was just about the dumbest thing I could have possibly done.

And the most wonderful.

I couldn't deny the energy slithering through my veins like some unholy power had been unleashed underneath my skin. My body wanted him. Every night that week, I'd slid my hand down underneath the waist of my sleep shorts when I thought about that kiss too long.

The wanting wasn't the problem.

It was the domino effect that came as a result.

And I had a really big "domino effect recipient" in the form of one ten-year-old brother. The front door opened with a slam, and I rolled my eyes because I'd told Theo a hundred times not to do that.

"The door, Theo," I yelled from the bathroom.

"You dressed?"

"Yeah, you can come back."

He ran into the bedroom, face flushed and eyes bright with ... something that looked a lot like he was about to get in trouble.

I set my brush down, hand settling onto my hip. "What is it? Why do you look like I'm about to get mad?"

He grinned. "Maxine is out front."

"Okay," I said slowly. "I thought she was just dropping you off because she had plans."

Theo glanced at my clothes and sighed heavily. "I guess that's fine."

I looked down. Short black cotton shorts. A mint green tank top with a hole in the hem. "Fine for what? I'm cleaning the house today."

"Why would you shower before cleaning the house?"

Because I'd been grouting tile flooring at the store's bathroom all morning, and he did not understand that kind of dirty.

"Why are you policing my behavior?" I shoulder-checked him as I moved out of the bedroom. "Is this a pre-teen thing?"

He laughed, running past me down the hallway and yelling for Maxine. "She's coming. Get ready."

"The hell is going on?" I said.

My phone vibrated in my pocket, and when I saw another unfamiliar number— similar to the last two I'd received asking for me to accept a call from the jail—I swallowed a frustrated scream.

"I don't *want* to talk to you," I muttered, shoving the phone onto the console by the back door where I could pretend ignorance. My mother had her own little compartment in my head, and it was really easy to hide her away from all the others currently fighting for the front row.

A car door slammed, and I peered out through the front window, but all I saw was Maxine's monstrous silver sedan.

She called out to someone.

I slipped a hair tie off my wrist and wound my damp hair into a knot at the base of my skull, and my hands froze in the air when I heard the newcomer respond to Maxine.

You have got to be kidding me.

I scrambled over to the front door and peered through the screen from the corner, where they couldn't see me.

That was when I saw him. He rubbed the back of his neck, one of his clearest signals of discomfort. Maxine patted his arm.

"It'll be fine. Trust me." I heard her say.

Her being the traitor that was determined to undermine my entire life plan.

"Maxine, you sneaky little snake," I whispered.

Briefly, I looked over at the framed photo of my grandma Black and mourned the hole she'd left behind in our life. If she was alive, I thought ...

But the thought faded almost immediately. If Grandma was still alive, she'd be plotting right alongside Maxine with a gleeful smile on her wrinkled face. More than once, she warned me that I'd regret the day I asked Hunter to leave me alone. And she tried to warn me before he packed up and moved to the other side of the country.

I didn't listen.

Her warnings didn't ring as loud in my head as my own. I might miss him. But allowing him the chance to choose something else, something better than any life I could offer him, didn't seem like anything I could possibly regret.

To Grandma, it was melodramatic.

To Hunter, it was excessively harsh.

But neither of them had my mother breathing down their neck. Neither of them had lived a front row seat to the kind of chaos and destruction she could wreak upon people's lives.

"Those Buchanans," she'd said the first week she was out of jail. The first week she stayed with Grandma and me. The only time she met Hunter. "They look like they've got money."

She was drunk at the time. Claimed later she didn't mean anything by it. But I saw the way she eyed him. His clothes. His car.

And to me, it didn't matter if she was drunk or high or stone cold sober. That part of my life—her—would never go away. Would never disappear.

I couldn't control her any more than I could control the weather. So I'd done the only thing that made sense at the time.

I pushed him away instead. At the time, it felt so noble. So right.

Until it just felt lonely. And miserable.

I wasn't sure I could fight that misery for much longer. Not now that I'd had another taste of him back in my life.

Maxine started toward the front door while Hunter tugged open the single-stall garage. I met her at the door with a fierce glare.

"Oh, put that thing away," she mumbled.

"If you tell me I should smile more, I will throw down, no matter how old you are," I told her.

She laughed, and my glare softened. For the time being.

"What is this?" I asked wearily.

Maxine waved me out onto the front porch, taking a seat on her walker. Hunter looked up at the sound, his eyes tracking slowly down the length of my body.

How did he do that? He made me feel like I was standing stark naked in front of him just by a single look.

Leave it to Hunter to have that elusive male superpower—the kind of unrelenting sexual energy that made my clothes want to disappear with nothing but a snap of his very talented fingers. I should hate him for it.

But I didn't.

I missed the things he could do. The sensations he could pull from my body.

Just as much as I missed talking to him at the end of the day. Listening to that slow, deep voice read to me with my head settled on his lap.

"I know you think this should be easy," I told Maxine. My eyes stayed on him.

Hunter hadn't moved. He was waiting for something ... permission. Or a tantrum. I could probably flip a coin, honestly. Either felt like a good option.

Maxine shrugged. "You love him. He loves you. You're the one making things harder than they need to be."

My gaze moved to her. "So you stick your nose in my business? Force the two of us into these situations of your own making?"

"Yup."

I gave her an incredulous look. "You're not supposed to admit it out loud."

"Bullshit." She pulled a handkerchief out of her purse and dabbed at her chest and neck. "You know what I'm doing. So does Hunter. Can't blame me either. Watching you two tiptoe around this makes me want to gouge my eyes out."

Theo joined Hunter, pointing out where the lawn mower was parked.

"He's here to do *yard work*?" I asked. "Seriously?"

Maxine smiled, serene and happy. "I paid for him fair and square, didn't I? I never said he was going to do work at my house."

Theo ran to the porch. "The grass looks awful, Iris."

"Maybe *you* should start doing it as part of your chores."

He gave me a look. "You told me no heavy machinery until I was twelve because you didn't want me chopping off any limbs by accident."

Hunter smothered a grin. Maxine nodded like she was in church and the preacher just said something particularly inspiring.

Honestly, one more of these setups, and she was dead to me.

I folded my arms over my chest. "Fine. But you get to help him, wise guy."

147

"Oh, didn't I remember to tell you?" He blinked up at me, the picture of innocence. "I'm spending the night at Maxine's."

My mouth fell open. "I *beg* your pardon?"

Maxine stood from her walker. "Got your bag, Theo? If we hurry, we can make that movie you wanted to see in Merryville."

"I—"

She tapped my chin. "Close your mouth, honey. You'll give the man ideas."

Hunter cleared his throat, and despite my growing rage at this whole duplicitous setup, my skin warmed at the warning I heard in that sound.

Maxine held up her hands. "My apologies. I meant no harm."

Hunter yanked the lawn mower out of the garage. "I think you've done enough for today, Miss Barton." He crouched down to check the gas cap, and my eyes locked onto the muscles shifting in his forearm under all that golden-tan skin. When his attention turned back to me, I snapped my gaze elsewhere.

Maxine made a pleased sound in the back of her throat.

"You will pay for this, Maxine Barton," I whispered softly.

She laughed. "I don't doubt it, little flower. It'll be worth every moment of retribution you can heap upon me."

Theo blasted back out onto the porch, his backpack gripped tight in his hands. "Bye, Iris!"

"Wait, did you grab pajamas? Clean clothes for tomorrow?"

He rolled his eyes. "Yes. I know how to pack clothes. I'm *ten*."

Watching them walk to Maxine's car, leaving me alone with Hunter—who was about to get sweaty and hot mowing my lawn ... my *actual* lawn, if I could pull my head out of the gutter for a moment—was too much.

It felt very much like I was sitting on top of a carriage, pulled by six great big, angry-looking horses, and no one thought to hand me the reins. Way too powerful for me to control. Too big to stop. All I could do was hold on and try not to get hurt.

Maxine sent me a satisfied smirk as they pulled out of the driveway, and my hands gripped the banister on the porch rail so tight that I was surprised my skin didn't split wide open.

Hunter sighed. "I didn't ... I had no idea she was planning this until she picked up Theo."

My jaw clenched tight, but I managed a nod. My lack of a reaction had his eyes brimming with frustrated heat.

And in turn, all I felt was frustration with myself.

I didn't know how to do this.

Any of it.

I was terrified. And excited.

I wanted to be around him, but I didn't know how to be around him and not want ... everything. I didn't know how to want everything, to *have* everything with him, without dealing with all the rest. Any time my thoughts jumped onto the carousel, it was impossible to get back off. They just went around and around until I felt dizzy trying to figure it out in a way I didn't hurt him more than I already had.

"I'm gonna"—I hooked my hand back at the house—"go do some work inside."

His eyes, dark and searing, never left mine.

Once I was safely back in the house, I sagged against the wall and held my breath, waiting to see if he would follow me in.

But the lawn mower started with a sputtered roar.

I blew out a breath. Right. It was better this way.

I managed to clean the kitchen, only glancing outside every five minutes or so as he pushed the lawn mower back and forth and back and forth. Most areas needed to be cut twice because the grass was so thick.

As I picked up in the living room, he started on the front. Back and forth, my eyes tracked his movements while I folded blankets, stacked mail, and dusted the bookshelf against the back wall. The chest of his shirt was damp with sweat, and when he'd finished the front, he cut the engine on the mower and stared at the house for a long moment.

My chest went tight because there was no way he could see me watching. Hell, I'd been dusting the same spot on the bookshelf for the last five minutes while I watched his arm muscles bulge, locked tight on the ancient mower handle.

They were coated with a sheen of sweat when he wiped at his brow.

I thought about what Maxine said. Maybe it really was as simple as she said. That because we loved each other, everything else would fall into line. Maybe I was complicating it because, at twenty, I'd determined that love couldn't possibly conquer everything. That the man I loved—without any choice in the matter—claimed that he'd love me forever.

The girl who didn't even really know what love looked like until she'd moved into this strange, wonderful little town.

My grandma taught me first about the kind of love I'd never known from my mother. I stared at her picture and thought about what she'd tell me right now if she were here.

And Hunter ...

I watched him exhale deeply and pull his gaze away from the house, then push the mower back toward the garage. Hunter had taught me the other kind of love. His love was patient and true. It was respect and passion and head-spinning desire. It was sweet. It was all-consuming.

And most importantly, his love was safe.

He made me feel safe.

I blew out a deep breath of my own, set the dust cloth down, and laid my hand over my heart, much like he'd done before he kissed me.

When I pushed open the front door, he had his back to the house, and I watched with a dry throat while he tugged at the back of his T-shirt and yanked it over his head. The muscles in his back shifted under all that smooth skin. The curved shoulders, the narrow waist, and the hips.

I must have made a noise—something unconscious—because he turned.

The smattering of dark hair over his wide chest narrowed to a thin line that disappeared into the waistband of his black shorts. The neatly stacked squares of his stomach held my eyes while they tracked up, the rounded muscles of his pecs holding my gaze for another protracted moment.

Hunter at twenty-one had been delicious enough.

Hunter at almost thirty-four ...

I wasn't entirely sure there were words in the English language to describe what the sight of him did to me.

He lowered his shirt and let me look my fill.

My hand was still gripping the front door, and I swallowed before trying to speak. "I've got iced tea inside if you want to come in."

Hunter's tongue licked along his bottom lip. Then he strode toward the porch, only stopping his long, sure steps once he stood over me. I hadn't moved an inch.

"That why you're inviting me in?" he asked, voice rough and heavy with desire. "For a drink?"

I let out a ragged breath.

"Because if it is," he continued, crowding even closer until my hand shook from wanting to slide up his stomach and over his chest, "I'll leave now. I can't be in there with you if that's all you want."

My eyes rose over his upper body, a slow ascent until they locked with his. "No, that's not why."

His jaw clenched. Hunter dropped his head, inhaling along my cheekbone until his lips were at my ear.

"Then you know what it means," he said, lips brushing against my skin. "If I follow you in there."

My body shook, and he noticed. "I'm scared," I admitted quietly.

"Why?"

"I don't"—I swallowed—"I don't want to mess this up again. I can't lose you twice, Hunter."

He hummed. His lips pressed a featherlight kiss to the edge of my jaw. "You won't," he said into my skin. "Invite me in, Iris."

I managed a jerky nod.

A sound rumbled low in his chest. Against my stomach, he was big. And hard. And I wanted him more than I ever had before.

"Good girl," he growled.

My fingers slid down the hot skin of his forearm until my fingers twined through his. He exhaled. So did I.

And I led him inside.

CHAPTER 18

HUNTER

*I*n silence, she led us into the hushed, dark house. Later, I'd catalog all the ways her home had changed. I'd study the space where she lived. Much, much later.

There were things we had to talk about.

Stories we needed to tell each other.

Those conversations, agreements, and understandings would come later.

Much, much later.

It had been twelve years, ninety-seven days, and some odd handful of hours since I'd had Iris Black in my arms, and I wasn't waiting another second.

We cleared the door, and I slammed it shut, swinging Iris around until she was in my arms. Our mouths met immediately, a tangled battle for dominance of my tongue and hers, the soft give of her lips underneath mine, and the sharp nip of teeth.

She moaned, her body trembling lightly as she wound her arms tight around my neck.

Her body had changed as the years passed, and even though I was sure I was gripping her too hard, my hands too demanding and moving too quickly, I yanked the strap of her tank top down and filled my hand with the soft, warm weight of her breast. There was more flesh there now, more to touch and taste and suck and bite, and I wanted all of it now.

Iris tore her mouth away with a gasp, her back hitting the wall next to the stairs with a thud. I rolled my palm in a circle, lightly against the tight bud of her nipple, and she sank down until my thigh wedged between her legs.

"You feel so good," I growled into the curve of her shoulder. Then I scraped my teeth along the tender line of her collarbone. She scraped her nails up my chest, and I hissed.

Iris cursed, foul and guttural, when my thumb and forefinger tugged at her. Unable to wait any longer, I ducked my head down and sucked her skin into my mouth. I groaned as I pulled back, and she rolled her hips against my thigh. Her shorts rode up, and my other hand pushed up through the opening.

"Hunter," she whimpered. Her hands shoved into my hair, tugging my face back up to hers. Her tongue slid hot and wet and slow against mine, and I pressed her into the wall. Hard, hard, harder, there was nowhere else for us to go.

There was only one place I *wanted* to go.

Inside.

Inside her. The woman I wanted, had waited for, and would love for the rest of my fucking life. Probably beyond my life, even. Whatever afterlife existed— heaven or any other names that earthly religions could call it—I'd spend that loving her too.

I slanted my head, devoured her mouth like a starved, wild beast, and she met me stroke for stroke, kiss for kiss. My hands couldn't stop moving and thread into her damp hair, tugging the thing that kept it held back. When it tumbled around her shoulders in a tangled mane, I fisted the long, dark length with a hard tug.

She broke away from my mouth with a shocked gasp.

"Here?" I asked. I licked along her jaw while she panted. "Am I taking you here?"

Her pupils were huge and dark as she stared up at me. Her head nodded jerkily. "It's here or the floor, buddy. We can move to a bed later."

I laughed against her mouth when I kissed her again. But my laughter stopped when her hand slid between us, curling around me. She dipped her head and sank her teeth into the meat of my shoulder. I was sweaty from being outside, and my girl loved it. She dragged her nose along the line of my chest, sucking at the base of my throat like she could inhale me whole.

I cursed under my breath, rolling my forehead against the wall, my hips snapping forward at the movement of her wrist. Then I plucked her hand away and took a moment to study the small flower tattooed onto her wrist.

An iris, the petals filled in with black ink.

I dropped a sweet, soft kiss there and then anchored her hand to the wall above her head. "Later," I said.

For a moment, as I pressed my thigh hard between her legs, her eyes fluttered shut, and I could see just how much this was affecting her. How close she was to hurtling over the cliff.

Her breathing picked up speed, her hips riding my leg, her back arching in a sensual curve, which pressed her chest closer to mine. Her breasts pushed against me, and I wanted to dive my mouth into the space between them again.

"Open your eyes, Iris," I commanded. "Watch me while you go."

Like someone had to pry those eyes open, she did as I'd asked. Iris took her pleasure from my body like I was an instrument built solely to please her.

Before the night was over, I'd show her exactly how well I could.

But for now, with my hands gripping her wrists so she couldn't touch me, I sucked her bottom lip into my mouth and a low moan built in her throat, a flush coating her chest.

Her eyes locked with mine, Iris visibly fought the instinct to toss her head back and pinch her eyes shut, but when her movements twitched and rolled, I knew she was close.

I rolled my hips, tightening the grip of my hands on the delicate bones of her wrists, and she came with a long, delicious, sighing moan.

"My beautiful girl," I exhaled. "Look at you."

I'd lose my mind if she laid so much as a single finger on me. There was nothing but a fire inside me, something hot and raging out of control. It had teeth and fangs and trembling muscles, and there was nothing left to hold back.

Iris slumped against the wall, and while she caught her breath, I shoved at the waist of her flimsy shorts. She looked drugged as she raked her nails down my back, pushing my own shorts down too. I kicked them off, and she fumbled until one of her legs was free. Her shirt was off one shoulder, and she ripped it over her head.

My hand curled around her bottom until I had enough of her flesh in my hands that I could boost her up against the wall.

"Please," she begged. She was mindless, a writhing creature trying to pull me inside with her legs wrapped tight around my waist.

I kissed her deep and hard, and she clung to my shoulders.

When I broke away, she gripped the sides of my face with her hands.

"I've missed you so much," she said, close to tears. Her eyes were shining and bright, and I rolled my forehead against hers.

Instead of telling her I missed her, because she knew, I fitted my lips between hers in a kiss so sweet, so light, that my body shook from the restraint that it took to keep it that way. I let her weight shift to the angle of the wall, the position of my body holding her up, and I slowly pushed my hips forward.

Not even halfway, I paused, and sweat beaded on my forehead. The sensations were too much. Too hot. Too good. Too tight.

And I wondered, for just a moment, if I loved her too much.

I pulled back.

She gasped, pupils dilated, pulse pounding wildly in her throat. "Hunter."

I locked eyes with her. "I love you," I told her.

Her lips curled in a smile.

Snap.

My hips sliced forward in a single, endless thrust, and she tossed her head back on a scream.

Iris held on while I exorcised all the days and weeks and months and years of missing her. My back was on fire. My thighs burned from the effort of holding us there.

And I wanted to exist in that single moment of mind-blistering pleasure for the rest of my life.

She was perfect for me—my counterpart for all the sides of myself that I'd never been able to show, never been able to indulge.

Again and again and again, I pushed her higher with each rough movement. I dropped my head into the curve of her neck and said all manner of things that I'd kept buried.

That I loved her.

That she was perfect.

I missed her.

She was my future.

And I'd do anything—*anything*—to have her like this for the rest of my life.

Her muscles went tight, locking with the kind of tension that heralded another explosion, and that was when I pushed in again, biting down on her neck.

She sobbed my name, her arms wrapped so tight around me that I wondered how she could even breathe from how closely we embraced. Heat crawled up my spine, a white-hot ball of delayed pleasure that I'd held at bay until she tightened around me again.

One more sharp snap of my hips and the liquid, golden glow spread all the way out. I shouted into her skin while it poured through me, to the tips of my fingers and down my legs.

I sank down onto my haunches, careful to keep my grip around her. Iris peppered kisses all over my face, sliding her lips over mine in a luxurious, slow kiss that felt like *more*.

It felt like we might not get very far before something started again.

"Holy shit," I exhaled.

She laughed, kissing my jaw. My throat. The corner next to my mouth.

For a few moments, all we did was breathe. Held each other. And it was perfect.

Iris hummed. "This can't be comfortable."

I kissed her shoulder. "It's really, really not."

She laughed.

Carefully, she straightened, shifting off my lap with a hiss. Then she stood, stark naked and looking like she'd just been banged senseless against a wall.

Iris held out her hand, and with a grin, I took it.

Once I was standing over her, I studied her eyes, cupping her face in my hands.

What I saw eased that remaining thread of tension I hadn't even realized I was holding on to.

I saw peace. Contentment. Desire.

And I saw love.

"No regrets?" I asked quietly.

She shook her head. "My body will regret that position tomorrow when I wake up, but that's it."

With a laugh, I kissed her.

"Now what?" She curled her hands around my back, then slid them down, cupping my ass with a devious grin on her face. Her fingers squeezed.

I hummed, pushing her hair away from her neck. I kissed the edge of her jaw. "Now ... we go to the shower."

"Really?"

I licked the line of her neck. "If you didn't notice, I'm a little sweaty."

"Oh, I noticed," she purred, sliding her hand slowly across my stomach, up my chest, then back down. "Am I allowed to wash your back?"

"Among other things."

With the sound of her laughter echoing down the hallway, I swung her in my arms, strode naked through the house, and settled her onto the bathroom counter while the water heated.

Her eyes glowed, and when they did, my entire heart felt whole. For the first time since I'd walked away, *I* felt whole.

The bathroom slowly filled with steam, and she caught my hand while I tested the water's temperature.

"I love you too," she said quietly.

I had to close my eyes, wrap my arms around her and just ... exist. Soak in the moment that I'd waited so long for.

It was dangerous to allow someone that much power over you, but I'd never known any other way to love this woman. And even knowing that she could wreck me all over again, I pulled her off the counter with our mouths sealed, my heart open, and dove straight back in.

CHAPTER 19

IRIS

"These are new," I said.

He grunted. I kissed the spot I'd just discovered, a smattering of freckles along his back, high up on his shoulder blade. The sun was filtering weakly in the bedroom, giving me just enough light to study his body in great detail.

"So are these," I whispered, trailing my fingers across the muscles in his arms.

Hunter's eyes were closed, his arms tucked underneath the pillow beneath his head, but his lips curled up in a tiny smile. I was perched on his ridiculously muscular ass, my legs straddling his body while I traced the planes of his back and arms and neck. Sometimes, it was with my fingers, and sometimes my lips or my tongue.

We'd left the bed once, sometime around nine the night before. Perched on the kitchen counter and wrapped in a bed sheet, Hunter fed me slices of apples, a bowl of grapes he'd cleaned, and we shared some sharp white cheddar cheese and cold rotisserie chicken. Between bites of food, we'd ask each other questions, filling in the gaps of time that we missed.

"Thirtieth birthday," Hunter started.

I smiled. "The last birthday before my grandma died." He slid a hand soothingly across my back. "She made that vinegar pie I love. She and Theo and Maxine sang 'Happy Birthday,' and it was the most god-awful version I'd ever heard in my life. I was so happy," I whispered. "The only thing I wished for was more birthdays like that."

Hunter swept his thumb across my cheek when I shed a tear. "I'm sorry she's gone. She was a wonderful woman, and she loved you so much."

I nodded. "I was lucky to have the time with her that I did. That's why I moved back not long after I got Theo. I knew he needed time with her, too."

"Smart," he murmured. "Must've been hard for her to see another grandchild go through what you did."

The entire night had been perfect. And I wouldn't let it be spoiled by mentions of *her*. I simply nodded, giving him a sweet kiss.

"Favorite Christmas memory," I said.

The look he gave me at the subject change was knowing, but he didn't comment. Hunter always knew when I didn't want to talk about my mom, and he never pushed.

His jaw worked as he finished his bite of chicken. "Probably my first one in Seattle after I finished grad school."

My fingers traced the line of his nose. "What did you love about it?"

"Everything," he admitted. "My parents came to visit because they didn't want me to be alone. Connor and Sylvia were with her family, and Levi was in college, busy with something. We drove through the light display at Spanaway Park, shopped at Pike's Market, saw the nightly snowfall at Snowflake Lane—"

"Nightly snowfall?" I asked with a smile.

He nodded. "Fake snow, but it's fun when you're not used to getting much at Christmastime."

I slid my arms around him while he told me about all the things he loved from that year. It would've been two or three years after he left Green Valley. And before he met his ex-wife, if I read between the lines correctly.

Samantha. I knew her name now. Knew enough about her that I felt a strange sort of sympathy for a woman who tried to love Hunter but never really had his heart. It was something he'd told me once, a long time ago. That was how it worked in the Buchanan family. You could meet someone else, even care for them, but they wouldn't be quite right for you. Something would always feel slightly off-kilter, an edge of discomfort to any relationship that was not with The One. I believed it now.

I didn't back then. Not really.

"It sounds amazing," I said quietly. I'd only ever experienced Tennessee Christmases. My scope of experience was so limited compared to his.

He kissed the top of my head. "It was. There was a lot I loved about living in Seattle."

With a deep breath, I pulled back. "Will you go back?"

Hunter's forehead furrowed. "To Seattle?"

Slowly, I nodded. My heart churned, and I braced myself that he might never have had plans to stay.

"No," he answered immediately. His hands cupped my face. *"No.* I'm staying here. I'll find a job, I can teach here or Merryville, or if I have to, I'll drive into Knoxville."

My relief was cool and sweet and instant, and he laughed at the way I sank against him.

"Maybe we could visit someday," I said shyly. "I'd like to see it."

Hunter smiled, a dimple appearing in the shadow of his dark stubble. I tucked my thumb into that dimple, then leaned forward to drop a kiss there.

He turned his head, sliding his lips over mine, licking at the seam of my mouth until I opened with a sigh.

No one had ever kissed me like Hunter.

His kisses satisfied me in a way that I never thought existed before or after him. It didn't matter to me that he'd kissed someone else, not anymore. And it didn't matter that I'd done the same. As his tongue slid sweet over mine, his firm lips turning demanding and rough as our hands slid over each other's bare skin, I knew that *our* kisses were the ones that held magic.

If I closed my eyes, I could imagine it like a silvery, pulsing cloud around our bodies. Its own living thing, capable of turning the whole world upside down just from the touch of his mouth on mine.

He knew when to take those kisses deeper, how to tilt his head to the side, to pull breath into his lungs so we didn't have to stop. He knew when to keep them sweet and slow and decadent, tasting my lips like I was the most delicious thing he'd ever consumed.

We kissed for a while like that—the sweet, slow kind, tasting of apples and grapes—and his hands slid under the wrinkled sheet so he could gather me fully into his arms.

In fact, we never stopped touching for the whole night.

When we slept, short snippets of exhausted dozing, I was tucked tight against his chest, or he was curled around my back, arm anchored firmly around my waist. When one of us finished napping, we used our hands or mouth to wake the other.

Once, Hunter woke me by sliding under the sheet, using firm hands to push me onto my back and pry my knees apart. I came awake to his head between my legs. I shoved the sheet down before gripping his hair in my hands because if a girl got woken like that, she wanted to see his eyes locked tight on hers when he feasted and feasted and *feasted*.

When he finished, he prowled up my still-shuddering body, licking a line around my belly button and taking my mouth in a searing kiss before he notched himself between my thighs and started moving in slow, slow rolls of his hips.

Each movement was deliberate, a gradual build until our chests were slick with sweat as he continued to push into me.

It was the opposite of the hallway because when I thought he'd move faster, he didn't. He'd slow again until my head thrashed frantically on the bed. Hunter would grin into my neck, telling me to be patient. To wait. To let it stretch out.

When I locked my thighs high on his sides and urged him forward with my hands on his buttocks, he chuckled darkly.

"Soon," he whispered into my ear. "Soon, my love."

"Now," I begged.

When he wouldn't move faster, when he started slowing even more, I shoved at his shoulders until he rolled onto his back with a booming laugh.

His laughter stopped, though, when I braced my hands on his stomach and lowered myself down.

Hunter's hands held my hips with bruising strength, and as I rolled my body over him, he muttered curse words through gritted teeth. When we came, it was at the same time, me on a sigh and him on a low groan.

We napped again, each subsequent round slower and sweeter because our bodies could hardly take any more.

But it didn't stop us.

We had twelve years of missed nights like this, driven by a mindless determination to make up for every single one of them.

When I couldn't handle anymore, and he couldn't either, we settled on soft, sweet explorations of each other's bodies. That was how I woke him, charting the topography of his muscled back, finding each freckle and muscle he hadn't had before.

My fingers moved from the freckles across his shoulder, down along his sides, and the skin tightened.

"Ooh," I whispered, "are you still ticklish?"

He buried his face in the pillow. "No."

I grinned. "Do you want me to get off you so you can go back to sleep?"

He glanced at me over his shoulder. "No," he answered with a smile.

Happily, I stretched myself over his back, inhaling the warm, smooth skin while he dozed again. My hands coasted over his shoulders and arms, and I couldn't help but marvel at the perfection of his body. He'd always loved to work out, lifting weights with his brothers when they weren't hiking or playing basketball. Clearly, he hadn't lost that love over the years.

I must've closed my eyes because I woke to the great mountain of a man underneath me, stretching his arms out and groaning.

I slid off his back, notching myself against his chest when he rolled over.

That was when his stomach growled.

I laughed, kissing over his heart. "Do I need to feed you?"

He shifted, burying his face between my breasts, sucking at the skin he found there. "I think you did a few hours ago. It was delicious," he growled.

I smacked his back, and he laughed.

Hunter set his chin on my chest and stared up at me. His hair was a disaster, the stubble on his chin deeper and darker than it had been the day before, and his lips were probably as puffy as mine from hours of kissing.

He'd never looked better.

"You know what sounds perfect?" he asked.

I traced the line of his lips. "A shower, four ibuprofen, and twelve hours of sleep?"

He grinned. "Besides that."

"Tell me."

He dropped a featherlight kiss onto the side of my right breast, nuzzling his nose into the warm flesh.

"A blueberry muffin and some coffee," he murmured, eyes locked on mine as he brushed his lips over the edge of my nipple.

I knew what he was asking for. And what it meant if I said yes. It wasn't a quiet meal in my quiet kitchen. It was a declaration—showing up to the bakery in the same car on a Saturday in the early morning hours. He'd want to hold my hand as we waited in line. He'd want to kiss me across the table, no matter who was there or could see.

I pulled his face up to mine and gave him a slow, sweet kiss. "I think a blueberry muffin sounds perfect to me too," I whispered against his lips.

The smile he gave me in answer was one I'd remember on my deathbed. It was amazing how quickly the past could be mended and erased over the course of one night with him. Those years apart had already faded into something fuzzy and abstract.

We dressed, managing to keep our hands off each other while we did. He opened the car door for me, grinning when I laughed at his show of chivalry. And when we pulled in front of Donner Bakery, meeting at the front of his car, he held his hand out.

His eyes were calm, everything about him so sure.

It used to intimidate me that Hunter never questioned our path. It was less scary now, something I didn't question.

It was easy to slide my palm over his, our fingers winding together as we walked toward the entrance.

The door opened with the jangle of a bell, and every eye in the place locked onto us when we took our place at the back of the line. He curled his arm around my back and dropped a kiss on the top of my head.

From the cash register, Joy's face popped around the side, her eyes brightening when she saw us.

She gave me two thumbs-up and a beaming smile that split her face right in half.

I laughed under my breath, shaking my head at this strange little turn of events. A few groups of women whispered amongst themselves, and I knew that by the end of the day, half of Green Valley would know we were together.

And this time ... everyone knowing my business felt perfectly right to me.

CHAPTER 20

IRIS

*a*s I inched closer to the store opening, I learned that Green Valley residents didn't care much for waiting. We made progress on the store, dusting shelves before filling them with jars and candles and jewelry holders, and placing rugs and vases filled with bright green-tipped stems around the space. I swear, half the town would randomly drop by just to "see how things were going."

Maxine and a few friends from church came on Monday morning while Hunter and I put the finishing touches on the small bathroom in the back of the store. Thankfully, they showed up *after* he'd finished sliding my shorts down, instructing me to keep my hands on the sink while he took me from behind, our eyes locked in the mirror and his hand covering my mouth. But my flushed face must have given me away because Maxine gave me a knowing grin.

I wasn't apologizing for it, though. The first night—with Theo gone at Maxine's —was the only one we'd had fully and totally alone with a bed at our disposal. So we took our pockets of privacy when we had them, even if it was in the store bathroom, thank you very much.

The phone calls, at least for the past few days, had stopped, and I was able to breathe just a little bit easier because of it.

My days were an exhausted blur, but having him there with me seemed to make them easier and not harder like I'd imagined.

He continued tutoring Theo, and all I received were glowing reports from Hunter and the school counselor. A few more comprehension tests and they'd clear him to move on to fifth grade. He helped Maxine shuttle Theo back and forth, even when I didn't ask him to. And oh Lord, I'd heard about it for days when Theo was able to join Hunter and his brothers when they played basketball at the park.

He brought me food to ensure I was eating well as the store inched closer and closer to completion. He let me put him to work, and to my surprise, he and Grant got along quite well.

It surprised Hunter too.

"He's a good guy," he said quietly after Grant and his guy had finished installing the point-of-sale counter he'd built for me. It was a beautiful, massive thing made of white oak and was so fricken heavy that it could probably outlast just about anything in the entire town.

I finished wiping down the counter, adjusting the white vase filled with fresh flowers that he'd brought from his momma's garden. "He is," I said.

Hunter screwed a light bulb into the small lamp I'd purchased for the end of the counter. "That why it didn't work out with you two?"

My eyebrows rose. Other than one brief conversation the first night, we hadn't touched on the matter of our pasts. It seemed like we'd both made peace with the existence of other people in the years we'd been apart.

"Among other things."

He considered that quietly.

"But that's not why it didn't work out." I set my elbow on the counter and turned toward him. "Obviously, I have a thing for nice guys."

Hunter smirked, and when he glanced in my direction, his dark eyes held a wicked gleam. He moved, sliding behind me so he could push the hair off my shoulder. He kissed my neck. "I'm not that nice," he said against my skin.

"Don't distract me with sex." I wiggled my hips when he wrapped a strong arm around my hips. "You're the one that brought it up. And yes, you are."

"That's not what you said last night."

I smiled. "I can hardly be held accountable for what I said when you had my hands pinned on the bed, and you wouldn't let me turn over."

Hunter's laughter had my heart churning warm and melty in my chest.

Just as I was about to turn in his arms and indulge my desire to kiss him sense-less, the door to the shop opened, and the new bell I'd installed jingled happily.

Hunter straightened, his arm dropping from around my waist. "Sylvia," he said with a smile. "Good to see you."

His sister-in-law, very pretty and very pregnant, waddled her way into the store. "Oh my Lord, look at how cute it is in here! I swear, you're gonna get me in trouble with Connor once this place opens."

I smiled, smoothing a self-conscious hand through my hair. Why was it that every time someone showed up, Hunter was trying his very best to get us caught for public indecency?

"Thank you," I told her. "Feel free to look around. We've got most of the stuff out at the moment. I'm just waiting on a few last big pieces of furniture and Grace's photos. And we're planning a soft opening next week for friends and family, so I'd be happy to email you the details if you want to come."

Her eyes darted happily between Hunter and me. "I'd *love* to come for the friends and family event."

He sighed, coming around the counter to drop a kiss on her cheek. "How's my niece or nephew treating you?"

She groaned, rubbing a hand over her belly. "I can't believe I've got six weeks left. My back's been cramping up the last few days something awful."

"Did you call your doctor about it?" he asked.

Sylvia waved him off. "You sound like my husband. It's nothing. Just hitting the point when my body feels like it's been taken over by an alien force, and there's not much I can do about it anymore."

"When does Connor get back from Chicago?" Hunter asked.

She blew out a breath, wincing as she started rubbing her lower back. "Four days."

"Maybe you should go stay with my parents. In case your back gets worse. That way, we can help you if you need it."

I watched them quietly. Hunter, despite being gone for so long, had an easy, natural way about his relationship with the woman married to his brother. He told me it was because Sylvia had been part of their family for so long. She and Connor met early in high school and had been together ever since.

Apparently, this family love legend wasn't full of angst and drama for everyone.

Sylvia rolled her eyes playfully. "Y'all act like women haven't been giving birth since the dawn of time. I'll be just fine. Now, shoo, so I can talk to your Iris for a minute. You two have been staying so busy here that none of us have gotten a chance to spend any time with her."

Hunter gave me a look, and I nodded. The fact that he checked had my heart going all soft and mushy. Sliding back into a relationship with him was as easy as breathing, but I still didn't know how to be a part of his family.

The first time, we were so young, and I could hardly imagine sitting down to a picture-perfect family Sunday dinner. Passing steaming plates of food while they laughed and talked and shared.

It was foreign to me, as good as being dropped into an alien planet. I'd been to his home, of course, but in passing. Enough to meet his parents and his siblings, and the rest of our time was spent at my grandma's, and in the woods and parks around town. In the aisles of the library where we picked books and curled up in a chair together to read.

Now there were moms and cousins and sisters and girlfriends trying their hardest to get to know me, simply because they knew how deep his love went. Sylvia's eyes had no ulterior motive nor angle she was trying to use.

"What's going to go here?" she asked, motioning to the big empty space in the middle of the store.

"I'll show you," I told her with a smile. I tapped on the screen of my phone and pulled up the picture I had bookmarked from the shop in Nashville, then turned it around so Sylvia could see.

Her face lit up. "It's *gorgeous*. I've never seen a couch like that."

"My grandma had one just like it when I lived with her," I said. "I've never seen one since, and it felt like fate when I saw this one for sale."

"What happened to your grandma's couch?"

My smile got a little tight at the edges. "Someone staying with her ... ruined the upholstery. Couldn't be salvaged."

Sylvia sighed. "It's such a shame when old pieces like that get destroyed."

I hummed. "Indeed."

Shame was a good word for it. Nellie had been crashing on that couch for about a month and got drunk one night, lighting a cigarette when Grandma and I were asleep. The following morning, she claimed the burn holes were an accident, but I didn't believe her. My grandma didn't have much in the way of discretionary income, not with both of us staying there, so the couch was dumped instead. The church gave her a donated couch about a week later, something nice and clean, but it wasn't the same.

And more than anything, replacing that one beloved thing that Nellie destroyed, it felt like a small way to honor my grandmother.

But Sylvia didn't need to know any of that. She rubbed at her back again.

I pointed at a display of small jars with crisp black-and-white labels. "I can't vouch for it myself, but this cream is supposed to work wonders for back pain and restless legs, and the woman who makes it said it's the only thing that helped her sleep for more than two hours when she was pregnant."

"I'll take three jars," Sylvia said.

With a laugh, I snagged one from the shelf and pulled the top off. "She uses lavender in it, and I love that smell, but not everyone does."

Sylvia sniffed when I held the jar out, her eyes closing. "Oh my. That smells like heaven. Make it four."

"Not that I don't appreciate a big sale, but I think four jars would last you until the baby's fifth birthday."

She had a sweet laugh, and there was something kind in her eyes that I found myself wanting to ask her everything now that she was in front of me. Whether it had scared her when Connor told her he fell in love with her as soon as they met. But I knew I wouldn't because I was the only one now, the only person who found their way into this family—with their perfect matches and soul mates—and then voluntarily left it. Left him.

"Francine wanted to come with me," Sylvia confided, walking with me toward the sales counter. "But I told her she wasn't allowed to scare you away."

I blew out a breath. "She wouldn't, but thank you for thinking I might need some time."

My iPad wasn't set up yet, another big purchase I was waiting on as I paid a billion contractors for all the work they'd done, so Sylvia fished some cash out of her purse and slid it across the counter. "You and Hunter probably feel enough pressure on this second time around. You don't need us sticking our noses into it just because we're glad to see him happy again."

Sylvia's face scrunched up in a wince, and she pressed at the side of her belly.

"Are you sure you're okay?"

"I'm fine. I'm fine. Baby is just pinching at my side is all." She waved her hand. "Either way, I thought you could use some breathing room."

I gave her a wry smile. "Oh, I think between Maxine and Fran, we've moved well beyond the nose-sticking part of our reunion."

Sylvia groaned. "I heard about what they did. We really do have the most notorious busybodies in the entire world living here, don't we?"

Hunter was across the store, organizing some tools back into the box he'd borrowed from his dad.

"Maybe," I said quietly. "But I can't argue with their results."

Sylvia sighed, a happy little sound, and my face went bright pink. I covered my cheeks with my hands, and it made her laugh.

"Well, if you've forgiven them their blatant interference, maybe we could have you out for a girls' night. Fran, me, Grace, Joss, and Magnolia try to have dinner together once a month. Just the Buchanan girls."

The Buchanan girls.

My stomach went weightless with the implication. And my heart ached with a hidden yearning I didn't know I still held on to. That someday, I'd have a family that big. That welcoming. I finally let myself imagine what this would mean for Theo. He'd have uncles and aunts, and a loud, chaotic house full of people to celebrate Christmas and Thanksgiving. He'd have cousins. Grandparents.

And I very much did not want to burst into tears because Sylvia invited me to dinner, so I let out a deep breath, not looking back up at her until I could speak clearly. "I would love—"

Sylvia's face went a little pale. "Oh."

"What?"

She tilted her head, glancing down. When she looked back up, her eyes were huge. "I ... I'm not sure if I just peed myself, or if your water can break in a much less dramatic fashion than they show in the movies."

"Your water just broke?" I asked, rushing around the counter.

Hunter sprang up from the floor and was at her side in an instant. "Are you sure?"

Sylvia nodded jerkily. "Mm-hmm." Then her eyes moved to mine. "Iris, I am so sorry. I just ... left amniotic fluid on your pretty new floor."

"Oh, my goodness," I said with a laugh, "there's nothing to apologize for. I told Hunter I wanted small-town life to happen here, and ... you're just kicking us off with a bang. No one will *ever* top this."

She laughed, but her whole demeanor had changed in an instant. Sylvia Buchanan looked scared.

Hunter had his phone to his ear, and I heard him leaving a voice message for his brother, then he hung up and immediately made another call.

I gripped her hands. "Hunter will take you to the hospital, all right?"

She nodded. "Connor isn't here," she whispered, her voice quaking.

"He will get on a plane as soon as he can," I assured her. "And you know these things can take a long time."

Sylvia nodded. "I know."

I did a quick mental calculation. She'd mentioned six weeks left. "And ... babies are pretty fully developed by this time, right? He or she just might be a little small."

Hunter laid a hand on her back. "Mom is gonna meet us at the hospital. She's calling your parents."

"Okay." She exhaled slowly. Some color had returned to her cheeks. "I don't have ... I don't have anything except my purse."

"Do you have a hospital bag at your house?" I asked.

She nodded. "It's in the nursery. Connor thought I was crazy for packing it already."

"Can Fran pick it up on her way?" I asked Hunter.

He shook his head. "She's coming from Knoxville. She and Dad were doing some furniture shopping."

"My parents live right by the hospital," Sylvia said, wincing again. "It's out of their way to drive to our place." Her eyes, big and wide, turned to me. "Will you bring it for me?"

"Of course," I breathed. "I'll be there as soon as I can lock up and make sure Maxine is good to watch my brother."

Hunter gave me a hard kiss, ushering Sylvia out to his car, and I let out a deep exhale when they were off.

"Goodness," I whispered.

After taking a mop to the floor, and making a call to Maxine, I did a quick sweep of the store to turn off lights and make sure everything was locked up before heading over to Connor and Sylvia's house. It was a cute home—blue siding and white shutters, two stained Adirondacks bracketing the cherry red front door.

The Buchanans, a sign proclaimed just above the doorbell, and I touched my fingers to it before I let myself in. Their home was exactly as I'd imagined it, based on Sylvia's personality. Warm and inviting, a sense of ease and comfort in all the furniture and bright, cheerful décor.

The nursery was decorated in a soft, pale yellow, an antique-looking bassinet was tucked into the corner, and I imagined it had been in someone's family for a very long time. The bag was sitting on the floor where she'd told me, and I gave the room one last wistful look before I hopped back in my car.

Hunter and I had never talked about kids, only that we wanted them someday.

At eighteen, nineteen, twenty, that future had felt so far off, and it was never anything that needed to be decided.

And now, all I could imagine was carrying his child. Growing a family with him, integrating ourselves into the history that he brought to our relationship, breaking my patterns.

Something about the nursery had me wiping quiet tears as I drove because we would've had that family by now. If it weren't for my own fears and the choices he made because of them.

No matter how insatiable Hunter and I were with each other right now, we couldn't ever really make up for the lost time. And maybe we'd forgotten that. We'd buried the past so deeply that distracting ourselves with sex, with the love we still felt, seemed like a healthy way to move forward.

But I wasn't so sure anymore.

I was walking into the hospital, the bag tucked over my arm, when my phone rang. It was a Nashville number, not the area code from the jail, so I answered.

"This is Iris."

"Iris, this is Sam Cummings. I was your mother's court-appointed lawyer. I'm not sure if you remember me."

I did. He wasn't awful. He'd helped connect me with Child Protective Services after she was arrested, but even with that, his voice was not what I wanted interrupting my day.

"Sam, this isn't a great time. Can we schedule another time to speak?"

"This won't take long." He cleared his throat. "You've been ignoring your mother's calls, I hear."

I smiled, a thin, annoyed smile that I desperately wished he could see. "I sure have. I don't really have much to say to her."

"She's getting out next month."

My heart dropped with a thunk, frozen solid at the base of my stomach. "What?"

"Good behavior," he said smoothly.

"Oh, for fuck's sake," I muttered under my breath. "I'm just hearing about this now?"

"You would've heard about it earlier if you'd answered her calls."

The snide tone in his voice had me clenching my teeth. "I want nothing to do with her, Sam. And I know that doesn't surprise you."

"It doesn't," he conceded. "But I wanted to let you know, so you can tell your brother."

"She does not get him back," I said fiercely.

"I didn't say she wanted him. All she told me is she wants to talk to you."

"I'll do my best to remember that," I told him, then hung up before I lost my temper.

Rage always felt like a particular waste of emotion to me. Maybe because I was raised by someone who could pull it out of me quite easily. I'd learned at a young age that anger did nothing but make me feel helpless. I couldn't control that emotion, no more than I could control my mother.

She manipulated people with every conversation and every interaction.

She never cared about the consequences of her actions. Never cared about how they spiraled out of control.

She stole from people. Regularly. Sometimes she got caught, but most of the time, she hadn't.

But no matter what manipulative, selfish, illegal things she did ... Nellie was *always* the victim in her own life. She never took responsibility.

And I couldn't help but wonder if the timing of her release—just as Hunter and I found each other again—was some elaborate test of this fateful love we shared.

Numbly, I made my way up to the maternity floor, and by the time I stepped off the elevator, I was fighting angry tears. From where I stood, I could see into the waiting room. It was filled with Buchanans. Hunter stood shoulder to shoulder with his youngest brother Levi. They smiled at some story Grace was telling. Levi's fiancée, Joss, was next to him, holding her stomach as she laughed. Fran and Robert were seated across from another couple, and the woman looked so much like Sylvia that it must've been her parents.

I couldn't go in there.

Not feeling that way.

That helpless rage was cold and prickly and uncomfortable, and I wanted to lock it away before being part of such a happy, hopeful moment. I walked to the nurses' station just by the elevator. "Can you take this to Sylvia Buchanan's room?" I asked.

The nurse smiled. "Sure thing."

I strode quickly back to the elevator before Hunter saw me, tapping out a quick text so he wouldn't worry.

Me: Just dropped off the bag to a nurse. Stay with your family. Just had something come up, and I have to go pick up Theo.

He didn't respond until I'd slid into the driver's seat of my car and set my forehead onto the steering wheel.

Hunter: Everything okay?

Me: Nothing to worry about. Just can't stay, and I didn't want to interrupt.

Me: Keep me updated on Sylvia.

Hunter: I'll come over when I'm done here.

Me: Sounds good.

Carefully, I slid my phone into my purse. I wanted it away from me. Because every time that ringer went off, I'd know it was her. I never wanted my past to affect my future ever again. But I wasn't so sure I could stop that from happening any more than I could stop loving Hunter.

CHAPTER 21

IRIS

"*An* inmate from Davidson County Correctional is attempting to place a collect call. Do you accept the charges?"

From where I sat on the couch in my family room, I could see my reflection in the gold-framed mirror sitting on the antique buffet that held my grandma's china. All the furniture was the same as she'd left it. And even if she'd left me a million dollars, I would have kept that donated couch and that mirror and that buffet because they represented the very best parts of my upbringing.

They represented happiness and warmth and love. Not that I felt any of those things while I told the operator that I would accept the charges.

I felt nothing.

The woman in the mirror was blank-faced. Her dark hair was slicked back off her face, a smooth ponytail down her back. And her eyes were vacant. There wasn't a single spark of emotion anywhere to be found, the necessary side effect of traveling down this particular path. It was a skill I'd honed from the age of ten.

When I saw her do something illegal.

When she asked me to help.

When she screamed at me for being selfish when I said no.

When she was taken away in handcuffs.

They all required the same thing—complete and utter emptiness.

If I was able to close off my emotions, then she couldn't see what she did to me. That wall between her and my emotions was my survival, and I hadn't had to use it in over four years.

"Hey, sweetheart." Her cigarette-rasped voice came through the speakers.

The face in the mirror was unmoved, not a single flicker of reaction. "Nellie," I said.

My voice was a placid lake, smooth as glass.

"You haven't been taking my calls."

"I haven't."

She exhaled, annoyance heavy in the sound. "Not a very nice thing to do to your momma."

"Is there something you wanted to talk to me about, Nellie?"

It took years of therapy for me to understand the kind of boundaries that I needed with her. Why that wall in my head wasn't something to apologize for. In fact, I never apologized to her for the way I spoke to her and held her at bay. She hated that because she'd lost the ability to manipulate me.

"I'm getting out early," she said, voice cheerful.

"Your lawyer told me."

"You living in your grandma's house? I heard I missed the funeral." She made a dramatic sighing noise. "Guess I should pay my respects when I get out. Not that she was ever much of a good mother to me. She never trusted me, always thought the worst of me."

Something snarled dangerously in my head, pacing sharp-clawed and angry underneath that glass-smooth lake, and I pushed it back down below the surface.

"I know that's not why you called me, Nellie. Please get to the point."

She sighed. "She leave you any money?"

My jaw twitched. "Just the house. You know she didn't have much."

It was mostly true. There was some money left in her accounts when she died, but once all her affairs were settled, the little bit left went into a small savings account for Theo that he wasn't even aware of. It was in my name because I didn't trust Nellie not to try to get her hands on it.

"I won't be able to get a job when I get out," she said. "Not easily, at least. Assholes never give us a second chance when we're trying to live right."

"Mm-hmm. I wish you luck with that."

She made an exasperated sound. "Lord, you don't have to be such a bitch, Iris. I'm your mother. The least you can do is help me. You have no idea how hard it is being where I am."

"You're right," I said smoothly. "I don't know what it's like."

"How's the kid?"

My jaw twitched again.

There were two buttons she knew to push when she wanted a reaction out of me. Grandma was the first.

Theo was the second.

I let out a slow breath. "You and I won't be discussing Theo. He's loved and taken care of, and that's all you need to know."

"He's *my* son, you know," she drawled. "If a mother wants to take her kid back, no judge in the world will stop me."

My fingers trembled, and I clutched at the edge of the couch.

You don't even love him, I wanted to scream. She didn't know that his favorite color was red. That he didn't like butter on his waffles. That he always slept on his stomach with his head underneath his pillow. That he hated thunderstorms and always wanted to sleep in my room when they rolled in.

She didn't know any of the things that made him the most amazing kid in the world, but she knew the most important thing possible.

That I loved Theo.

Just like she'd once used my love for Hunter to see if it could benefit her somehow, she had no hesitation doing the same thing with her own son.

My throat was tight and achy, an invisible hand clamping down on it until I had to remind myself that I could breathe just fine.

"You're right, Nellie. Theo is biologically your son, but I am his legal guardian. You are a convicted felon, and I don't have so much as a parking ticket. If you're going to challenge me for custody," I said, the snarl beneath the surface clawed its way up, and I felt the shake of it in my bones, "you better prepare for the fight of your fucking life."

She clucked her tongue. "Calm down. You always get so dramatic about things. Just ... help me get my feet under me when I get out of prison, and you can keep him."

My breath was coming in short pants, my chest heaving as I lost the grip on the wall holding everything back.

It wasn't even a wall, really. It was a dam holding back the ocean.

You can keep him, she said. Casually, too. Like she was talking about some left-over food.

I sank down, my trembling hand holding my forehead. "What do you want?"

"I don't want to come around there any more than you want me. Give me something so I can rent an apartment, maybe float me for a few months until I can find a job." She went quiet. "But I will come around. I'll come and spend *lots* of quality time with the kid if that's not something you can manage."

I hated her.

I hated that she was my mother. That I had anything in common with her.

That my sole branch on my family tree was Nellie Black, with her lies and her selfish nature, and her complete lack of a moral compass. I wasn't sure I'd ever be able to reconcile it.

"Define something," I said wearily.

She sniffed. "Twenty thousand."

I laughed. I couldn't help it. "You've lost your fucking mind, Nellie. You think I have an extra *twenty grand* lying around?"

"Whether you do or don't isn't my problem, sweetheart. I get out in a few weeks, so you've got plenty of time to figure that out."

The sound of a car pulling into my driveway snapped me upright.

Hunter.

"I have to go," I told her. Without waiting for a response, I disconnected the call. Striding from the couch into the kitchen, I cranked the water on in the sink. It was ice cold when I splashed it on my face, and with my hands gripped on the edge of the counter, I took a few slow deep breaths to calm myself.

Hunter had been at the hospital all day, his last update letting me know that Connor got on a direct flight from Chicago and would likely make it in plenty of time for the baby to arrive.

He didn't knock before he came in. "Iris?" he called.

I exhaled shakily, trying desperately to keep the dam up. "In the kitchen."

He was grinning widely when he walked into the room, and I wanted to burst into tears.

"Edie Rose Buchanan, all five pounds and two ounces of her, made her official entrance into the world today."

He swept me into an embrace, humming against my mouth as he kissed me.

"A girl?" I whispered. The idea of it, so sweet and innocent, swept away so much of the dirty feeling that I'd been left with after my phone call. "I thought Buchanans always had boys."

He laughed. "Well, little Miss Edie decided otherwise, and she's got her uncles and her grandpa wrapped around her perfect little finger."

Hunter set me down. Fishing out his phone, he turned it so I could see a picture.

My breath caught. In the first shot, Hunter was holding a tiny, wrapped bundle, but instead of smiling at the camera, he was looking down at his niece like she'd just solved world hunger. In the next picture—still tucked against Hunter's arm—

Edie was wearing a giant pink bow on her wrinkled forehead, a true inauguration of a Southern-born girl, and she was impossibly small, with perfect bow lips and a little button nose that looked an awful lot like Sylvia's.

The next picture was Fran and Robert on the hospital room couch with their sons surrounding them and Edie cradled in a beaming Fran's arms.

Something about it broke my heart in a way I'd never really experienced before.

Instead of just feeling shame that my family—if you could call it that—was so many universes away from his, I experienced a bright, violent pang of desire.

They warred for the top spot.

The man I loved—he was so happy. I smiled up at him as he told me about her labor. Connor made it just as she started to push, sprinting into the room and throwing his duffel bag at Levi's head. About how Fran and Sylvia's mom couldn't stop weeping as they heard the baby's first cry from where everyone waited in the hallway.

How Grace crowed with victory at not being the only Buchanan girl any longer.

My eyes filled with tears as he spoke.

He stopped, curling a hand around the back of my neck. "What is it?"

"I love seeing you this happy," I told him.

And it was the truth.

The kind of love he was experiencing—had experienced his whole life—was such a fucking gift. And he deserved it.

Not that I had done anything to deserve Nellie as my mother, but I had my grandma. And I had Theo.

And now, I had Hunter. I wanted to grow a family like that with him.

I wanted our life to end with him and me holding a grandchild, surrounded by people we loved in a cramped hospital room. And no one could take that away from me, not this time.

The urge to chase away the shadows of my day, to grab onto whatever sweet happiness he'd brought into the room with him, was like someone dropped a match into a pile of dried kindling.

Hunter showed only the slightest hint of concern at the shift in my mood, but when I rose on my tiptoes to suck his bottom lip into my mouth, that concern fled.

He slanted his head, his tongue tangling with mine as my arms wrapped around his neck. The groan he let out was a pleasant surprise and maybe a little shock, but God bless him, Hunter got with the program very quickly.

I clutched his back as he deepened the kiss, and he wrenched my shirt up, sliding his hand underneath my bra, demanding and sure in his grip and the way he swiped his thumb over the tip. I whimpered at the way he acted without hesitation. How he knew exactly what would feel good to me.

He knew when I needed slow and sweet, knew when I needed hot and hard and relentless.

This was the latter.

"Are we alone?" he asked.

I nodded, tearing at his shirt. I sighed when he tugged it over his head. "He's at Maxine's for another hour."

He shoved his hands down the back of my shorts, filling his hands with my flesh, kneading his fingers there. "An hour in an empty house? We could do a lot with that," he whispered against my mouth. "Where should I start with you?"

Hunter growled the words, and it took everything in me not to mount him right there in the kitchen.

"I want you over me," I told him. His eyes flared, fingers tugging at my shorts. "We start in the bed."

He wouldn't slow me down, wouldn't drag me down from the high I was chasing with him.

I didn't want to lose this surety of what our future could—would—look like. That it was something I could be a part of, use the good things he brought into my life as a way to baptize myself of the past. Even if the sins hadn't been mine.

And if Hunter slowed us down, I'd have to admit, again, that it was too easy to bury ourselves in this rekindled chemistry.

I pushed him down the hallway, stripping my clothes as we went. He almost fell over trying to take his pants off, and the laughter bubbling up in my chest made me feel even greedier, like I was just on the cusp of losing it all over again.

When we were naked, Hunter took a moment to simply stare after pushing me down on the bed.

"You're so beautiful," he whispered. His hand settled on my stomach, his fingers spread wide, and he slid it up, over my breasts, coasting across my ribs. But the touches were too light, too sweet. I sat up and wrapped my fingers around him.

He hissed, prowling over top of me as his mouth devoured mine. His teeth tugged my lip, his hands rough and greedy now. I sucked on his tongue while he used his hands on me, one finger and then two in slow, dexterous movements that had me panting into his mouth. But I wanted to go with him, so I pulled his hand away. Hunter sensed my mood, looking deep into my eyes, clearly searching for an answer to a question he hadn't verbalized.

"Please," I begged.

He braced my knee against his chest. "Please, what?"

I gripped his forearms while he teased me. My fingers dug into his skin, and I finally managed coherent words. "Please, Hunter, just love me."

His forehead furrowed. "Always."

Whatever he was looking for, he saw it as I was staring up at him. Maybe he saw my mindless need for him, the way only he had been able to make me feel this way, or how the bigness of what I felt for him didn't scare me anymore.

"Always," he said again as he slid my thigh up over his shoulder. I was helpless, unable to move, and it was perfect.

That was how he took me.

And took and took and took.

I was sobbing his name after a few minutes. He looked ferocious with sweat sliding down the side of his face.

I braced my hands on the headboard, arched my back up, and it changed the angle in a way that tore the breath from my lungs.

With snapping, hard movements of his hips and sucking deep kisses against my skin that felt dirty and raw and perfect, Hunter Buchanan gave me exactly what I needed.

He took it all away just by loving me.

CHAPTER 22

IRIS

"You're working *again*?" Theo asked. "I'm getting bored at Maxine's house. She stopped letting me play video games for more than an hour because she says they're going to rot my brain."

I laughed as I rinsed out his cereal bowl and tucked it into the dishwasher.

"Not working. I just need to head downtown to meet with Grandma's attorney because I have a couple of questions for him."

"Mr. Haywood?" Theo asked.

I nodded.

"What do you need to meet with him for?"

Theo wasn't watching me as he asked because I'd met with the kind older man a lot after Grandma died. She'd worked with him on her estate paperwork, making it a smooth, seamless process for me to move into the house and be able to close out all her accounts.

But I'd promised my little brother honesty.

I sat at the table and laid my hand on his arm. "Can I talk to you a second?"

He sat up, eyes wary at the tone of my voice.

"No lies, right?"

Theo nodded.

"I had a call from Nellie's attorney yesterday morning."

His mouth flattened into a straight line. "What did he want?"

I exhaled slowly. "Nellie is getting out of jail early, and he wanted to let me know."

For a moment, Theo showed no reaction at all. It was an eerie replica of my own facial expression just before I talked to her.

Then the tips of his ears turned red. So did his cheeks. "Am I going back with her?"

I sank onto my knees in front of his chair, my hands gripping his arms. *"No.* You are staying here with me."

He breathed out in a hard puff. "Swear it?"

"Yes, I swear it." I sat up so I could hold his face in my hands. "Listen to me. I am your legal guardian. I have a home and a business, and we have support here. You are not going anywhere, do you hear me?"

"But she could still ... she could still try?" His voice wobbled.

I shook my head. "You and me, kid. That's it. I don't care who tries to separate us. They will *always* lose."

He threw himself into my arms, and his frame trembled while I made soothing noises into the disarray of hair on top of his head.

The force of my love for him was so big that it was hard to keep it contained in one person's body. I'd pay Nellie whatever she asked for, and that was why she'd done it.

In that way, I was the best kind of predictable to her. She didn't ask for the house or my business. She'd asked me to trade for something that was infinitely more precious than either of those.

Nellie traded on the one commodity she'd always been short on—the ability to love a child more than anything else.

I kissed Theo's forehead. "That's why I'm going to talk to Mr. Haywood. He's Grandma's attorney, and it's his job to help us. I just need to make sure that everything is in order, and there's nothing she can do."

Theo nodded, swiping furiously at his damp cheeks. "Okay."

"Maybe don't tell Maxine just yet, okay? I want to talk to Haywood first."

"You'll tell Hunter?" He sniffed noisily. "Aren't boyfriends supposed to help with stuff like this?"

This kid. He would be the death of me. It was so easy for him. You ask people for help when they're in your life. But the reality wasn't that simple.

He'd never even asked me to confirm that Hunter was my boyfriend—or whatever label we were going by. He simply accepted it because he liked Hunter. He respected him. And Theo saw the change in me when we were together.

But this ... this wasn't so black and white.

I paused before answering. Tell him what? That I was about to drain my savings account, my entire safety net, because my mother was blackmailing me? I could hardly think the words, let alone imagine saying them out loud. Not just to him, to anyone.

I'd take it to my grave if I could. Because if Theo ever found out, it would break his heart in a way I wasn't sure I could ever fix.

"You let me worry about telling Hunter and Maxine, okay? Let's just ... keep this between us until I get it figured out."

He held out his pinky. I wrapped mine around it.

By the time I dropped him off at Maxine's, his eyes were clear again, but I worried about how he might backslide with the knowledge that she might reappear any day.

Hell, *I* was trying not to backslide. It was a different sort of tension, one that you couldn't understand unless you'd lived in that kind of chaos growing up.

When I arrived at the offices of Haywood and Haywood, I felt marginally better.

This was an action I could take, something preemptive, something in my control. I pushed open the heavy wooden door and did a double take when I saw the younger Haywood standing by the front desk. Tucker, if I remembered right.

He smiled. "Morning. Come on in."

"I'm, uh, I have an appointment with your father."

Tucker gestured toward the first office. "My dad came down with something last night, I'm afraid. He thinks he's dying, but my mother informs me it's nothing but a man cold. He'll be fine, but that means you're stuck with me for today if that's all right with you."

My hesitation was clear, and he gave me an encouraging smile.

"You're Iris, right?" he asked. "Iris Black?"

I nodded, hand tight on my purse strap. "Your father just ... he was a great help with all my grandma's estate work. He knew a lot of the important background for some of my questions today."

Tucker smiled again. He was tall and broad, even taller than Hunter, and honestly, he was so handsome it was a little hard to look him straight in the eye. "I took a brief read through your grandma's file, so I think I know all the salient points." He paused. "And I promise, all of our conversations are protected by the attorney-client privilege. I won't share anything with anyone unless you ask me to."

There was the unspoken worry, and his calm, steady delivery helped ease the tightness in my chest. "No one knows what I'm about to talk to you about," I said. "Just my brother."

"No one will hear about it from me." Tucker's eyes were full of understanding. He lived with Grace Buchanan and had since just after they started dating. I could see why they were a good match. She was all fire while he was steady and sure.

I blew out a breath. "Okay."

Once we were settled in his office, Tucker took copious notes as I explained the legal situation I found myself in. His forehead furrowed when I told him about Nellie's phone call and her request.

"That's extortion," he said quietly. "If you had proof, she'd have another felony on her record."

"I know."

He let out a slow breath. "Anything else?"

I shook my head.

Tucker leaned back in the big leather chair, his eyes trained somewhere on the back of the wall as he processed what I'd told him. With his hands resting across his stomach, he tapped his fingers.

"And you don't want to see her face charges for the blackmail?"

With a shrug, I answered honestly. "I just ... want her out of our lives. There's nothing but my word against hers that she said it. And even if she did get charged, there's no telling what her sentence would be. Say she catches the judge on a good day. He makes her pay a fine and gives her two years. She could be out after one on good behavior." My voice cracked. "And Theo and I start this bullshit all over again because my mother is a horrible person."

Tucker slid a box of tissues toward me. "You're probably not wrong," he said gently. "Tell me what you want to do, and we'll figure out a way to make it happen."

I balled a tissue up in my hand after wiping under my nose. "I'm going to give her the money. And I want her to sign something that says she'll never come back for Theo. Ever."

Tucker eyed me carefully, and even though I didn't know him well, I knew he was struggling with choosing his words.

"Out with it," I said wearily.

"It's my job to help you think through all angles. And sometimes that means asking tough questions to figure out the best course of action." He sat forward in his chair and took a deep breath as he folded his hands together. "Are you sure you want to let your mother win this round? That's a lot of money, and I worry she'll think she can tap that source again in the future because you're giving in to her now."

My stomach trembled a little at the thought of letting Nellie win anything. But Tucker couldn't possibly understand. No one did. Not until they walked in my shoes or had lived my life. I closed my eyes and pulled Theo's face to the front of my mind—his floppy hair and skinny arms and blue eyes—and I smiled.

"That's how much I love my brother," I said. Opening my eyes, I settled back in my chair and met his gaze unwaveringly. "I will do anything—pay any amount —to keep him safe from her. If she asked for double, I would've found a way to make it happen, but I'm glad she didn't. If I say no now, and I allow her to fight me for him because my pride can't handle giving her a check, it doesn't matter that I'd probably keep Theo in the end. My brother would be terrified beyond belief that there's even a slight chance he'd go back. I will spend *every* penny to my name to save him from that feeling, and I will sleep just fine at night when I do."

Tucker smiled—a quiet, subdued smile—and then picked up his pen.

"Sometimes, we just need to hear the why," he said. "And I like that one."

My exhale was slow and shaky, but my stomach had settled, and my resolve was firm.

At the look in my eye, he nodded. "I'll need to brush up on some similar cases, but I can write up a document that provides her consent for you to independently adopt Theo. It's a less intense legal process than termination of parental rights while still giving you what you need."

"Okay, that sounds good."

"Can you afford to pay her?" he asked. "I hate to do it, but I have to ask."

I rolled my lips between my teeth. Going through my banking records was my next step. Add up what I'd spent on the store and what was outstanding. "I have savings. It'll just about tap 'em out, but with my loan for the store, I should be able to swing it." My eyes welled up. "As long as no roofs or furnaces or cars need to be replaced any time soon, we should be okay. We've lived on less."

That was the thing about being an adult, being responsible for someone other than yourself, putting down roots somewhere. There was always something that needed to be fixed. There were always broken bones and doctor's bills and school projects that cost money.

Tucker tapped his fingers on the desk, pausing before he spoke. "Have you told Hunter? You know he'd help you."

He said it so carefully that I lost my battle with the first few tears. I shook my head.

"Not yet," I whispered. "Imagine telling someone you love that you come from something this ugly. If I thought I could keep it a secret forever, I would," I admitted with a dry laugh. "Trust me, I know how bad that sounds."

Tucker didn't answer. He simply listened with that steady, kind look in his eyes.

"I love him too much to start our relationship out that way. So I'll tell him once everything is settled and done. He'll ... he'll try to fix it for me. To take care of it. And I need to do this on my own. She's my problem to solve." I sucked in a quick breath. "You can't even imagine what she's like."

Tucker studied me. "It must have been hard to grow up with a parent like that."

A tear dripped down my chin, and I used the balled-up tissue in my hand to wipe it away. "Imagine walking through a minefield every day. One wrong step and ... *boom*. The only good that came from all those explosions was that I got to live with my grandma Black."

He smiled. "And that's when you met Hunter, right?"

I nodded. "Moved here when I was sixteen. Met him a year later."

"You don't have to tell me if you don't want to talk about it." He grinned. "I know how those Buchanans work when they meet their person. It's a ... pretty unstoppable force. When you see them all together, it's hard to argue with, even if it doesn't make a damn bit of sense."

"I never got to know the rest of the family very well," I admitted. "Back then, it was hard for me to be around them—a family so perfect."

"Oh, they're not perfect," he said. "But they do love each other. And that's much more important." He gave me a long look. "And they'd love you too, if you let 'em. They'd love you through something this big and this ugly without batting an eye. If you choose not to tell Hunter right away, I can respect your reasons. But as your attorney and someone who knows that family, I think you should."

"I'll think about it," I said, the only thing I was willing to concede. Tucker wasn't wrong. But he wasn't a truly unbiased source either.

He promised to get back to me in a couple of days with a document for Nellie to sign—if I was actually able to get her to agree. I shook his hand, and when we walked from the office into the lobby, I stopped short at the sight of Grace Buchanan reading on the leather couch next to the front desk.

Her smile was immediate when she saw me, but then it dropped just as fast. "Are you okay? You've been crying."

I exhaled a laugh, wiping under my eyes. "I'm ... fine. Everything will be fine. Just needed to go over some estate stuff for my grandma."

Tucker was behind me, so when Grace studied her boyfriend's face before settling back on mine, I wondered what she saw.

"Okay," she said slowly. Then she leaned forward and gave me a fierce, tight hug. With her hands on my shoulders, she locked eyes with me. "I know he won't tell me shit about what you talked about, but if you need backup or someone's tires slashed or like ... if I need to shank someone, just blink twice, and I won't ask any questions." She tilted her head. "Well ... maybe a couple, if you go the shanking route."

I laughed. "Thank you, Grace. I appreciate the offer."

"Anytime," she said seriously.

"And thank you, Tucker," I said.

He smiled. "I'll talk to you soon."

I left the office, somehow feeling even more emotionally drained than when I'd shown up. A text from Hunter was waiting on my phone, and I wanted nothing more than to ignore all my responsibilities, go seek him out, and hide in his arms for the rest of the day.

Hunter: Just saw your car parked on Main Street. If you get this in the next couple of hours, I'm at the library if you want to find a couple of new books with me.

. . .

Instead of answering, I drove straight there even though I knew I didn't have time to stay. I stopped into the bathroom to splash water on my face, a sad attempt at mitigating the time spent crying in Tucker's office. But I managed, and that was all that mattered.

It didn't take me long to find him once I walked into the main area of the library, and I took a moment to study Hunter before I approached. He was wearing black-rimmed reading glasses, one ankle propped on the opposite knee, a thick book resting comfortably in his lap.

I loved him so much.

I loved that he came to the library to read an old book instead of scrolling mindlessly on his phone. I loved that the rest of the world saw the quiet, contained man and that I was fortunate enough to see what simmered underneath.

Hunter must've felt the weight of my stare because he glanced up. A soft smile played over his lips as he closed his book and set it on the table next to his chair. I walked toward him, heedless of who was watching, and settled myself onto his lap, my knees tucked up against his chest while he wrapped an arm around my back.

Hunter kissed me with a deep hum. "Well, hello to you too."

I rubbed my nose against his. "I can't stay long. I've got boring things to work on."

"Want some help?"

I shook my head. "It's bank stuff. You stay and read your book."

Hunter brushed a thumb over my cheekbone. "Need a hand at the store when you're done with your banking?"

"Not much to do there today. I still don't have anything from that lady in Merryville. She's the last vendor I'm waiting on. It's all the blankets and scarves. They won't take too long to set up."

"And your furniture," he reminded me. "Weren't we going to go to Nashville for the couch and the matching chairs tomorrow?"

My heart sank. "I think ... I think I'm gonna wait on those."

His brow furrowed. "Why?"

199

Because the couch and the chairs would take a healthy chunk out of my savings account. It was something I could justify when there would be leftover funds. But spending five grand on some pretty places to sit—in light of what the rest of my money was being used for—felt like a selfish thing to do.

"It's just a lot of money," I finished lamely. "I've spent more than I thought on the renovations. I'll get something else. Eventually."

His eyes searched mine. "You okay?"

Slowly, I nodded. "Didn't sleep well last night. Maybe I can find time for a nap today."

"Call me if you want company," he murmured, brushing another kiss over my lips.

I smiled, unable to help it. "Hunter Buchanan, if you joined me for a nap, that would defeat the purpose entirely."

He grinned. "I'll be good, I promise."

When I laughed, a librarian cleared her throat in the row next to us, a sharp, disapproving sound.

"What are you reading?" I asked him, voice dropped into a hushed whisper.

He grabbed the book and settled it where I could see the title. When I saw something about phonemic fluency, I gave a deep, dramatic sigh. "I can see why you're so riveted."

Hunter laughed quietly. "It's riveting if you're trying to help kids read better."

I leaned forward to set my lips on his. The simple act of breathing him in helped calm whatever riot was churning in my chest. The sharp throat clearing happened again, and his mouth curved into a smile.

"I've never been kicked out of a library," he whispered, "but I think you might break that streak if you keep it up."

I pecked his lips again, standing carefully off his lap. "I'm going."

"See you later?" he asked, trailing his fingers over mine.

I nodded.

"Want me to bring dinner for the three of us?" He curled his pinky around mine. "Or maybe I could do some steaks if your grill works."

"He cooks too," I murmured, leaning down for one more soft kiss.

"Do you mind?" a voice drawled. "There are children in here," she hissed.

I straightened, giving the older librarian a patient smile. "I'm going."

The sound of Hunter's laughter echoed in my head as I left the library, and I held on to that sweet sound as long as I could, trying to keep the feeling with me as I drove to the bank.

Unfortunately for me, it didn't help.

CHAPTER 23

HUNTER

*H*ands full of take-out bags from Daisy's Nut House, I almost didn't hear Theo call my name.

"What'd'ya get me?" he yelled. He was at the neighbor's house, using their full-size basketball hoop.

"Cheeseburger and fries."

That earned me a big grin.

"I'll be in in a minute," he said. "Almost done with my game."

"Your sister in there?"

He nodded, running toward the hoop to toss in an easy layup. "She's cranky, though," he said. Theo widened his eyes. "Like, really cranky."

"Duly noted." I gave him a smile, but it was just for show.

Something was wrong, and I'd known it from the moment I got to her house the day before. Our sex was always insane—passionate and explosive—and she always matched my readiness. But there'd been an edge to that, something frantic that was unsettling.

Iris was hiding something. And I wasn't sure if she was hiding something from me or using me to hide from something. I didn't like either option because it triggered a whole slew of memories from the first time we broke up.

She'd done both, and as a young man so blindly in love with her, I never considered pushing her on the why when I registered what she was doing.

I took a deep breath before I walked into the house. Maybe Theo was exaggerating. Maybe the crankiness was because she was tired. Or she hadn't eaten enough today.

But through the screen door, I had a clear sight line to the dining room table. Iris had her back to me, the table covered in binders and statements, and her laptop opened to what looked like a bank account page. She had her elbows on the table, her chin resting in her hands as she stared at everything in front of her.

I opened my mouth to speak, and that was when she said, "I hate her."

Her voice was hushed, not meant for anyone's ears, and my brow bent in confusion at the anger I heard. Not just anger, the resignation.

I clenched my jaw because if it was about her mom, she'd rather gouge her eyes out with a pencil than talk about Nellie.

Taking a step back from the door, I let a few seconds pass before I called out, "Dinner incoming."

Papers shuffled, and the legs of her chair scraped across the floor. "It's open."

She met me by the door, holding it open with a restrained smile.

"Almost done working?" I asked.

She lifted her chin, offering her mouth for a quick kiss. "Mm-hmm."

The laptop was shut, and she'd moved the loose papers into the now-closed binder.

"You said you've got bank stuff going on? It's not the loan for the store, is it?"

Iris followed me into the kitchen, and we unloaded the take-out containers onto the small kitchen table. "No, it's not the loan," she said. "Just ... other stuff. It'll be fine, though."

A peek into the first container showed the salad she wanted, so I handed it to her. "You sure you don't want any help? I'm no accounting major, but I did have to deal with my share of budgets at the school."

"No, it's okay." Iris washed her hands, glancing at me over her shoulder. Her smile was tired. "Does Theo know you're here?"

"He said he'd be in soon."

"What'd you order?" she asked.

Subject officially changed.

Frustration simmered, and I had to remind myself that after such a long separation, no matter how well I did know her, there was still an adjustment period. "The chicken wrap. Cheeseburger for Theo."

She shook her head. "He'd eat them every day if I let him."

Even though the subject was changed, and it might not be smart, that look in her eye gutted me enough that I couldn't let it go.

"What's wrong?" I said.

Iris froze.

I approached slowly, easing my hands up the sides of her arms. "What's wrong?" I repeated a bit more gently. "I can see it right here." Using my thumb, I traced over the graceful arch of her eyebrows. "And in your eyes."

Those eyes met mine, and there was so much sadness there that my discomfort snapped straight into deep, deep worry.

"Talk to me," I told her. Iris moved into my arms, burying her face into the side of my neck. Her body shook, only the slightest tremble, and I tightened my embrace, kissing the top of her head. "Whatever it is," I said, "you can tell me. All I want is to be there for you."

"And you are. But it's not that simple," she whispered. "And it's ... it's not about us. I promise."

Her head lifted, and she followed that promise with a soft kiss, something meant to soothe. I sank into it because I'd never deny Iris moments like this. My hands swept along her back, and Iris pulled back just far enough to brush her nose against mine.

"That doesn't make me worry any less," I told her.

She pulled out of my arms, and her eyes looked red again. "I don't mean to frustrate you," she said. "I've gotten used to dealing with this stuff on my own, you know? It's a hard habit to break."

"Stuff like what?"

Iris closed her eyes, rubbing a hand over her forehead. But she didn't answer.

I blew out a hard breath, and her eyes flashed open. Iris studied my expression warily, her chest rising and falling on rapid breaths.

"Is it your mom?" I asked quietly.

Wrong question. Or, rather, the right one. And I knew it because it was like something snapped shut behind her eyes.

In an instant, she was completely closed off.

"Don't do this." I cupped her face in my hands. "Iris."

"Don't do what?" she said.

"Don't shut down. You can talk to me."

Her chin wobbled, and her eyes went bright and shiny, but she remained quiet. We stood like that for a long moment, and finally, I let my hands drop.

"This isn't a burden anyone else can take from me," she whispered. "I know you want to, but you can't."

Frustration boiled over. "What I want is for the woman I love to trust me with something important."

"This isn't about trust," she said. The whisper was gone, and her own frustration bled into her words. "It's not about you at all."

"I didn't say it was."

"Didn't you?" She crossed her arms over her chest. "Then *trust* me when I say this is separate from us. I want the man I love to believe me when I tell him something important. Something true."

"It doesn't feel very true," I told her. "It feels like you refuse to tell me something about her. And if it's hurting you this much, I should know. Because I can help."

"No, you *can't*," she yelled. "You can't help. You can't save me from it. I have it handled because she's always been my problem to deal with. She has always been my cross to bear."

A tear slid down her cheek, and she dashed it away with an angry hand.

My heart battled my pride. That was always what it boiled down to with Iris. She had my heart forever. But when push came to shove, she didn't let me all the way in. Pride demanded I give her space and take some space for my own reasons.

I couldn't force her heart.

"I wonder something," I said slowly.

She stayed stubbornly quiet, arms folded tight over her chest.

"I wonder what she did to you that your default is always to push me away like this when she's involved."

Her face went pale. Her pulse fluttered wildly at the base of her neck.

"And I wonder if you'll ever believe people will help you, show up for you, shoulder those burdens with you simply because they love you. Not because they have to. Because they want to." I shook my head. "You can ask me to be there for you for no other reason than I love you."

She stared down at the floor, and her hands clenched into fists. I wasn't sure if that was anger, sadness, or she was trying to keep from reaching out to me. All three options had my heart feeling just a little bruised. For her. And for me. Because I wasn't sure what to do with this.

Theo banged through the front door. "I know! I know!" he yelled. " I'm going to wash up. You don't need to remind me."

Iris lifted her head, and her eyes were dry.

The control she had over her emotions in moments like this cut me down to the bone because she wore the same look on her face the last time she told me to go.

"I'm not going anywhere," I told her quietly. "But I think you'd enjoy your dinner more if I left."

She rolled her lips between her teeth, giving me a tiny nod.

I closed the remaining steps between us and slid my hand down her hair, laying a soft kiss on her forehead. "I hope you know," I whispered, "just how much I love you. Yes, I want you to trust me, but I want you to trust in something else."

Her hand fluttered onto my chest, laying over my heart. "What?"

"You are separate from her too," I said.

She inhaled sharply, her fingers pressing into my skin.

I kissed her forehead again. "Will you call me?" I asked.

Against my chest, she nodded.

And I walked out because I knew if I saw her face, I'd stay. I'd always stay if she wanted me there, and she also knew that.

But there was something else that was equally true. Every time we made strides in our relationship, it was because someone nudged her in my direction.

I needed Iris to take a step on her own.

CHAPTER 24

HUNTER

"*I*t's not about the mom."

The ball sailed over my head, sank neatly into the hoop, and my brother's fiancée beamed proudly at the bewildered look on my face.

"What do you mean it's not about her mom?" I said, struggling to catch my breath. "This is always the thing that she won't share. It was back then too, before I left. Her mom is the reason she pushed me away, even if she's never actually said those words."

Levi dribbled around me, bouncing a pass to Joss, who caught it. She played by wheelchair rules, settling it into her lap for two strong down pushes on her right wheel, stopping to toss the ball in a perfect arc for another three.

We used to do this at least once a week when they lived in Seattle, and I was glad we were all back in the same place again—even if Joss had a terrible knack for shooting better than I did.

"Pretty," Levi said, bracing his hands on her chair handles for a kiss.

"Can you not make out while we're in the middle of a relationship talk?" I asked.

Joss pushed at Levi's sweaty chest with a laugh. "Don't be jealous just because you and Iris have your heads up your asses in equal measure."

"'Scuse me?"

Levi whistled.

"You do," she said, then she shrugged. "That's how relationships go. But you're expecting her to change a lifetime of patterns at the first bump in the road, and I'm sorry ... it doesn't work that way when you've got truly complicated family dynamics."

Normally, I had these conversations with my brothers. However, Connor was still at the hospital with Sylvia and Edie. They needed a little bit of extra monitoring after coming so early.

When Levi asked if I wanted to join him and Joss to work out at the park, I said yes, desperate to get someone else's take.

Joss reminded me a lot of Iris, which was maybe why I'd immediately felt so comfortable around her when they moved out to Seattle by me. In moments like this, when she had no problem serving up brutal honesty, I wondered just how much my brothers held back in their advice.

Joss pivoted her chair in my direction and set her hands on her lap. "When did this happen again?"

"About two days." I took a seat on the bench next to the court and wiped a towel over my face. "I thought she'd call me the next day, but it's been quiet."

Levi and Joss shared a look. My brother settled onto the concrete next to Joss's wheelchair. "What worries you about it?"

I set my elbows on my knees and stared down at the ground for a moment. "That I'll always have to be the one knocking down her walls. We were so young the first time we were together, and I didn't push at those moments when I knew she was keeping that part of herself separate from me. But maybe I should have."

"So what if you do?" Joss asked.

My head lifted, my gaze meeting hers. Joss's eyes were a piercing blue, and they were relentless in their intensity.

"What if you do have to?" she repeated. "What if you'll always have to be the one who has to remind her that those walls are safe to come down? That you'll be there no matter what's behind them? What if you do?"

"I—" I swallowed. "I would do it then. But aren't I allowed to be frustrated about it?"

"Of course," Levi said. "No one's saying you can't. But ... maybe you need to remind yourself that the way Iris deals with stuff about her mom is not about you. It has nothing to do with you."

Joss laid her hand on Levi's shoulder and gave him a soft smile.

"I learned that from you," my brother said to her.

She leaned over, and he gave her a quick kiss. When her gaze moved back to mine, she gave me a rueful grin. "I didn't always handle big feelings well, Hunter. But the moments I lashed out at Levi or kept some truth about my feelings hidden from him were no reflection on who he was as a person. It was never about doubting his love or doubting him." She sighed. "Having a complicated relationship with your mom ... it bleeds into so many aspects of a young woman's life."

"I just want her to talk to me about it," I said. "We've missed so many years together, and it's hard to see her shut down so soon after we found each other again. I feel like we've made no headway. Like we're going to end up right where we were before. Where she pushes me away, and I'm put in a position where I have to decide whether to respect her need for space, or I keep pounding on a locked door."

Again, they traded a look. Joss glanced back in my direction. "I think I'm about to say something that might really piss you off."

"Oh, good." I sighed.

"You didn't spend twelve years apart because Iris pushed you away." She sat forward in her chair. "All that time apart was because you were afraid."

Levi dropped his chin to his chest.

A shocked exhale slipped out of my mouth. "You seem to have an awfully strong opinion about it for someone who wasn't there."

"I wasn't there," she agreed. "But I know you, Hunter. One of the best parts of when we moved to Seattle was the time we got with you. And because I had that, I saw you with Samantha." She paused, shaking her head a little. "I have an opinion because I can see the difference in you now that you're here and you have Iris."

My jaw clenched.

"So tell me I'm wrong," Joss continued. "I *know* how this works. Your heart never wavers. You meet her, and you know, and it's right and wonderful. Buchanan love at first sight family legend, *blah, blah, blah*. But that doesn't mean there aren't other parts of you that don't get in the way. The fact that you love her doesn't mean you aren't just as culpable in those years you missed. All those years that you now think should be erased"—she snapped her fingers—"like that. Get over yourself, Hunter. You're not the only wounded party here. You left her. You *married* someone. You proved her fears right, and I don't blame her one fucking bit for having a problem opening up right away."

I stood from the bench, my stomach in knots, my heart chugging uncomfortably.

I wanted to scream at her, tell her she was wrong, that she had no fucking right to say any of this to me. My hands shoved into my hair, and I tightened my fingers into fists. A useless outlet for my frustration.

I dropped my head back and stared up at the sky.

"Fuck," I roared. "Isn't this supposed to be easy? Isn't that the point of all this? That we have this"—I tapped my chest with a fisted hand—"this thing inside us. What's the point of knowing who we're meant to love if it's still this damn hard?"

Joss was watching me with sad eyes, and so was Levi.

"I left her," I said, gripping my head in my hands. "I left her because I thought I was doing the right thing, and the entire time I was gone—every fucking day without her—it was like someone was twisting a knife around my insides. I couldn't stand the thought that she would ever feel trapped in this thing that I felt." My breath shuddered out of my chest, ragged and uneven. "I couldn't handle the thought of going back, and she wouldn't care. That it wouldn't mean anything that I missed her or that I'd been miserable." As the admission flowed out of me, all that anger ebbed. My whole body slumped in defeat. My voice sounded like I'd chewed glass, like the words were making me bleed from the inside out. "I didn't go back because I was afraid of what I'd find." I met Joss's gaze unflinchingly. "And no one has been brave enough to tell me that."

Joss brushed a trail of tears off her face, giving me a tiny smile. "It wasn't fun if that helps."

I exhaled a shaky laugh. "A little."

"Have you told Iris any of that?" Levi asked. His fingers were twined through Joss's.

I shook my head. "We've talked about our years apart, but I think we were both afraid to touch that particular topic. Like it was too big to tackle when we were so wrapped up in just ... loving each other again."

"Yeah, don't think we don't know what you were doing in that bathroom when we got to the store," Levi drawled. "We know you were *wrapped up*."

Joss held her hand out to me, and I took it. "I speak from experience," she said. "If she's working that hard to protect herself, she's got a really good reason. A lifetime of experiences that made that armor necessary. And you may have to chip away at it for the rest of your life, but I promise, she will never feel safer than when she's with you."

Leaning down, I wrapped an arm around my future sister-in-law and kissed the top of her head. "Thank you," I said quietly. "I needed to hear that."

She grinned. "I will hand you your ass anytime it's remotely necessary."

"My girl," Levi said proudly.

I exhaled heavily, checking the time on my watch. "I'm gonna go shower, then see if she's home." I smiled at Joss. "Not to knock down any walls," I told her. "Just to remind her I'll be there when they come down."

"There's hope for you yet, Hunter Buchanan," she said sagely.

Back in my car, I checked my phone and the screen was still empty of messages or calls. But instead of adding a weight to my chest, I simply felt a renewed determination to get to her.

There was no promise, no guarantee that any of this would be easier, simply because of how certain I was in my feelings. That was always my biggest mistake. Certainty didn't take the place of needing to put in the effort.

I pulled my car into the driveway at my parents', pulling straight up to the door of the garage apartment.

The door was unlocked when I went to use my key, and I figured my mom needed to get in for something.

But the lamp next to the couch was on, and I could've sworn I'd turned it off. Tossing my gym bag onto the ground next to the door, I peered through the window over to my parents' house, but it looked dark.

"Hi."

Her voice was quiet and unsure, and when she stood from the foot of my bed, her eyes were wide, her hands clasped loosely in front of her. My copy of *The Alchemist* was in her hands, the one she'd found on my nightstand.

At the sight of her, my heart soared.

I was ready to seek her out, remind her that I'd be there as long as it took to lower those walls. But seeing her there, taking a step in my direction, my heart settled in my chest.

I walked toward her with a small smile. "I was just coming to find you."

Her lip quivered. "Were you?"

I nodded.

"I'm glad," she started, then paused to gather herself, "I'm glad I beat you here then."

My arms ached to hold her. But this was something we needed, something we should have done right at the beginning.

"Why?" I asked.

Iris let out a deep breath, taking a quick glance down at the book in her hands. "You told me once that all paths, all the signs in your life would lead you right back to me."

My chest hurt from all the things pressing up against it. "I did. And I meant it."

"You missed something, though."

My eyes burned at the sure, steady look on her face. "What?"

Iris took a step, holding the book out.

Carefully, I took it, brow furrowed in confusion.

"Look," she said quietly.

With a deep breath, I flipped through the pages, my body stilling when I saw a glimpse of her neatly formed handwriting toward the back.

Whatever path you're on, whatever signs guide your steps, I will never walk apart from you again. I'll be with you because you *are my heart.*

My voice was rough and uneven, my vision blurry when I looked back at her. "I should've fought harder for you, Iris," I whispered. "I'm sorry I didn't. I'm sorry my fear kept me away for so long."

I didn't stop the tear because she'd earned that from me. She shed them too, silent tracks down her smooth cheeks, reaching up to brush mine away. I covered her hand with my own, pressing a fervent kiss to her palm.

"I'm sorry I told you to leave," she said. "And I'm sorry that I didn't fight for you either. That I let *my* fear do this to us."

After setting the book down, I curled my hand around her neck, my fingers tangling in her hair. Her eyes fluttered shut as I slowly pulled her into my arms.

She slid her hands around my back and curled them up by my shoulders as I folded her tightly into my embrace. My head bent over hers where she pressed it into my chest, and together, we exhaled.

Sometimes, forgiveness needed big flashy displays and gestures that could easily play out on the big screen.

And sometimes, it was this.

It was a quiet embrace, refusing to hide from the hurt that we'd caused each other.

It wasn't loud or for anyone else's consumption. It was saying the words *I'm sorry* and meaning them.

Sometimes, the pain tricked us into thinking it was more complicated than that. And love made us think that it wasn't necessary.

Both were wrong. And for too long, Iris and I fell prey to listening to both voices.

I kissed her temple, smoothing the hair back from her face as she raised her chin.

"That wasn't so hard, was it?" she said.

A smile tugged at the edge of my lips. An incredulous laugh came out in a puff of air.

Twelve years. Two broken hearts. And a lifetime that had passed between those two things.

"Nah," I said. "Easy as can be."

Iris's smile broke open, wide and bright.

I cupped her face with both hands, settling my mouth over hers for a slow, sweet kiss. She was still laughing softly as I did.

This kiss tasted different than any we'd ever shared. Better than the first and sweeter than any that had come before.

I sipped at her top lip, then her bottom, my heart swelling impossibly big when her tongue teased at the seam of my mouth. I chased it with mine, sliding my fingers into her hair so I could angle her head to the side.

Iris broke away first. "I love you," she said against my lips. "I'll never shut you out like that again."

For as happy as the kiss had started, I heard the knot of emotion in her words.

I kissed her.

Once.

Twice.

Rolling my forehead against hers, I sighed. "I love you too. And I'm not going anywhere."

For the first time, it felt like Iris and I were choosing each other at the exact same time. There wasn't one racing ahead of the other, no imbalance in our feelings, no catching up to be had by the other person.

This was us, meeting on the path with clear eyes and unwavering belief in what we had.

I bent at the knee, swept her up in my arms, and strode toward the bed. Iris curled her arms around my neck and settled her head on my shoulder despite the short trip.

That was not what this was about.

There would be no rush, no hurtling toward some unseen finish line that ended with us sweaty and panting.

All I wanted, all I'd ever really wanted, was to remove all the barriers between us. So that was what we did.

She sat quietly on the bed while I peeled her shirt off, smiling up at me when I discarded mine.

"Stay right there," I told her, dropping a hard kiss on her waiting mouth.

While I locked the door and checked it again for good measure, she removed her bra, setting it on top of her slowly growing pile of clothes. Iris slid back on the bed as I pushed my shorts and boxer briefs off.

A small smile played around her lips when I jerked my chin, motioning for her to move off the bed.

The way we moved toward this inevitable reunion was a stark contrast to all the previous ways we ended up in bed. I yanked back the covers, settling on my back, hand wedged under my head while she crawled over me. Her body stretched over the top of mine, and I slid a hand up the lithe nakedness of her back. She pressed her nose against the side of my throat and inhaled greedily.

Her hands trailed along my stomach and over my chest, and she set her chin over my heart, watching me with big eyes.

"I like being naked in bed with you," she said.

I laughed, and it made the mattress shake. Iris buried her head into my chest again, cheeks pink.

She smacked my stomach. "You know what I mean."

I gathered her closer. "I do." Then I kissed her softly like we had all the time in the world.

Because we did.

She shifted on the bed, laying her head in the same position as mine, and she settled her hands underneath the pillow.

Gently, I let my fingertips trail over the line of her nose, over her cheekbones, and across the delicate cupid's bow of her upper lip.

"She called me," Iris said softly. "A few days ago. And I was embarrassed."

I stayed quiet, and when Iris removed one of her hands from beneath the pillow, I slid my fingers between hers, pulling our hands up to my mouth so I could drop a kiss over her knuckles.

And that was how we stayed, bodies pressed tight, hands entwined, while my love poured her heart out. Her fear and her shame and her determination to change the ugly past where she'd been born. She wrung every drop of what she'd been feeling into that bed while I listened.

I'd catch all of it.

By the time she was done, her throat was raw, her eyes red from crying, and I'd never loved her more.

Wrapped up in my arms, Iris fell asleep like that, and I lay awake for a while longer, trying to decide if we'd ended up better and stronger for the distance we'd gone through.

With my lips pressed against the silky skin of her forehead, I knew I'd never know for sure. If we would've ended like this, just as strong and just as sure.

All I knew was that I was exactly where I was meant to be, no matter how we got there or what circular path we took.

That was how I drifted off to sleep, with Iris in my arms and the heart in my chest as whole as it had ever been.

CHAPTER 25

HUNTER

*T*ucker, Grace, and I took one of the booths up against the window. From where I sat, the thick plait of Iris's braid was in my direct line of vision. As much as I wanted to see her face, this was the seating arrangement that made the most sense. We'd picked a booth across from hers and one back so that the three of us could easily watch the exchange without being obvious.

The coffee cup in front of her was full, but she'd yet to take a sip from it. Too nervous, I suspected.

All week, she'd been edgy and a little quiet. Last night, she woke me in the middle of the night by tugging my arm over her waist, tucking her legs between mine, and burying her face in my chest the way she liked.

We'd spent quite a few nights that way since our overdue conversation in my apartment, talking quietly in the dark, making up for lost time in a different way. When she wasn't making finishing touches on the store—just days away from her friends and family opening—and I wasn't tutoring, we'd started easing Iris into life with the Buchanan family.

Grace and Magnolia—my cousin Grady's girlfriend—brought her dinner at the store one night and helped her decide on final décor placement and jewelry merchandising. Whatever that was, it was *important*, as I'd learned when I asked a question that earned me three equally intimidating glares.

She and Joss and my mom went for coffee at Donner Bakery, and apparently, it made Joy cry behind the cash register to see them together. Something she hadn't even done when Iris arrived with me.

Theo was able to join me, my brothers, and my dad while we fished on Bandit Lake. She cried when we left her house with her brother belted safely into my dad's SUV.

Happy tears, she'd assured me.

As I watched the entrance of the Merryville diner, I couldn't help but wonder if we'd have more tears before this day was over.

Tucker took a sip of his coffee, arm slung over the back of the booth so his hand could rest on my cousin's shoulders. "That her?" he asked.

The woman exiting the rusted-out pickup truck was rail-thin, with bottle-blonde hair and Iris's eyes. Their bone structure was eerily similar, and even though I hadn't seen Nellie Black in twelve years, she'd aged considerably.

Iris's head turned to stare out the window, and even though I couldn't see her fully, I knew that wall was back up.

And now I understood why.

"We're right here," I said, loudly enough for her to hear.

Iris gave a slight nod and faced forward again. Nellie came through the front door, speaking briefly with the young woman working at the hostess stand. Then her gaze moved around the restaurant, coming to rest on Iris with a polite smile to the server.

My stomach was in knots, so I could only imagine how Iris felt. Tucker said something in a low, quiet tone to Grace so that it wasn't painfully apparent we were listening to every word that was about to be exchanged.

Nellie approached the booth, and for a moment, I worried that my blatant staring would catch her eye, but she was only concerned with Iris.

"Look at you," she said. "You haven't changed a bit. You look just like I did at your age."

Iris's shoulders moved on a deep breath. "Have a seat, Nellie. I got you some coffee."

Her mom mumbled her thanks, adding a couple of packets of sugar, studying Iris as she stirred it in. "You buying me breakfast too?"

"That depends on you." Iris folded her hands in front of her.

Nellie huffed. "Aren't you going to ask me if it's good to be out of prison? You don't seem very excited to see your mother."

"I didn't meet you here to make small talk. I'm here because you asked me to pay you off so that I can keep Theo." Iris paused. "Let's not pretend this is a happy reunion."

Nellie whistled. "You've gotten some bite in the past few years. You used to be nicer to me."

"Thank you."

"I didn't mean it as a compliment."

Again, Iris smiled. "I took it as one, though."

After a long drink of her coffee, Nellie set the mug down and spread her arms out. "You're the boss. If I've gotta play nice to get some bacon and eggs, why don't you lay it out for me? I don't have much in the way of discretionary income right now," she said quietly, "as I'm sure you can imagine."

"How much did you have in your account when they did your discharge?"

Tucker explained all of this to me while we waited for Nellie to arrive. The day she left prison, she would've been given all of her personal effects and "gate money"—whatever money was in her prison account from the work she'd done during her time—or at least fifty bucks to be able to purchase a ride wherever she was going.

"A few hundred." She tapped the side of her mug. "But it's only going to be harder for me to find a job now."

"Breaking the law over and over will do that to you."

Nellie's eyes narrowed, and I blew out a slow breath. Tucker, still pretending he was talking to Grace, spoke under his breath.

"I thought she wasn't going to antagonize her."

My eyebrows went up on my forehead. "That was the plan."

"If that was my mom threatening my brother, I'm pretty sure I'd have ripped her face off by now," Grace said sweetly. "I give Iris credit for being as calm as she is."

Tucker squeezed Grace's shoulder.

Iris cleared her throat, reaching into her purse and withdrawing a plain white envelope. But she kept it in her hands.

Nellie's eyes tracked it with a wild gleam of anticipation.

I thought I'd hate her. That I'd feel a vengeful sort of anger. But I just felt sad. For Iris, and Theo, who'd done nothing but be born to a selfish woman who couldn't think past her own wants and needs.

"Is that what I think it is?" Nellie asked.

Iris nodded. "Every penny you asked for."

Nellie huffed incredulously. "I didn't think you'd say yes."

She held out her hand.

But the envelope stayed tight in Iris's grasp. With her other hand, Iris pushed a manila folder to the other side of the table.

"What's that?"

"A paper I'd like you to sign."

Nellie's eyes narrowed. "What paper?"

"Read it."

As she scanned the first page of the document, her eyebrows shot up. "Consent to adopt? He's ten. You're already his legal guardian. Why would you need me to sign this?"

Iris leaned forward. "I don't *need* you to. That's the thing."

"I don't understand."

Tucker's face was intent, listening to every word Iris used, something we'd talked about the entire drive to Merryville.

"If you give your consent to allow me to privately adopt Theo, I don't need you to go in front of the judge to terminate your parental rights." Iris held her mom's gaze without so much as a flinch, and my arm itched to wrap around her shoulders. "It's easier for both of us. Because you don't want him any more than I'm willing to give him up."

Nellie exhaled in an irritated puff. "This is the thanks I get for asking my daughter for a little help getting on my feet?"

"You asked me for twenty thousand dollars and threatened to have him taken away if you didn't get it. That is blackmail." She tapped the manila folder. "This is the way I feel comfortable helping you out right now. But it's not a condition of the money."

Nellie folded her arms and gave Iris a confused look. "Then what the hell is it?"

Iris leaned forward. "It's a promise. Between you and me. You take this money, give me your signature in return, and stay the hell away from us. I don't want to see you, I don't want to hear from you, and if you so much as breathe in Theo's direction, I'll take everything I know about you to the great state of Tennessee. Care to see if you could do a third stint in jail for the shit that went unaccounted for?"

"I can challenge your status as his legal guardian," Nellie said.

Iris nodded slowly. "You sure could try. And you'd lose. I have a business, I have a home, I have friends, and ... I have family in Green Valley." She paused, turning her face to the side, as much as a glance toward me as she could manage. "Unlike you, I will do anything to keep Theo safe. Even if it means draining every penny of my savings account in the process."

Nellie worked her jaw back and forth, eyes locking again on the envelope.

"You must really hate me, Iris."

Iris inhaled slowly, then she shook her head as she expelled the breath. "I don't hate you, Nellie. Even when I wanted to, or said that I did." She shrugged. "I just wish you were different," she said simply. "This is your chance to prove that you can be."

If I didn't know it before, I knew it then, sitting in that small diner in Merryville. Iris Black was the strongest woman I'd ever met.

Underneath the table, her leg bobbed rapidly, and I knew that I was right earlier. Before this day ended, Iris would have a few more tears to shed. As much as I wished I could've sat by her side, it was so much more important that she face Nellie alone.

Nellie studied her daughter, but she had the same fixed expression on her face as Iris. Maybe a trait they had in common, which Iris would hate.

"D'you have a pen?" Nellie asked quietly.

Iris held one out to her. The pen was a gift from my father, and it was heavy, something I'd used since I graduated college. I carried it with me everywhere I went. Nellie studied the pen, the black and gold detailing, eyes catching on my initials engraved onto the side of the pen. She rolled her lips together, twisted the pen, and scrawled her name along the bottom.

Iris's frame sank in relief.

Tucker sighed, eyes closing once the folder was closed.

Grace grinned. "She didn't even need us."

I glanced back at Iris. While Nellie dug for something in her purse, Iris looked over her shoulder and gave me a quick wink.

I smiled. "No, she just needed to know we were here. That's all that matters."

Tucker finished his coffee. "I can notarize it." He looked back and forth between Grace and me. "You two can serve as witnesses."

Over the rim of my mug, I eyed Tucker's phone, sitting facedown on the table just next to Iris's elbow. Nellie hadn't looked twice at it.

Once the manila folder was back in her possession, Iris took a deep breath and extended the envelope.

Nellie took it. "Thank you."

The gleam was gone from her eyes, and I wondered how long this subdued sense of selflessness would last.

Iris watched her mother run a finger over the edge of the paper as Nellie popped the envelope open to double-check the amount. Iris's face stayed even when Nellie's lips curled up in a tiny, pleased smile.

"I think you can buy yourself breakfast with that, Nellie."

She slicked her tongue over her teeth. "Suppose I can."

Nellie stood from the table and tucked the check into her purse. "So that's it?" she asked.

"Goodbye, Nellie," Iris said. "Good luck with everything."

"You really mean it," her mom said quietly.

Iris nodded. "It's time for a fresh start. For both of us. I don't ever want to see you again after this."

Nellie gave her daughter a long, unfathomable look, and I held my breath, wondering what she might say next. But nothing came. Probably because she didn't have the decency for any sort of emotionally poignant goodbye. Instead, Nellie nodded crisply and left the diner without a backward glance. I was out of the booth in the next heartbeat, as was Iris.

We met in the middle, my arms engulfing her immediately. She sank into my embrace. "Holy shit, it worked," she breathed.

I kissed the top of her head. "It worked. He's yours."

Iris beamed up at me. "He's mine."

I slid my palm down the silk of her braid, tugging at it until her face was tipped up toward mine. Our kiss stayed soft and sweet and short. When I pulled away, Nellie was in her truck, staring through the windshield at us with a blank look on her face.

Iris pulled away, her eyes glowing. She wound her arm around my waist, smiling at Tucker and Grace. "Thank you for the use of your phone, Tucker. And for all your help."

He notched two fingers to his temple in a salute. "Hey, thank the state of Tennessee for being a one-party consent state for recording conversations. Now there's nothing she can accuse you of should she have a change of heart."

Grace sighed. "It is so hot when you go all lawyer-y."

Tucker laughed, tugging her closer for a kiss.

I pressed my nose to the top of Iris's head to breathe her in, and she looked up.

"A fresh start, huh?" I asked.

She nodded. "Sounds good, doesn't it?"

I kissed her upturned lips. "Yeah, it does," I whispered, mouth brushing hers. "Let's go home and get working on that. Don't you have a store to open today?"

Iris laughed. "I do. Wanna help me?"

"Always."

CHAPTER 26

IRIS

I couldn't stop fidgeting on the short drive from my house to the store.

"Deep breaths," Hunter said, his wrist resting casually on the top of the steering wheel.

I did as he asked, only feeling the slightest settling of the butterflies fluttering through my stomach. "What if no one shows up?"

He turned to me with a crooked smile. "You really think that's possible?"

"No." I smoothed my hands along my denim-clad thighs. "Maybe I should have dressed up more. Who wears jeans and a tank top to a store opening?"

"Iris."

His voice was so calm and steady and deep, and I pinched my eyes shut at the subdued amusement I heard there. "I know, I'm freaking out."

Hunter slid his hand over mine, his long thick fingers bracketing mine.

It anchored some of those nerves, and I was able to pull a slow, steadying breath into my overworked lungs.

Gawd. You'd think I'd just run a marathon for how out of breath I was.

"I just want it to be perfect," I told him.

His eyes held so much love. "It will be."

"How do you know?" I whispered. My throat ached from all the emotions I was holding back. The day had been so big already, clearing the hurdle of Nellie, of any possible legal trouble she could cause Theo and me. It was an embarrassment of riches to assume that this other big thing could go off just as well.

Easing the car to a stop at a red light, he moved his gaze from the windshield over to my face. "Because this is what you're meant to do. Everything you've done has brought you here."

Surging across the seat, I gripped his face in my hands and planted a searing kiss on his lips. "I love you," I told him. "But I will kill you if you make me cry."

He laughed. "Duly noted."

I closed my eyes as he made the last turn. "I can't look."

"I think you should," he murmured.

Carefully, I peeled my eyes open, my mouth falling open when I saw the line. The entire block in front of the store was full of people. I saw Joy and Maxine, some of my neighbors, Jennifer Sylvester Winston, and a few others from their family. Some of Maxine's friends from church. Bobby Jo MacIntyre and her husband. Magnolia and Grady. Grace and Tucker. And right in front of the doors, holding flowers, was Hunter's family, Theo centered right in the middle of them.

A gorgeous balloon arch, which had not been there the night before when I locked up, covered the entryway to the store. It was shades of ivory and silver and gray, settling into solid black balloons at the base. "What?" I was maybe possibly going to black out. "Who?"

He squeezed my hand. "It was Grace and Magnolia's idea. Joss wanted us to do something more practical, so she opted for alcohol you can drink later."

I laughed, even as my eyes burned hot and insistent with tears.

"I will not cry," I said fiercely. "I will *not* cry yet, Hunter Buchanan, and you can tell them that."

Hunter laid a hand over his heart. "As soon as we get out of the car. But ... just wait there."

I gave him a look. "What for?"

"Trust me," he said, eyes locked on mine.

Slowly, I nodded.

Hunter grinned, quick and bright, and the sight of it had my heart somersaulting. Honestly, that was all it took, and I wanted to climb him like a tree. It was stupid how much I wanted him. How much I loved him. How perfect he was for me.

I blew out a slow breath while Hunter parked, jogging in front of the car so he could open my door.

The crowd waiting yelled and whistled when I got out of the car, and even if it sort of made me want to crawl back into the car and hide, it was the most surreal, happy moment of my entire life.

"They're all here," I whispered, tears threatening the edge of my eyelids.

Hunter curled an arm around my shoulder and pressed a kiss to the top of my head. "For you."

With his hand in mine, we walked across the street. Just before we approached the curb, Hunter nodded at his parents. His mom grinned, and arm in arm with Robert, they left the waiting crowd and walked toward us.

She swept me in a tight hug. "We are so proud of you, honey."

"Please don't make me cry," I begged her in a choked voice.

Fran laughed, her eyes shiny when she pulled back. "I try not to make promises I can't keep."

Robert laughed, as did Hunter.

I smiled at them, then mouthed, *"Thank you,"* to Magnolia and Grace, who traded pleased smiles.

"Are y'all ready to go in?" I asked.

There were cheers and scattered applause, and I caught Maxine wiping a knuckle under her eye.

Hunter set a hand on my back. "One more thing," he said into my ear.

When I glanced up at him in question, his parents moved to the side. So did Connor and Sylvia, and Levi and Joss. They'd been dead center in the crowd, blocking the entrance with Theo. And when they moved, I saw the bright flash of emerald green.

Right in the center of the store, exactly where I'd pictured it, was my grandma's couch. I strode forward, mouth hanging open.

"How did you ...?"

Fran flanked me on one side, Sylvia on the other with Edie tucked safely in her free arm. "Consider this our *Welcome to the family* gift," Sylvia said quietly.

"Your grandma would be so proud of you, Iris," Francine said, rubbing her hand along my back. "She may not be able to be here for you, but we always will be, and we want you to know that."

And right there, in the middle of Main Street, in front of the whole damn town, I burst into tears.

CHAPTER 27

HUNTER

*F*ive hours later, Iris and I slumped on the green couch. My cousin Grady was sprawled on the floor. Magnolia stood behind the cash register, wiping down the counter as Grace flipped the sign to *Closed* behind the last customer.

"Holy shit," I groaned. "I don't think I can move."

Iris settled her head on my shoulder with a yawn. "I'm going to sleep until next week."

Magnolia cleared her throat delicately. "Unless you hire someone before tomorrow, you won't be sleeping for a while."

I felt Iris's cheeks widen into a smile. "We did good tonight, huh?"

Grady lifted his head. "I hike for a living, and I don't get this tired."

I laughed. "Working retail is a little different, isn't it?"

He settled his hands on his stomach. "Wake me up when it's time to head home, Magnolia."

She glided over to my cousin, holding out her hand. "It's time to go home now. I need to get these heels off."

He stood, dropping a kiss on her upturned mouth.

"I can't thank you guys enough," Iris said. "I never would have survived today without you."

Grace plopped onto Tucker's lap, where he was settled in one of the armchairs. "That's what family is for."

Iris snuggled under my arm, pressing her face into my chest. I kissed the top of her head.

My family slowly trickled out, heading home with hugs and more thanks and boxes full of the extra cupcakes that we'd served from Donner Bakery.

Iris locked the door, leaning her forehead against the glass with an audible, heavy sigh. And even though my body protested any sort of movement that wasn't stretching out on the nearest soft horizontal surface, I stood from the couch to wrap her in a hug.

She clutched my back, and we stood there in the quiet space, arms tight around each other.

"You were amazing," I told her. "All day. Every part of it."

Iris turned her chin up, and I snagged her mouth in a kiss. She hummed happily. "Thank you," she whispered.

"You can thank me by turning off those lights," I told her.

She grinned. "Here?"

"Of course you'd think I mean sex," I murmured, kissing her as she laughed. "I am too tired for anything of the sort, woman."

But she did as I asked, flipping off all the overhead lights until all that was left was the small lamp on the wood countertop at the back of the store. I tugged her toward that green couch, the one she'd wanted so bad, and because I knew we'd fit, I settled on it and opened my arms.

She laughed under her breath, carefully climbing over my body so she could settle into my arms, tucked between my side and the back of the couch.

"Remember when we used to cuddle exactly this way when your grandma had this couch?" I asked quietly.

Iris hummed, settling her hand over my heart. "I do."

"I like when you answer like that," I spoke into her hair.

"Why's that?" she asked coyly.

I pinched her side, and she laughed. "You damn well know why."

She set her chin on my chest and stared up at me, eyes soft in the dim light. "Tell me anyway," she whispered. "Please."

My hand slid over her cheek, my thumb brushing her cheekbone, then tracing the line of her bottom lip. "Because someday soon, Iris Jean Black, I'm going to ask you to marry me." I let out an unsteady breath as her eyes shimmered with unshed tears. "I won't be able to wait long. I hope that's okay."

Shakily, she nodded. "That's okay with me."

"Good." My fingers wove into the silk of her hair. "I want to stand in front of our friends, our family, your brother, and I want to hear you say them while I put a ring on your finger." My voice deepened, and a single tear slipped down her cheek. "I've dreamt of you saying those words to me, and I can't wait to turn that dream into the proudest moment of my life."

She pushed up, kissing me sweetly, tasting like her happy tears.

I settled my arms around her waist and held her close, breathing her in.

We fell asleep like that, on the green couch, in the place we called home.

And nothing had ever felt better.

EPILOGUE

IRIS

Six months later

There was something occasionally terrifying about your life turning out in a way that was almost too good to be true.

Hunter moved in with Theo and me about a month after the store opened because we didn't see the point in waiting. He hogged the bed. Ruthlessly tugged the covers in his direction when he slept. Thankfully, it was just another reason to stay tucked into the nice, warm little crook against his chest.

He had more books than we had bookshelf space and a collection of dress shirts larger than my entire wardrobe. The first thing he did after moving in was paint over the purple on my old bedroom walls to create an office space for himself, one entire wall lined with bookshelves so that we could move the stacks and stacks that had taken up residence in our bedroom.

He and Theo ganged up against me with regularity, but I only pretended to be annoyed by it. My brother was so damn happy that it took everything in me not to burst into tears when I watched them play basketball in the hoop Hunter installed in the driveway. Or go fishing with Hunter and his brothers and their dad. Or when Fran and Maxine started teaching him how to knit.

Hunter sang in the shower, a little off-key and a lot loud, and sometimes I banged on the bathroom door when I couldn't hear myself think.

It was those moments when he'd laugh, and I'd fight the urge to join him.

Life was sweet, the kind of happy that didn't feel precarious anymore.

He woke me with a kiss every single morning, and it was when I started settling into the realization that I could finally relax.

He got a job at Green Valley Public Schools that fall, teaching middle school English, and he absolutely loved it.

All the big things in our lives locked into place so seamlessly that even the small things that annoyed us about each other felt like exciting little discoveries.

Sometimes.

"You cannot be serious," he said.

I set my hands on my hips. "I hate it. It's not going up on our walls."

Hunter gaped, gesturing to the framed artwork he brought home from a garage sale. "It's a classic. This lady had no clue how much it was worth."

"It's ugly." I tilted my head. "It looks like someone dumped a can of paint over on accident and decided to call it modern art."

Hunter set his jaw, and once that stubborn light filled his dark eyes, I knew we were going to battle this out.

Theo glanced between us, then lifted his hands. "I'm outta here. Yell for me when it's safe to come back inside."

"It's safe *now*," I called after him. "That painting is going back into someone's garage."

With a frustrated growl, Hunter bent and scooped me up over his shoulder, marching out of the family room. I pinched his side, my hair dangling down.

"Put me down, you big bully."

He didn't, maybe because my delighted grin was evident in my voice as I said it. His hand tightened on my thigh. "Give it one week. You'll fall in love."

"Not a chance. I already let you put up that horrible photo in our room."

Hunter sighed.

The photo in question was probably the worst in existence that had ever been taken of me, the day he proposed—about three months earlier.

Hunter dropped to one knee while we were on a simple picnic. There was no fancy fanfare and no big skywriters or groups of people popping out behind the trees to surprise us.

It was him and me on a beautiful fall day with the smell of changing leaves in the air.

I burst into sobbing, red-faced tears when he slid the vintage diamond onto my shaking finger, and he held me while I cried through my reaction.

It was happiness and excitement, and the kind of relief that makes you feel like you unlocked a thousand pounds of pressure from your soul.

Even if Hunter and I never got married, if I never wore his ring on my finger, I would've been completely happy. But I wanted to be his in this way and wanted him to be mine.

Because he wanted to remember the day, after I wiped my face and we kissed for a while, he wrapped his arm around me and tugged me into his side to snap a picture of our faces pressed together.

"That horrible photo," Hunter drawled, as he set me with a bounce onto our bed and stared down at me, "is my favorite one in the world."

I stretched my arms over my head and waited for him to join me. "I look a mess."

His eyes warmed. "That's why I love it."

Sitting up, I tugged on Hunter's hand until he toppled onto the bed next to me.

After months of doing this, we settled into our favorite spot seamlessly. His arm under my neck, around my shoulder, me on my side with my leg over his.

Today, though, instead of staying on his back, Hunter turned onto his side so he could slide his lips over mine in a long, luxurious kiss.

I opened, waiting for his tongue to slide hot and wet over my own, but he pulled back, dropping kisses on the tip of my nose and the curve of my cheekbone.

"Despite your terrible taste in modern art," he murmured, "I do love kissing you, Iris Black."

I smiled. "Despite *your* terrible taste in modern art, I can't wait for you to call me Iris Buchanan."

His breath was audible, sucked in through gritted teeth, and his big hands tightened on my body when I said it. Whenever we talked about our wedding, only four months away and about a month after Joss and Levi would finally get married, it lit some proprietary caveman side of Hunter that I thoroughly enjoyed.

Hunter's lips sought mine, ferocious and firm. His muscles under my hands were unyielding as they coasted over his chest and shoulders. The kiss felt endless, with biting and sucking and rolling hips. Slick tongues and soft moans. Riding that perfect tipping point of just before we started tearing at each other's clothes for a quick, fierce bout of lovemaking while we had the house to ourselves. But it stayed innocent enough because doors were open and unlocked, and we were not trying to traumatize Theo with our sex life.

His hands did slide up under my shirt, playing with the strap of my bra, but he didn't take it any further.

He slowed the kiss and pulled away, a speculative gleam in his eye.

"What?" I asked.

He pecked a kiss on my lips and settled on his back.

"I have an idea," he said.

"As long as it doesn't involve that monstrosity in the family room, I'm all ears."

He pinched my ass, laughing when I yelped.

Hunter soothed the spot with his hand. I smacked it away.

"You were saying," I prompted.

He hummed, chest expanding on a deep inhale. "I was."

Snuggling into that chest, I closed my eyes and breathed him in. The words he chose started somewhere deep beneath his ribs, and the vibration of them was pleasant against my ears.

In fact, I was so wrapped up in feeling what he was saying that the words didn't register for a moment.

I snapped my head back, eyes wide. "You want to what?"

He smiled softly, sliding his hand over my cheek, weaving his fingers into my hair. "I want to adopt Theo after we get married if that's okay with you."

My eyes glossed over, a disbelieving laugh springing out instantly. "What? *Yes*, that's okay with me."

His smile widened. "Good." He leaned down to kiss me, laughing against my mouth when I gripped his head with both hands and ramped that kiss up about ten degrees with my tongue and a helpless whimper that he was even real, and he was here, and he was mine forever.

Hunter gentled the kiss, wiping his thumb under my eye to catch a tear that had escaped. "I thought maybe we could ask him before the wedding. Make it part of the ceremony. Then we can end that day as Hunter and Iris and Theo Buchanan." His eyes were searing in their intensity. The conviction of his love for us. "Our family."

Too impossibly happy to believe, slightly terrifying in how good it all was.

I wrapped my arms around his neck and hugged him as tightly as I could manage until the muscles in my arm shook. "Our family," I repeated. Then I pulled my head back, our eyes locking. "I still want babies, though."

His grin was wolfish. "Good."

"A couple," I whispered, sipping at his bottom lip. When I nipped at the flesh with my teeth, he growled, hands curling around my ass until he tugged me tight to him.

"Maybe more than a couple," he answered, voice rough and uneven, his hard length pulling an ache from my body.

"Door's unlocked, buddy," I said, pecking his lips. "Don't get any ideas."

Hunter laughed, the sweet sound of it curling around my heart. There were no walls anymore. No boxes to keep pieces of him and me separated.

Everything was wide open, the future something bright and wonderful.

And it was just getting started.

SECOND EPILOGUE

HUNTER

Three months later

"So how does it work?"

I glanced at Theo. "What?"

He took a deep breath, glancing around the table at me, Tucker Haywood, my cousin Grady, and my brothers. "The Buchanan family love curse."

Even though we were surrounded by people, loud music, and laughter—it was a wedding reception, after all—the four of us went still as statues.

Levi's eyes widened. "How'd you know about that?"

Theo shrugged. "I just heard my sister talking about it over there. I'd never heard about it before tonight."

My brothers and I traded a loaded look, and I cast a grin in the direction of the *over there* he was referring to. Where we were seated a few tables over with the groom, Iris was at a circular table with the bride. A burst of happy laughter came from their table, and my heart warmed at the sight of Iris having so much fun with Joss, Magnolia, Grace, and Sylvia.

241

Joss was telling them a story, her arms waving wildly, and when I glanced over, my brother studied his brand-new bride with contentment clear in his eyes.

One month, and I'd be able to do that too.

Our wedding wouldn't be as big as Joss and Levi's—half of Green Valley was dancing and laughing underneath the fairy lights strung across the field holding their reception. For me and Iris, it would be family and a few close friends.

But this night—for my brother and the woman he'd loved since he was a teenager—was perfect.

Levi tore his gaze from Joss and leaned forward to brace his elbows on the table. He'd ditched the tie once the reception started, and it was hanging around his neck. "What'd you hear them say?"

Theo took a deep breath, blowing it out with comically puffed cheeks. "They were talking about how they thought it worked. How it might have started back when the first Buchanans moved into Green Valley."

Connor nodded. "Did they have any good ideas?"

He shrugged, tugging at the collar of his dress shirt. "Nothing that made any sense. Something about a secret wishing well that was actually magic, or maybe someone cast a spell hundreds of years ago or something. But … the whole thing just sounded a little …" His eyes darted around the table again. "Nuts."

The men seated with me all smiled in turn, probably thinking through all the ways they'd experienced our strange little family love legend. But no one said anything, clearly deferring to me for this one.

In the months since I'd moved in with him and Iris, I could say with relative ease that my best friend and constant sidekick was an eleven-year-old boy. Now that he'd started school—dominating fifth grade like I knew he could—we didn't get to hang out quite as much together, but conversations like these were my favorite.

Theo was inquisitive, brutally honest, still cursed like a frat boy, was impossibly sweet with his sister, and made me laugh more than anyone I'd ever met. I already loved him like my son, but soon enough, it would be legal—and I couldn't wait.

"I'll tell you what we know," I said. "Which isn't much. But you've got to promise to keep it a secret."

He nodded, blue eyes wide and serious. "What happens if I tell someone?"

My cousin Grady set a hand on his shoulder. "You get struck by lightning."

"*Really?*"

"Ignore him," Tucker said.

"Is he full of shit?" Theo asked.

Levi burst out laughing. Connor choked on his beer.

"He is," I answered. "But you've got to treat this information carefully, you know."

Theo gave me a serious nod. "I promise."

I told him the story in the exact same way that our dad had told us.

"We don't know how it started, Theo. And we don't know why. But as far back as anyone can remember, the men born into the Buchanan family have had one thing in common. When they meet the person they're meant to love for the rest of their life, they know it *immediately*. Love at first sight." I glanced over at Iris and felt that familiar tug in my soul—the absolute rightness of her. "Real love too. Not just attraction or chemistry. But the person who's your complete, perfect match."

He sank back in his chair, mouth hanging open. "Nuh-uh."

Levi nodded. "It's true. I met Joss when I was seventeen. The moment I laid eyes on her, I just … knew." He smiled over at her again, studying the sight of her in the beautiful white dress that she wore. "Nothing had ever felt so right in my entire life."

Theo furrowed his brow, listening as each man around the table gave a simplified version of how they'd fallen in love. When his attention settled back on me, he still looked confused.

"And it was like that for you too?" he asked quietly. "With Iris?"

It was my turn to study the love of my life. She wasn't wearing the white dress— not yet. Tonight it was a beautiful deep green, and it made her eyes glow in a

243

way that had my knees a little weak when she came out of the bedroom. From where I sat, the diamond on her left ring finger glittered under the lights.

"Yeah," I answered. "Felt like something missing clicked into place when I met her."

Theo went quiet for a moment, and I nudged his knee with mine under the table.

"What is it?" I asked.

"You were apart for a long time, though."

Slowly, I nodded. "We were. Falling in love so young doesn't mean it'll always be easy. Your sister and I just had to be patient. Work through some big stuff in our lives before we were ready to be together again."

Theo exhaled heavily. "All right. That's good to know."

Levi grinned. "What makes you so curious, Theo?"

Theo shrugged. "Well … if it happened for you when you were young, then I could meet her any day. I figure I'm one of the Buchanan men now, so I better keep an eye out."

I settled a hand over my chest, trying to absorb the emotional impact of what he'd just said. Levi's eyes went suspiciously shiny as he nodded. "Yeah, Theo. You just might have to do that."

Tucker and Grady and Connor all smiled and gave small pieces of advice to Theo, who absorbed it like a sponge. In just a few short months of being part of my family, he'd blossomed under all the attention.

My mom and dad spoiled him rotten.

His new uncles and aunts were just as bad.

And as for me … he'd tucked himself firmly into my heart, and moments like this just cemented why.

A cool hand slid over the back of my neck, and I looked up to find Iris smiling down at me.

"Hey," she said.

I pushed my chair back, and she read the wordless invitation for what it was, settling on my leg where I could wrap my arm around her waist. I gave her a soft kiss, and her lips curled into a smile against mine.

"Gross." Theo sighed.

Levi laughed. "You're at a wedding, man. Bound to see some kissing."

"Yeah, I figured it would just be you and Aunt Joss, though. I see them kiss enough at home."

I kicked at his foot, and he kicked back, a devious grin on his face.

"What were you gentlemen talking about over here?" Iris asked. "It looked awfully serious."

Theo and I traded a look. With a raised brow, I decided to let him answer as he wanted.

"We were talking about love," he said.

Iris's smile widened. "You got someone you want to tell me about, Theo?"

He shook his head. "Not yet. But … it sounds like I'll know pretty quickly once I do. Right, Hunter?"

Iris's gaze met mine, and I smiled. "Yeah, you'll know."

She kissed me again, and even if I'd get a million more of her kisses before my life was over, they never felt like anything less than magic.

And maybe that was what love was, no matter how fast or slow it found you.

Each and every one of us had found a little piece of that in a world that didn't seem to believe in it anymore.

No matter where it came from or how we managed it, that love was the best part of our lives. And the best part was still to come.

Because now … we just got to live it.

The End

Author's Note

If you're just joining along with the Buchanan family for the first time, or if you've been here since Levi met Joss—thank you.

Writing this family for the past four years has been a tremendous honor, and I'm so grateful for all the messages (so, so many messages!) asking when Hunter would get his happily ever after.

When I came up with the idea of the Buchanan love curse, I never intended to explain it. I didn't think it would add anything to the individual love stories to know the full scope or how it started or why. To me, there was something a bit more beautiful about it, if it remained a mystery.

Each book in this series challenged me as a writer in a different way, and I'm so grateful that Penny allowed me the opportunity to stretch those creative muscles in the amazing universe that she's built.

I'll definitely leave a bit of my writer heart in Green Valley, on the Buchanan's front porch. Thank you for coming along with me on this wonderful adventure.

ACKNOWLEDGMENTS

First and foremost, I have to thank the incomparable Penny Reid. While she continually tells us she's not our boss in this Smartypants Romance venture, she *is* our fearless leader and I could not respect and love her more after taking part in this experience for the last four years. The time, energy and passion that she's invested into every single author who has passed through the Smartypants universe is incredible.

Getting the email that she was approving my pitch for a Donner Bakery series (and Baking Me Crazy) was a pivotal one in my author journey. I am so grateful that she's allowed me to stretch and grow and challenge myself as writer in this world, and surrounded me with the most amazing, intelligent, kind, funny women in the process. My fellow Smartypants authors (and the women who run it alongside Penny) can never, ever get rid of me now. Sorry not sorry.

As always, thanks to Kathryn Andrews for being the best plotting partner in the world and always rolling with the punches when I decide (again) to change the story because something doesn't feel right.

To Kelli Collins for doing an amazing job with dev edits, and seeing the nuance where I fell a little short.

To Piper and Brooke and M.E. for diving into Dramione with me (IYKYK), and talking through some of the stuff in this book along the way.

To Najla Qamber and Joseph Cannata for creating cover magic.

To Jenny Sims and Kelly Allenby for cleaning up the mess.

To Tina and Michelle for keeping my author life in order.

To my READERS. I love you, I love you, I love you. Without YOU, I couldn't do this job. This job can drain your cup with frequency, but what fills it back up again is seeing you fall in love with the characters.

Rejoice in hope, be patient in tribulation, be constant in prayer.
Romans 12:12

OTHER BOOKS BY KARLA SORENSEN

(available to read with your KU subscription)

The Wolves: a Football Dynasty (second gen)

The Lie (Faith Pierson's story)

The Plan (Lydia Pierson's story)

The Crush (Emmett Ward's story)

The Ward Sisters

Focused

Faked

Floored

Forbidden

The Washington Wolves

The Bombshell Effect

The Ex Effect

The Marriage Effect

The Bachelors of the Ridge

Dylan

Garrett

Cole

Michael

Tristan

Three Little Words

By Your Side

Light Me Up

Tell Them Lies

Love at First Sight

(Published by Smartypants Romance)

Baking Me Crazy

Batter of Wits

Steal my Magnolia

Worth the Wait

ABOUT THE AUTHOR

Photo cred: Perrywinkle Photography

Karla Sorensen is an Amazon top 10 bestselling author who refuses to read or write anything without a happily ever after. When she's not devouring historical romance and Dramione fanfic or avoiding the laundry, you can find her watching football (British AND American), HGTV or listening to Enneagram podcasts so she can psychoanalyze everyone in her life, in no particular order of importance. With a degree in Advertising and Public Relations from Grand Valley State University, she made her living in senior healthcare prior to writing full-time. Karla lives in Michigan with her husband, two boys and a big, shaggy rescue dog named Bear.

Stay up to date on Karla's upcoming releases!
Subscribe to her newsletter:
http://www.karlasorensen.com/newsletter/

Website: http://www.karlasorensen.com/
Facebook: http://www.facebook.com/karlasorensenbooks
Goodreads: https://www.goodreads.com/author/show/13563232.
Karla_Sorensen
Twitter: http://www.twitter.com/ksorensenbooks
Instagram: https://www.instagram.com/karla_sorensen/

Find Smartypants Romance online:
Website: www.smartypantsromance.com
Facebook: https://www.facebook.com/smartypantsromance
Twitter: @smartypantsrom
Instagram: @smartypantsromance
Newsletter: https://smartypantsromance.com/newsletter/

ALSO BY SMARTYPANTS ROMANCE

Green Valley Chronicles

The Love at First Sight Series

Baking Me Crazy by Karla Sorensen (#1)

Batter of Wits by Karla Sorensen (#2)

Steal My Magnolia by Karla Sorensen (#3)

Worth the Wait by Karla Sorensen (#4)

Fighting For Love Series

Stud Muffin by Jiffy Kate (#1)

Beef Cake by Jiffy Kate (#2)

Eye Candy by Jiffy Kate (#3)

Knock Out by Jiffy Kate (#4)

The Donner Bakery Series

No Whisk, No Reward by Ellie Kay (#1)

The Green Valley Library Series

Love in Due Time by L.B. Dunbar (#1)

Crime and Periodicals by Nora Everly (#2)

Prose Before Bros by Cathy Yardley (#3)

Shelf Awareness by Katie Ashley (#4)

Carpentry and Cocktails by Nora Everly (#5)

Love in Deed by L.B. Dunbar (#6)

Dewey Belong Together by Ann Whynot (#7)

Hotshot and Hospitality by Nora Everly (#8)

Love in a Pickle by L.B. Dunbar (#9)

Checking You Out by Ann Whynot (#10)

Architecture and Artistry by Nora Everly (#11)

Scorned Women's Society Series

My Bare Lady by Piper Sheldon (#1)

The Treble with Men by Piper Sheldon (#2)

The One That I Want by Piper Sheldon (#3)

Hopelessly Devoted by Piper Sheldon (#3.5)

It Takes a Woman by Piper Sheldon (#4)

Park Ranger Series

Happy Trail by Daisy Prescott (#1)

Stranger Ranger by Daisy Prescott (#2)

The Leffersbee Series

Been There Done That by Hope Ellis (#1)

Before and After You by Hope Ellis (#2)

The Higher Learning Series

Upsy Daisy by Chelsie Edwards (#1)

Green Valley Heroes Series

Forrest for the Trees by Kilby Blades (#1)

Parks and Provocation by Juliette Cross (#2)

Story of Us Collection

My Story of Us: Zach by Chris Brinkley (#1)

My Story of Us: Thomas by Chris Brinkley (#2)

Seduction in the City

Cipher Security Series

Code of Conduct by April White (#1)

Code of Honor by April White (#2)

Code of Matrimony by April White (#2.5)

Code of Ethics by April White (#3)

Cipher Office Series

Weight Expectations by M.E. Carter (#1)

Sticking to the Script by Stella Weaver (#2)

Cutie and the Beast by M.E. Carter (#3)

Weights of Wrath by M.E. Carter (#4)

Common Threads Series

Mad About Ewe by Susannah Nix (#1)

Give Love a Chai by Nanxi Wen (#2)

Key Change by Heidi Hutchinson (#3)

Not Since Ewe by Susannah Nix (#4)

Lost Track by Heidi Hutchinson (#5)

Educated Romance

Work For It Series

Street Smart by Aly Stiles (#1)

Heart Smart by Emma Lee Jayne (#2)

Book Smart by Amanda Pennington (#3)

Smart Mouth by Emma Lee Jayne (#4)

Play Smart by Aly Stiles (#5)

Lessons Learned Series

Under Pressure by Allie Winters (#1)

Not Fooling Anyone by Allie Winters (#2)

Out of this World

London Ladies Embroidery Series

Neanderthal Seeks Duchess by Laney Hatcher (#1)

Well Acquainted by Laney Hatcher (#2)

Made in United States
North Haven, CT
16 April 2023

35516770R00159